PRAISE FOR THE DELIGHTFUL ROMANCE NOVELS OF

Judith O'Brien

ONE PERFECT KNIGHT

"Ms. O'Brien mixes a little Hollywood, a little Disney, and a little literature into the cauldron of this Arthurian legend to create a magical adventure that frolics through medieval Camelot and the streets of New York. Don't miss the fun."

—*Romantic Times*

"Imaginatively romantic, you'll enjoy the fast pace and charismatic characters of *One Perfect Knight*."

—*Rendezvous*

TO MARRY A BRITISH LORD

"Ms. O'Brien demonstrates she has the talent to be the next superstar."

—Harriet Klausner, *Affaire de Coeur*

"A delectable tale of love and intrigue with lively bits of humor. . . . Delightfully entertaining."

—Betty Babas, CompuServe Romance Reviews

"For readers who enjoy historical stories about England, royalty, and the aristocracy, this one is for you. . . . Well researched, well written, and well worth the read."

—*Rendezvous*

"Full of wonderful characters, several romances, a little mystery, a forbidden love, and a surprise ending. Judith O'Brien just keeps giving readers what they want—a good, strong, well-crafted, clever and witty read."

—Kathe Robin, *Romantic Times*

"O'Brien's books are a delight."

—Helen Holzer, *Atlanta Journal*

ASHTON'S BRIDE

"Lush descriptions, vivid characters, and strong emotional writing combine to make this an unforgettable novel."

—*Rendezvous*

"I was captivated from the very first page. . . . Poignant, powerful, utterly compelling and so very heartwarming."
—Brenda Joyce, author of *Splendor*

"This tender, funny love story will haunt me for a long time. . . . I feel as if I've discovered a rare and charming new treasure to add to my list of favorite authors."
—Teresa Medeiros, author of *Nobody's Darling*

"Judith O'Brien has a wonderful sense of humor and she knows how to combine it with the kind of drama, fantasy, and romance readers cherish."
—Deborah Smith, author of *A Place to Call Home*

"Quite simply, a must-read."

—*Publishers Weekly*

RHAPSODY IN TIME

"Her characters are wonderful and so believable that readers can't help but cheer them on. Time travel has a new voice, and her name is Judith O'Brien."
—Maria C. Ferrer, *Romantic Times*

"*Rhapsody in Time* is an exciting time-travel romance that pays homage to the New York City of the Roaring Twenties. Judith O'Brien has gifted the audience with two dynamic lead characters and a fast-paced romance."
—Harriet Klausner, *Affaire de Coeur*

Books by Judith O'Brien

Rhapsody in Time
Ashton's Bride
Maiden Voyage
Once Upon a Rose
To Marry a British Lord
One Perfect Knight
The Forever Bride

Available from POCKET BOOKS

JUDITH O'BRIEN

THE FOREVER BRIDE

SONNET BOOKS

New York London Toronto Sydney Tokyo Singapore

This book is a work of fiction. Names, characters, places and
incidents are products of the author's imagination or are used
fictitiously. Any resemblance to actual events or locales or persons,
living or dead, is entirely coincidental.

An *Original* Publication of POCKET BOOKS

A Sonnet Book published by
POCKET BOOKS, a division of Simon & Schuster Inc.
1230 Avenue of the Americas, New York, NY 10020

ISBN: 0-671-00041-1

First Sonnet Books printing October 1999

10 9 8 7 6 5 4 3 2 1

SONNET BOOKS and colophon are trademarks of
Simon & Schuster Inc.

Tip-in illustration by Gregg Gulbronson

Printed in the U.S.A.

For my son, Seth, a bundle of skinned knees and smiles, an endless supply of jokes and laughter. You bring joy to everything.

Now will you clean your room?

THE FOREVER BRIDE

Prologue

∞∞∞∞

$\mathcal{I}$t was a quiet night, the pale green leaves and just-sprouting blooms of springtime perfuming the air with lush, floral scents. Although it was not a full moon, the brilliant sliver hanging in the black night with the radiant glittering stars provided enough light. There was no need for the lantern in his bag.

His destination was the fancy frame house outside of town, beyond the streets south of Grand that were illuminated by street lamps or well traveled by coaches and pedestrians. No, this location was well away from the city bustle—just above Sixty-first Street, near the old Treadwell Farm, a place of shanties and stray livestock. Remote though the house was, it was lit from within by gas lamps and boasted running water. It was a new idea, created by the house's owner, the reservoir of gas fuel just beyond a pretty retired arbor behind, and a water pipe connected to the well.

In spite of the seriousness of his mission he could not help but admire the house in its beauty and simplicity. Grand though it was, with over a dozen large rooms within, there *was a cleanness and purity of line that pleased his aesthetic sense. It was indeed a fine house, almost classic in the dimness of night.*

As he had expected, there was a single light burning on the second floor. It was her bedroom. The new bride, fresh from London.

And she was alone, all alone.

The burlap bag suddenly seemed heavy, and he clutched it so tightly his knuckles grew white.

He knew what he had to do, and he moved swiftly. There was no need to fear detection—they had seen to that earlier. The neighbors, distant though they were, had been called out of town. He himself had helped to forge the letters, cleverly directing the families to relations dozens of miles away. And much to his secret pride, the letters had worked beautifully.

Now all he had to do was to pin the note to the door, the warning so carefully phrased. That accomplished, he reached back into the bag and began to set the . . .

The explosion blew him off his feet, then a mighty *whoosh* followed by indescribable heat and the sound of shattering glass as the panes blasted from the windows.

What had happened? Stunned, the bag now consumed by fire, he staggered to his feet and faced the house.

Great tongues of flame were leaping from every window like giant vipers.

In shock, he stood, and then came the noise. The scream. The banshee shrieks of the dying woman.

Should he do something? This wasn't supposed to happen! It was to be a warning, that was all!

And then he saw the horrible vision, the slender figure through the upstairs window, now as bright as the sun, the silhouette and her flaying arms and the hair, all of the hair, rising and dancing like a mermaid's mane in the ocean. And *then there was nothing but the flames. The screams were gone. The dancing mermaid had vanished.*

He must run, to be as far away from this place as possible. But his feet wouldn't move, like trees planted with deep roots in the road before the exploded house.

He couldn't move.

Opening his mouth to scream, nothing was emitted, not a single sound but the flames and the crackling of timber and the shattering of glass and furniture within.

He couldn't breathe. He couldn't breathe. . . .

And then, as always, he awoke, drenched in sweat, his heart pounding.

He was in his soft bed, the down feathers and the sweet-smelling linens and the plump pillows.

Gasping for breath, he didn't bother to light a lamp. He would fall back asleep now, soon enough. He would sleep, just as he had every night since last spring.

The night he killed Amanda O'Neal Stevens.

1

New York City, 1849

They closed the window curtains and waited for the ghost to arrive.

"Are you prepared to see your husband now?"

The widow nodded once, twisting her thin silver wedding band. "I do not know what to say," she whispered, and then smiled just a little. "We were married for eight years, and now I do not know what to say."

Celia Thomason placed her hand on the young widow's wrist. "I understand, Mrs. Jenson. But your husband will be the same man, maintain the same character as he did before his passing. You needn't be shy."

"Don't people get better?" She cleared her throat once. "What I mean is, after they have passed over, don't they become kinder and more God-fearing?"

Even in the plush, cool dimness of the front room parlor, with the heavy green draperies blocking the late-afternoon sun, muffling the sounds of brisk footsteps and rolling carriages and clip-clopping horses, Celia could see glintings of white in the widow's hair.

Yet she could not possibly have reached thirty—perhaps she was even younger than Celia herself.

Her eyes, though, were old and tired, a flat gray framed by lids of dry crepe, her thin lips pallid and taut. Chronological years were meaningless to a woman who had labored hard her entire life, only to be forced into more dire circumstances now.

It had been several months since her husband perished in an appalling accident. A longshoreman, he was unloading great juke sacks of coffee, each one weighing hundreds of pounds. Apparently he had not realized how precariously balanced the highest sack was, and when he tripped, the entire pile tumbled onto him, leaving his wife and three children nearly penniless.

With what small funds remained, Mrs. Jenson had come to Celia Thomason, noted spiritualist, to seek advice from her late husband. Most of the city knew of Miss Thomason's remarkable skills. At a time when spiritualists were pitching tents, collecting money, and fleeing by dawn, Celia Thomason was solid, permanent. After all, she worked from her aunt's respectable brick home just off Washington Square, and had been conducting séances for almost four months. Thus she had stability and longevity on her side.

"Sometimes souls do become kinder after they have passed. Now close your eyes, Mrs. Jenson," Celia instructed. Hesitantly, the woman complied. "We must think of your husband, the best elements of his character. Think of his smile."

The widow tilted her head, then after a few moments, shook it. "To tell you the truth, Hiram didn't much take to smiling on a regular basis. When he did smile, why I knew he had been sipping from the jug again."

"I see." Celia patted the woman's hand. "Then imagine his kindness to your children, his tenderness towards the babies."

The widow leaned forward, her brow drawn in concentration. The seconds seemed to yawn with the wait as Mrs. Jenson searched her memory. Finally she sighed. "Miss Thomason, try as I might, I can't recall any such moments. Poor Hiram suffered terribly from the bilious colic, and he thought the children made it worse, what with their noise and racket-making and all."

"I see. Well, then think of his tenderness towards you. When you were courting, and he was a romantic young man in love and . . ."

The widow shook her head again, eyes still dutifully closed. "He wasn't ever much on tenderness, Miss Thomason. Or romantic. I thought that would come in time, after we married, but . . . well. All that came were the children. No, Hiram had many good qualities, but he was not what one would call a tender man."

"Then dwell on those good qualities. Think of them one by one."

The widow nodded eagerly, then her face fell slowly. "Let me think," she began.

"As a provider?" Celia offered. "He was a good provider for his family, was he not?"

"Hiram could have been a good provider had he applied himself," the widow said softly. "But he wasn't much on business. More often than not I had to take the coins from his pockets at night when he came home after . . ." Her face reddened even in the darkness. "After a hard day of work, he said a man deserved a strong drink or two. So I would take the coins and use them to help with the eggs. I sell eggs and sometimes butter, you see, and more and more, we had to rely on the egg money."

"Of course." Celia squeezed her hand. "Then think of him at church, standing beside you and the children and . . . Is anything wrong?"

"Well, Miss Thomason, the only time I recall Hiram at church was a few months ago."

"Then think of that image!" Celia cried, relieved. "Think of him . . ."

"It was his funeral."

"Oh."

"But he was handsome, I will admit, in his clean shirt and all."

"Indeed. Well, then, is that how you would prefer to think of him?"

"I suppose so." She bit her lower lip. "His shirt was so nice and clean. His face was shaved so close it almost shined. I don't reckon his fingernails had ever been so tidy."

"Then let's imagine your Hiram all clean and shaved, shall we?"

The widow nodded and closed her eyes even tighter in concentration.

They sat in silence for a few moments, the outside street sounds a faraway din. The widow seemed to relax, adjusting to having her eyes closed, being in a strange parlor with plush carpet beneath her feet and the smooth mahogany table wood beneath her hands.

"Now I will summon my spirit guides," Celia instructed. "Hopefully they will help you communicate with your husband. Are you ready, Mrs. Jenson?"

The other woman nodded. "Yes, yes. I believe so."

"Very well. Keep your eyes closed while I reach out to the other side."

For more long moments both women remained silent. Then finally Celia's spoke in a much-altered voice, a deeper register with flat inflections, a peculiar monotone. It was a mechanical-sounding voice, as if operated by the gears of a clock. "The spirits are gathering now. They are bringing him, your husband . . ."

She jumped. "Is he here? Is he in this room?"

"Yes. Yes. The spirits say yes." She maintained the strange tone. "He is here to help you."

"Can you see him?" Her voice was rising. "Can I look?"

"No. Do not look now. But he's beside you, and the spirits say he is gentle and loving."

"Hiram?"

"Yes. It is Hiram."

"I'm so sorry about the shoes, Hiram!" The widow spoke into the air, winding her black-edged handkerchief into a knot. "Please don't be angry. I just want to make sure you're not angry, that you won't haunt me or the children. It wasn't our fault, the shoes!"

"Oh, he's not angry!" Celia rushed. Then she returned to the mechanical voice. "No. He wishes to convey that he is pleased. Wait a moment." As if listening to ghostly voices, she paused, then continued. "He is happy about the shoes."

"He is? About the shoes?" For the first time a note of skepticism crept into her voice. She stiffened and opened her eyes, glancing around the parlor. "Where is he, then? I don't see him. We were married for eight years, Miss Thomason. Why can I not see him?"

Celia's expression remained blank, her eyes wide and

unblinking. "The spirits say you were not ready yet for the glorious vision. But do not fear. Your husband will soon make himself known to you."

Then there was a noise, soft at first. "What's that?" The widow looked around the darkened room, to the settee, the wing chairs, the tea table. The somber wood trim added to the general feeling of fashionable gloom and clutter. Then she glanced toward the fireplace, cold and bare in spite of the November chill outside. Fires were never used during sessions, it was explained to the clients, as the crackling interfered with Miss Thomason's communication with those beyond.

Mrs. Jenson had located the source of the noise. A delicate blue and white porcelain vase on the mantelpiece was rocking back and forth, evenly, rhythmically. As she watched, her eyes widened. "What is that?"

"It's Hiram."

The widow gaped. "What's he doing?" Dropping her voice, her chin quivered. "What's he going to do?"

"He wants you to know he's here."

She swallowed, eyes riveted to the vase. And then in a flash, the vase popped off the mantelpiece, shattering on the glazed brick below.

"Oh Lordy!" The young widow jumped to her feet. At that moment a violin resting on a wing chair seemed to rise forward, as if it would have stood up and marched off the chair. Instead, the bow that had been beside it began to hover, then saw against the strings. A scratchy tune was heard, and Celia took hold of the woman's hand to keep her from fleeing.

"Please, let me go!" She tried to yank her hand away, but Celia tightened her grasp.

Then she stopped and listened, her face melting

from panic to puzzlement, then to recognition. "Miss Thomason, that was Hiram's favorite tune! I don't know the name of it, but he sometimes whistled it when he came home late at night."

"He wishes you to receive a message." Celia's voice, calm and commanding, rose above the uncertain squeaks of the violin.

Mrs. Jenson glanced away from the instrument for a moment as her eyes widened, staring at nothing, her brow lined in confusion. Then she looked nervously to the side, left and right, as if expecting something unpleasant to happen.

Celia did not outwardly react to her client's expression, but it was one she knew all too well. She had seen the same controlled stare, the sudden rigid tension, on women young and old, members of respected society as well as those who dwelled on the outskirts of town. Their social status mattered not. It was all the same, no matter who they were or how grand or humble their lives.

Like so many others, the young widow was every bit as terrified of her husband in death as she had been in life.

"What? What does he want?" Mrs. Jenson's roughened hand began to tremble.

Celia smiled, dropping the mechanical voice as she again spoke in her own warm tone. "He longs for you to be happy," she said simply.

"Hiram? You sure you got the right spirit?"

"He says he's sorry, so very sorry for all of the grief he caused you," she continued.

"He does?" Her voice was a mere sketch.

"Although he seldom told you, Mrs. Jenson, he

loved you and the children very much. And he was proud of what you were able to do with the butter and egg business."

"He was?" Slowly she sank back into the chair. "He never told me, not any of that."

"Well, he wants you to know now just how he felt. And there is something else, something he wishes me to convey to you most urgently. He wants you to remarry. He says there is a man . . ."

"No! That isn't true! I was always faithful to Hiram!"

"Of course you were! He knows that, Mrs. Jenson! He's always known that. But he believes you can find happiness with . . ." Celia closed her large, deeply set eyes. She paused for a moment, as if waiting for a phantom voice to give her the name. Then slowly she opened her eyes and looked directly into the widow's face. "He wants you to marry someone named John Tudlow."

All color drained from Mrs. Jenson's face. Her lips were white as she placed trembling fingertips against her cheek, as if reassuring herself this was real.

"Mr. Tudlow, he owns a dairy farm over in Brooklyn," she whispered. "He's been most kind to me and the children, buying our eggs for more money than they're worth. He even taught Seth, my oldest boy, how to whittle." She seemed to be speaking to herself as she sank back into the chair. "He's been most kind."

"Well, your husband says you should marry him. He'll take care of you and the children."

Mrs. Jenson remained motionless for a long while, and the color gradually returned to her face. And for the first time that afternoon—perhaps in a very long time—she smiled.

"Hiram's not mad?"

"Of course not. He wants you to be content and for the children to thrive. That is his deepest wish."

"Mr. Tudlow." She smiled, and then with an almost girlish giggle, she leaned toward Celia. "He's very handsome, Mr. Tudlow is. Not in a boisterous way, but he's quiet and kind. And he's taken the temperance pledge, he does not touch spirits of any kind."

"No spirits, Mrs. Jenson? Then you had better not tell him of this visit." The violin had settled back against the chair, and all was quiet in the parlor.

Mrs. Jenson gave Celia a blank look, then, slowly, she smiled again. "I understand! That was a jest—spirits and spirits!"

"Mrs. Jenson." Now Celia could not hide her pleasure. "I do believe you're going to be just fine."

The widow rose to her feet and looked around the room. "This is a lovely parlor, Miss Thomason. A very lovely parlor indeed. I've often wished for curtains on my own windows. Perhaps soon, quite soon." Then she straightened and opened a small drawstring bag tied to her wrist. "I don't have much, but here it is, all of the money that . . ."

"No," Celia lowered her voice. "No, please, Mrs. Jenson. I don't want any of your money."

"Excuse me?"

"Please. Keep it for you and the children. And maybe you could buy yourself a pretty new bonnet, or those curtains."

"But I thought . . ."

"Never mind what you thought." Celia pulled the drawstring tightly and pushed it gently back to the widow. "Just remember that you deserve happiness, and if you find it, well, that will be reward enough for both me and your late husband."

Dumbfounded, Mrs. Jenson allowed Celia to lead her by the elbow through the parlor and into the hallway. It wasn't until Celia opened the front door and the brisk autumn wind splayed across their faces that Mrs. Jenson stopped abruptly. The trees in Washington Square opened their leaves to the breeze, brilliant shades of copper and gold, and some children were playing ring around the rosie, hands clasped as they sang and laughed in a merry circle. A man and woman, their age impossible to determine, stood on the far edge of the square, heads leaning so close they were almost touching, and he took her hand and drew it to his lips.

The widow turned to Celia, her eyes searching. And suddenly she smiled. "Bless you, Miss Thomason." She squeezed her hand, and after a moment's hesitation, she wrapped her thin arm around Celia's shoulder in an awkward embrace. "Bless you." And then, as if embarrassed, she scurried down the front steps and onto the street, never looking back, clutching her black shawl about her shoulders, her head erect.

Celia watched the retreating figure as she crossed the square and wondered if she would ever see Mrs. Jenson again, or if she would move happily to the countryside of Brooklyn and start a new life.

Standing on the steps of the brick town house, Celia Thomason was a striking presence. Her very appearance was vexing to her Aunt Prudence, who had fervently hoped her niece would grow into a fetchingly short, plump woman with curves, preferably in the right places, and curls, preferably blond. Coincidentally, much as Prudence herself had been in her youth.

But Celia, who had lived with her aunt since the age of eight, had instead become a tall, slender young woman with thick reddish brown hair and brown eyes that seemed too large and too knowing for a twenty-six-year-old spinster. Growing up with such unfashionable physical characteristics had been a most unattractive act of defiance on Celia's part. And it was not as if there was nothing to be done about her appearance. To alleviate, if not rectify, the dismal situation, Aunt Pru had tried to convince Celia to sleep in curling rags, to hunch over to minimize her height, and to pad her figure with horsehair or cushions, even India rubber "hips."

"You have such a dainty waist," Aunt Pru would sigh. "But how can one see such a waist without a little help? Think of the padding as signposts, my dear. So that gentlemen can know where to look."

"Oh, Aunt Pru, if they don't know where to look by now, I can't help them. And I refuse to become a human road map."

According to Aunt Pru, as long as she remained unrepentantly tall and lanky, she would remain woefully single. What Aunt Pru did not know was that Celia had become determined to avoid marriage. Her experiences in the past few months had all but confirmed what she had long suspected, that only the rare marriage was a happy one. If no man wished to marry her as she was, well, that suited her quite nicely, thank you.

And in spite of her unfashionable figure, she'd had offers from several men. But most of them were widowers with a houseful of ill-behaved children. Celia knew very well that a wife was a less-expensive proposition than a housekeeper and governess. And once married, a wife could seldom leave, unlike a paid employee. No, Celia found nothing charming in the institution of marriage. Perhaps for other women, but not for Celia.

She stepped back into the house, closing the front door behind her as she rubbed her upper arms. Some good had been done during that last session, she thought to herself. The poor woman might find a measure of joy. That was a satisfying notion to Celia.

In the parlor she pushed back one of the thick drapes, allowing the misty white sunlight to fill that corner of the room. Now that light streamed into the room, the air of gloom lifted, making the parlor comfortable and inviting.

There was a rustling in the fireplace. Celia, consumed with the task of tying back the other side of the curtain, did not bother to glance over her shoulder as a large, booted foot emerged from the fireplace. There it dangled for a few moments, twisting at the ankle, followed by dust and grime and another large foot to match the first.

"Miss Thomason," came a muffled male voice, hollow as if from a great distance. "Can you lend a hand?"

She finished the tie with a satisfied pat and turned to the fireplace. "Certainly, Patrick." The sight was absurd, two feet hanging toes-outward from the chimney, and for a moment she grinned as the feet made a vague pedaling motion. Then with sure hands she pulled on both boots, and in an instant Patrick Higgens slid into the parlor.

"Sorry, Miss." He brushed the chimney dust from his shoulders. "So, did she enjoy today's show?"

Celia cringed at the words. "Yes, well."

A panel behind the chair with the violin popped

open. Aunt Prudence, her head a mass of steel gray ringlets, smiled. "What did we get, my dear? That one was worth five dollars."

"Ah, more than that! Ten, at the very least." Patrick, a sturdy young man with a face full of freckles, crossed his arms. "That was the right song, wasn't it, Miss Thomason?"

"Yes, it was the right song, Patrick. At least Mrs. Jenson thought so, and that is all that matters. Thank you."

"I was a bit concerned, Miss. You see, my sources told me that was the late Hiram Jenson's favorite tune, but they had only heard him with his fancy lady. It's called 'Slap the . . .' " His face reddened and he halted midsentence. Clearing his throat with a rolled fist at his mouth, he looked at both women and continued. "Whist, I thought. What if she's never heard the song, his wife? But she had heard it. Perhaps not the words, mind you, but the tune seemed to go well enough."

"Patrick, you were brilliant!" Aunt Pru patted the lad's shoulder. "And the bit about the dairy farmer, well. It was fortune itself that guided you to the corner that day, when the dairy farmer discussed marriage to the Widow Jenson with his friend. Nothing short of brilliant!"

Both Patrick and Aunt Pru beamed at each other for a few moments, savoring the triumph, as if waiting for a round of applause. They almost missed Celia's demure exit.

"Celia?" Aunt Pru called. "How much did we make on this one?"

"Well," she began, not looking at the pair as they stood together.

"How much?" Aunt Pru repeated.

Celia did not answer.

"She's done it again, Mrs. Cooper." Patrick whistled through his teeth. "She's done it again."

"Celia." Aunt Pru spoke the name as an accusation.

Celia shrugged. "She's a poor widow with children." Unable to look them in the eyes, she began to rearrange the crystal brandy decanter on a side table and brush imaginary dust from the lip of a sparkling glass. "They live near the Five Points, on the very edge of that terrible place, with the ruffian gangs and the pigs running wild."

There was a silence from the other two, and Celia realized she had failed to make an impact. "She's a poor widow with children," she repeated.

"She won't be a poor widow for long, now that she has her sights set on that Brooklyn dairy farmer. Now that we supplied her with a gentle push. That alone should be worth something." Aunt Pru placed her hands on ample hips upholstered in black damask. "Honestly, Celia, what are you thinking? This is the fifth time this week you have refused to accept fees from our clients."

Patrick shook his head. "And to think of all that work, wasted. And me in that cold dark chimney with the bellows, making the vase dance a jig."

"But it wasn't wasted, don't you see? This poor woman has slaved her entire life. Now her mind is at ease, and she'll find contentment. The children will be cared for, children who have known nothing but hunger and fear. She never would have made herself happy without some encouragement. Isn't that payment enough?"

The expressions on Patrick and Aunt Pru's faces

made it clear that no, indeed, that was not payment enough. Patrick shook his head once more and left the room, mumbling something in Gaelic. Aunt Pru waited until he was gone before facing her niece.

"We cannot live on air, my dear," she said to her niece. "When your uncle was alive, rest his soul, we had the luxury of not having to think about where our next meal came from. But, Celia, all of that has changed. While your uncle has provided for us quite handsomely, we must add to that sum in order to maintain the house."

Celia nodded, holding a passive expression as her aunt continued her monologue about responsibility and their future. She had perfected her speech over the past few months, so now it was a smoothly pat recitation punctuated by occasional hand-wringing and one or two sad tilts of her head.

Part of Celia listened with detached wonder. Poor Aunt Prudence had no idea how dire their circumstances really were. Yes, Uncle James, the sweetest and kindest of men, had indeed shielded them from all matters of finance. He kept them ignorant of financial reality. As they nursed him through his long, final illness, he had grasped her hand when they were alone and tried to speak, but his voice would not come. Instead of words, his efforts had formed wheezes and coughs.

But soon enough she learned what he had been trying to say. The information had been delivered not from gentle Uncle James, but from the three rough-looking men who appeared on the doorstep the very day of his funeral.

Their message had been quite simple. Uncle James had borrowed money—a lot of money—during the last years of his life. According to the toughest-looking of the three filthy brutes on the doorstep, a beefy man with a nose like an onion bulb covered with splotches and dots, Uncle James had gambled heavily on anything and everything, from international matters (he bet England would become the next state) to more local concerns (that Jeb Hankins's rooster could learn to talk).

Unfortunately, Uncle James was not a very astute speculator, and soon he was depending on these suspicious characters to lend him enough to keep up the household, to pay the servants, and above all, to keep his beloved Prudence from knowing the truth.

The end result was that if the estate—meaning Aunt Pru and Celia herself—did not repay his various loans in full by the fifteenth of December, they would all be destitute. The onion-nosed man had even waved the deed to the house under her chin for effect.

They had searched for that deed before her uncle had died. Now she knew why it was not to be found.

As much of a shock as that information had been to Celia, who kept Aunt Pru from hearing the men, the real surprise came when they informed her how much was owed.

By mid-December, they had to repay twenty-one thousand dollars. Cash. The vile man in the center showed her a contract, signed in the undeniable spidery hand of Uncle James. He had agreed to the sum, and to the fifty percent per annum interest.

It was now November, and Celia had less than a month to find twenty-one thousand dollars.

Unless Celia could find a way to repay the sum, everyone in the household—from the servants and their families to Celia and Aunt Prudence—would be destitute. She couldn't even attempt to sell some of the more valuable items in the house, for they were all accounted for in the contract he had signed.

Dear, sweet Uncle James, with his wispy white hair and his gentle blue eyes, always fastidious in his white starched stock and old-fashioned jacket, had bartered away their future on the off-chance that a rooster could talk.

From the moment Celia had heard the truth, she had decided two things. One, no matter what, she must do her very best to prevent Aunt Pru from knowing the truth about her husband. In her grief, the one fact that had been a constant source of comfort to her aunt had been the untarnished memory of James Cooper. Celia would not take that away from Aunt Pru. Not ever.

The second thing Celia had decided was that she would do everything possible to come up with the money. Perhaps she could do it, and the servants would never know, and Aunt Pru could rest easy in the notion that Uncle James had provided well for them before his death.

Beyond reaching the goal of twenty-one thousand dollars, Celia had no thoughts.

It hadn't seemed such an impossible task to accomplish six months earlier, when Uncle James first passed away. Initially she had been stunned—he had been a father to her since her own parents' death almost twenty years before. Although he had been ill for several years, the notion of Uncle James's being absent was quite overwhelming. Then she shook herself out of her sorrow and set about doing anything she could to make money, from taking in sewing to writing articles for the

New York Daily Dispatch under the name of Cecil Thomason. She even baked pies to sell, much to Aunt Pru's amusement.

The grand irony was that she was successful at everything she attempted—except making enough money to pay off the men. Her sewing was praised, her articles printed in full, and her pies became the mainstay at several fashionable levees. She was even informed that Mayor Caleb Woodhull had admired her apple pie served at a tea honoring heroes of the Mexican War.

But her total profits, the five cents here, the twenty cents there, an occasional few dollars, were all absorbed by the household like drops of water in an ocean. It meant nothing, did nothing to help.

Then, just when she was at her wit's end, something miraculous happened.

Aunt Prudence was entertaining some of her friends, mostly widows, all sitting primly with their tepid tea and lukewarm conversation. Celia stepped into the parlor, her hands still slick from working the crust on her latest batch of pies, and offered the women fresh cups of tea.

As usual, Mrs. Wheelen was discussing her favorite topic—illness and death.

"And I warned him," she stated in a hushed voice, as if the subject of her discussion was but a few yards away. "I told him he had something of the egg eye about him."

"The egg eye?" Celia repeated, unable to keep the mirth from her voice.

"Yes indeed. It is more of a hard-boiled egg eye, you see, all popped out and yellow." Mrs. Wheelen savored her words like a chef tasting the most sublime of delicacies.

"Heavens!" Mrs. Jarvis cried, her hand with its fingerless lace gloves covering her mouth. "How very unpleasant!"

"Unpleasant it may be." Mrs. Wheelen enjoyed a theatrical sip of her tea, pinkie finger waving in barely harnessed glee, before handing the empty cup to Celia. "The point is, within two days he was dead."

Celia reached for the cup, and the instant she touched it, it flew across the room.

There was a collective gasp.

"That was him!" Mrs. Wheelen's own eyes grew wide. "That was Old Ben! He said just before he expired that he would come back to see me!"

"The blacksmith?" Aunt Pru had winked at Celia. "Now why on earth would Old Ben the blacksmith come all this way just to visit you, Mrs. Wheelen?"

"But it was him! Haven't you heard about the goings-on with those Fox sisters upstate?"

Of course they had all heard. Everyone knew about Margaret and Katie Fox, young girls who were able to summon spirits at will. Those who attended their sessions swore the otherworldly tappings were genuine, that remarkable messages were being sent in code to the sisters, and from the sisters to the grieving survivors of those who has passed from this earth.

In this age of spectacular discoveries, from Mr. Morse and his telegraph machine to the harnessing of electricity, this seemed to be the most amazing feat of all. At last, death would no longer mean an end to joy. Finally man—or, rather, two farm girls—had conquered eternity itself.

Their fame had spread like a thunderbolt in the past year, and numbered amongst their ardent supporters

were some of the greatest thinkers of the day, including
Frederick Douglass and Elizabeth Cady Stanton. No
one was immune to the universal lure of communicating with the dead. No one could fail to be moved by the
promise of immortal love.

Now that interest had been piqued, and the Fox
sisters were unable to see everyone who longed for
their services, others began to rouse spirits, for a hefty
fee. There were posters pasted on every wooden fence
and free brick wall, advertisements in most every publication, offering the services of the newly named
spiritualists.

Celia reached over to Mrs. Timmons's cup, and that,
too, leapt from her hand. She was about to apologize—
clearly, the shortening left on her hand from the just-
finished piecrust had caused the cups to fall.

But the words never left her lips. Or perhaps they
had—it was impossible to tell. There had been a veritable cacophony of noise—shrill, excited. The subdued
parlor of the late James Cooper became a torrid world
of exclamation points and shouts.

Mrs. Timmons began to sob, stating that she would
pay ten dollars—anything—to hear one last word from
her dear George. Another voice, it had been impossible
to locate the source in the hectic din, was crying out to
a lost child.

Several servants entered, one with a dripping wood
bucket of water—assuming that the only event that
could cause such a commotion would be a swiftly
moving fire. But Celia had led the women from the
parlor in a frenzy, bonnets still on the chairs, tables
overturned, bits of cake and dainties crushed into the
carpet.

The three servants scratched their heads, righted the furniture, and removed the broken cups and saucers before they left.

Celia stood, dumbfounded, in the empty parlor with her aunt, teapot still in her hand.

Aunt Prudence seemed equally dumbfounded, until she asked a simple, fateful question.

"Dearest." She turned slowly to Celia. "Exactly how much did Mrs. Timmons say she would pay to speak to her late husband?"

Thus Celia Thomason, noted spiritualist, came into existence.

Finally, Aunt Prudence finished her sermon on responsibility and the virtues of hard work and perseverance. Celia glanced over her aunt's shoulder, where the daguerreotype of Uncle James was propped in its ornate gold frame. How much had that vanity cost? At the time he had complained about sitting still for so long during the exposure, of the vile chemical smells in Matthew Brady's studio on Broadway and Fulton Street. And even then he had been borrowing money from those men hand over fist, money that would go to pay the photographer at fifty percent interest. Even then he had set into motion the means of their ruin. Sweet, kind, oblivious Uncle James.

Yes, they had been successful with the spiritualist business, presenting Celia as the genuine article. It had started gradually, first with Mrs. Timmons. Word spread throughout the area, and soon people were coming from all over to seek the aid of Celia Thomason, and they always paid cash for the privilege. Not that she ever asked for it. The grateful customers simply expected to reimburse the fetching Celia and her thoroughly respectable aunt for their ministrations.

But Celia was far from comfortable with the business. There was an unmistakable air of deceit whenever someone would hand her the money, and she always wanted to push it back. Until that moment in the session, she could almost justify their unintentional trade, for she saw the relief in people's eyes, the tension leave their body as they heard their loved ones who had passed over were happy and content and returning their love threefold. The séances offered a chance to say a final good-bye, to utter words that were unspoken, to right petty or enormous wrongs.

Aunt Prudence went so far as to call their sessions "grief-reducers." She even maintained that most of their customers knew the tricks. Deep down they realized the sessions were fraudulent, but their overwhelming desire to believe kept them coming. Again and again individuals of the highest social rank as well as the more humble would return to Celia with further questions, more words they wished to share with those gone from this world.

Sometimes Celia wondered if she could really summon spirits. With the ardent thanks of comforted clients still ringing in her ears, she sometimes lay in her own bed, hoping to rouse her parents, dead now these twenty years. Maybe she could do it, she would whisper, closing her eyes and clutching a blanket in her fists. Please, please come to me, she would pray. Please, Mother, please, Father. I miss you. I cannot recall your features. Please come to me.

Then she would open her eyes and see nothing except the bedroom, if there was a full moon to illuminate. If not, she would see nothing but dark shadows that she could wish to be almost anything she pleased. Surely if she had any genuine talent, she could have seen her parents, or received one last message from beyond.

No, she was a fraud. There was nothing magic about her, no special talents sent from above or below or sideways or anyplace else for that matter. It was Celia and the clients in a darkened parlor, and from there it was nothing but trickery mingled with hopes.

And their trickery had required help. The task of transforming a pleasant room into a veritable theater of the dead took ingenuity and a lot of hard work. They soon learned that their own household staff could assist during the sessions.

The servants had thoroughly enjoyed the change of pace, especially Patrick, who proved to be surprisingly creative in devising an intricate pulley system to manipulate objects such as musical instruments, bric-a-brac, and occasionally one of the more spry maids swathed in yards of gauzy, ghostly white cloth. One maid, Ginny, made an especially convincing child due to her tiny stature, while Hannah excelled at women of every age and young men.

Patrick prided himself in the knowledge that from behind hidden panels or within the chimney he could make virtually anything fly with the finesse and elegance of a master puppeteer. It was a matter of honor, and the more challenging the assignment—the infant twins, for example—the more impressive his results.

Aunt Prudence had experimented with lanterns and slides, flickering images to project on walls or the ceiling. But those methods failed when the paper slides caught on fire, leaving one man to assume his gentle, God-fearing mother had been consumed by the flames of Hades. It took all of Celia's considerable diplomatic skills to coax him back to the table and believe that his elderly mother was, in fact, with the angels in heaven enjoying a festive bonfire.

The sleight of hand only took them so far, however. She needed more substantial information once the flash and brilliance of Patrick's show faded. For it was later, when the customers thought over what had happened, that they needed solid information upon which to cling. They craved tidbits to prove that what had happened was real, to mull over in the darkness of their own rooms and grant comfort in the cold of the night.

So it was Celia herself who orchestrated what she began to consider the most duplicitous deception of all—the Green Book. It started as a ledger of names and relations of the first clients gathered in the most obvious of ways, from the graveyard. Celia herself had gone to the Timmons plot and jotted down names and dates to help lend authenticity to the first sessions. The first Green Book expanded to include tavern gossip, newspaper clippings, information gathered from family Bibles when Aunt Prudence visited friends. They followed individuals to learn daily habits, gently pumped innkeepers and merchants with such a delicate touch they never realized how much information they were giving, if any. There were six Green Books now, all bursting with such details and personal information that they could become blackmailers if all else failed.

Indeed, all else had failed.

Yes, they had been successful. But because of the cost of their "productions"—the materials needed, the extra wages paid to the servants—Celia had been able to save only four hundred thirty-eight dollars. It was a terrific sum, to be sure. But not nearly enough to cover the twenty-one thousand due in a matter of weeks.

So it made no difference if Mrs. Jenson kept her few dollars. Celia would have to reveal the truth to Aunt Prudence and the servants soon enough. In the meantime, perhaps she could do some good yet, comfort a few more grieving individuals.

For in a matter of days, she would be unable to help anyone, including herself.

Aunt Prudence was waiting for a response to her sermon. Celia took a deep breath. Maybe she should tell her now, give her aunt a chance to reconcile the future, grim as it might be.

Celia was about to speak when there was a powerful rap on the front door.

"Good heavens." Aunt Prudence frowned, turning toward the mantel clock. "Do we have a five-fifteen?"

"No, we do not," Celia replied. "Mrs. Jenson was our last of the day."

She looked at her aunt in the unguarded moment of confusion. When had she grown so old? Her valiant attempts at holding on to youth were no longer effective, the artificial gaiety, the girlish curls of gray. Celia felt her throat tighten at the thought of telling her the truth. How horrible to be the emissary of such news. Celia's future was ruined, to be sure. But her aunt—it would mean the death of her future, but more devastating, the death of her belief in Uncle James.

A second knock was even more forceful, rattling the windows on the side of the door.

"Whoever it is seems to be using a tree trunk instead of the brass knocker." Celia smiled to her aunt. Aunt Prudence smiled back, and Celia touched her hand. "Please, Aunt Pru, you deserve a cup of tea. I'll get the door."

"Yes, well. Thank you, my dear." Aunt Prudence patted her niece's hand in return, and went toward the sitting room for her tea, relief etched on her plump face.

Perhaps they would be saved, Celia thought as she watched her aunt leave the parlor. Perhaps something miraculous would occur. Perhaps they would be saved.

Celia straightened and walked toward the front door, smoothing her hair and wondering who on earth could be on the other side.

She pulled the door open, anxious to avoid another set of ear-splitting explosions. For a moment she just blinked, for before her was perhaps the largest human she had ever beheld. He was facing away from her, and all she saw was an expanse of back covered with a dark green, two-tiered cloak which was flapping in the wind. He was tall as well as broad, and for a moment she just gaped at the sheer size of the man, almost monstrous, almost nonhuman.

Then he turned on his polished heels. "I am here to see Miss Thomason," he announced in a deep voice.

Celia opened her mouth to speak, but for the very first time in her life, no sound issued forth.

For the man on her steps was handsome beyond words. And he was also, just as clearly, full of barely restrained rage.

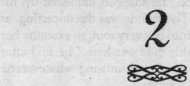

2

Celia wondered what she could have possibly done to evoke this man's anger. She had never seen him before in her life. Indeed, he was not the kind of man one could ever forget.

She bit back a sudden urge to beg forgiveness and promise to never do the deed, whatever it was, again. The man stood not a yard away from her with a stance and manner that all but proclaimed himself in supreme power. His face, though finely featured, even vaguely aristocratic, was set in such an attitude of fury she instinctively took a step backward.

"I repeat. I am here to see Miss Celia Thomason." He spoke with an accent. English, perhaps? His eyes were dark, darker even than her own, and his hair was a tousled mass of gleaming pitch black in the muted light. It was a disturbing impression, blazing eyes and wild hair.

It was an image she would never forget.

He tapped an impatient foot. "Is this not the correct address?"

"It is, sir," she finally spoke.

"So she has a voice," he snapped unpleasantly, his gaze raking over her. The feeling was disconcerting, as if he was able to peer into her very soul, to examine her existence. "It's devilishly cold out here," he said after completing his perusal, after dismissing whatever he found upon his initial scrutiny.

"It is, sir." What on earth had happened to her? She had always been able to think on her feet, to come up with a retort. It seemed he had squelched that ability between his powerful thumb and forefinger and flicked it away as if it were nothing but a tiresome gnat.

"May I inquire if Miss Thomason is presently at home?"

"She is, sir." *Oh, that was clever,* Celia thought. *So well-phrased and pithy. He must think me something of a wit.*

"Is she indisposed or ill?"

"No." Another stinger from Miss Thomason. Really, she thought crazily, she must write these jewels down, lest she forget them.

She took a deep breath. Then it came to her in one lucid, terrible revelation. He was there for the money. She could no longer push the realization to the back of her mind, no longer pretend it wasn't coming. There he was, the physical embodiment of their downfall. He would restate the date the money was due in full, a date already emblazoned on her mind. Or worse, he was there to hasten their end.

Of course that was it, the reason this man stood on the steps thus. Granted, he was far more presentable than the other three. This one had bathed within recent memory, and his clothing was obviously expensive.

Uncle James himself could not have found the slightest fault with the finely spun wool of the cloak or the blinding white linen of his collar.

This man was probably the mastermind behind the entire business, the king of the roughs.

Celia and her aunt's entire future would be forfeited to supply this man with yet more finery.

She stiffened, suddenly strong, for now she had a weapon of her own. Now she hated him.

"Who is it?" Aunt Pru called from the hallway.

No matter what, Aunt Pru must not meet this man. It would destroy her.

"I will see to it," Celia called back, reluctant to even turn her back on the stranger.

"A new vocabulary, I see," he said. "Excellent. Does it extend to 'Please enter'? As I believe I mentioned, it is too brisk for my liking outside."

Of course he wants to enter, Celia thought as she stepped aside. He wants to take inventory, Christmas being but a few weeks away.

Aunt Prudence was still in the hallway, and watched the stranger enter with a growing, silly grin.

"So handsome," she mouthed to Celia, her eyebrows peaked in delight.

Celia nodded and ushered him into the parlor as quickly as possible, closing the door behind her. His back was toward her for a moment, and again she was struck by the sheer size of the man. He could harm her easily, without so much as a crease in his suit or a wrinkle in his perfect brow.

Then he turned, mild surprise on his face. "Are *you* Miss Thomason?"

"I am." She nodded.

"I assumed you were a serving girl because of, well."

"Yes?"

"Because of your hair."

In spite of her new weapon of hatred, she was taken aback, curious about his odd comment.

"My hair?"

"Yes, well. You see, it has come to my attention that well-bred young women such as yourself"—he cocked his head in acknowledgment of her existence—"seem to be taking it upon themselves to redesign the human head."

"Pardon me?"

For a moment his features lightened, and he was no longer fierce but, indeed, rather interesting. Not exactly enticing, but somehow appealing. The effect remained as he continued. "Yes. Well, in London, as well as here, the more fashionable the woman, the more unnatural her hair. I believe you must know what I mean, Miss Thomason. The loops and plaits and twists." He made a vague motion around his own head as if describing a creature from Greek mythology. "One woman of my acquaintance reminded me so much of a dog I had as a youth, with flaps on each side like canine ears, that I kept on wanting to pat her head and slip her a morsel of meat from the table."

Something unexpected happened then. Celia laughed. Immediately she stopped, regaining her composure. This man was the enemy.

"But you, Miss Thomason," he went on, his eyes fixed on her now with uncomfortable intensity. "You dress your hair simply, the way most housemaids do."

She unintentionally reached up to touch her hair, fastened with a comb and some pins, and stopped halfway through the gesture, bringing her hands together in front of her deep blue wool gown once more.

"You have me at a disadvantage, sir. For I know not who you are, although I believe I know your business."

"Of course you do. The spirits have informed you, is that not so?" He pulled off one black leather glove, then another, his appearance again returned to the tightly wound anger of before. "It also surprises me that you answer your own door. Do you not employ servants for such tasks?"

"Yes. But I like to answer the door."

"During business hours?"

"Yes. If you will, during business hours."

"Now please clarify for me, I am embarrassingly ignorant of your profession and your"—he raised an eyebrow—"co-workers, if you will. Do the dead keep the usual hours? I was led to believe they preferred to do business at night, when their chains and ghostly moans can cause the most disturbance. Am I wrong?"

Celia crossed her arms and merely glared at him.

"So, you refuse to answer me, Miss Thomason?"

"No. I refuse to be mocked by you."

"Am I mocking you?"

Again she did not answer. For long moments they stood staring at each other.

He was, indeed, a wonderfully formed man. Had he not been so unpleasant . . .

"It was not my intention to mock you," he said at last. "But I am curious. Tell me what you know of me, what the spirits have conveyed to you in their mysterious ways."

At first she wished to ask him to leave. How dare he

quiz her, insult her? But she held on to her temper. This was not a man to cross, no matter how vile he was. If she had any chance of keeping some small portion of control over the ebb of the conversation, she would have to play along with his games of power.

So she smiled, and he seemed perplexed by her change of expression. She quickly began to speak, not wishing to let this brief moment of his awkwardness pass. "You have just arrived here from London, although you are not from there. You were educated at Oxford, yet you hail originally from Ireland. Outside of Dublin, I would imagine."

As she peered at him a thought came to her. There was something in his eyes besides the anger and the arrogance that made them flicker so darkly. It was something she had seen repeatedly of late.

He was grieving.

Her trade had also taught her how to read simple signs, obvious clues no matter who the person attempted to be. She had learned to read the truth. He was too old to be devastated by the loss of his parents, and at once she dismissed the thought of the loss of a child. This was not a man who had ever been married, much less a father.

A friend? No. The loss was something deeper, more compelling.

Combining it with her other intuitions, she came to her conclusion. "I am sorry, sir," she said softly. Hateful as the man was, she was unable to keep genuine compassion from her voice.

"You are sorry?"

"Yes." She reached for him, then halted. "I am very sorry for the loss of your sister."

The man's mouth opened, his eyes wide and befuddled, almost comical, and she continued. "And the reason you are here concerns the money. We both know the sum."

He seemed incapable of speech, and part of her realized this must be a very rare occasion indeed.

"What is the sum?" he said, his voice still full of command.

"The twenty-one thousand dollars."

He remained motionless and unblinking. The only outward sign that he was the least bit surprised was a telltale working of his square jaw, barely perceivable.

"Hmm." He tilted his head once. "Most interesting." Taking a deep breath, he looked around the parlor, seeing it for the first time. "Is that brandy?"

"It is, sir."

"May I?"

His question surprised her. Didn't they just clarify that he now owned everything in the house, including, of course, the brandy?

In two strides he was by the decanter, pouring out a measure of the liquor. He drank it in one single motion, then poured himself another before facing her.

"I told you I was in London," he said with a very slight smile, one eyebrow cocked. "When we discussed ladies' hair fashions, I mentioned London."

"Indeed you did," she confirmed.

"That explains one of your statements. Nothing mysterious, just a simple ability to remember what was said. Yet how did you . . ." he began. "You're good. You are very, very good." Then he stopped. "But you were wrong about the money."

"Was I?" she replied warily.

"Yes." He drank half of the glass. "You were off by half."

Celia kept her face relaxed as her mind raced. What game was he playing? Was he doubling the sum she owed? The mere thought of owing forty-two thousand dollars made her queasy.

Swallowing the rest of the brandy, he reached for the decanter, then stopped, placing the empty glass down on the table with such force she thought it would shatter, but it did not. "I do not intend to pay you twenty-one thousand dollars."

Celia felt her heart stop, then begin to pound with such ferocity she could barely breathe. Her corset was too tight. Way too tight. Why was it so tight?

"But you said yourself I was good, very good." Her voice was silky and even, almost fooling herself. What was she getting into? Why pay her? What was he up to? He must not be one of the thugs collecting the money.

"You are good, Miss Thomason." He seemed to be gaining strength just as hers was weakening. "But I refuse to be a victim of extortion."

At that her knees almost buckled. He, the victim?

There was another long pause as he stared unblinkingly at her, and as bits and pieces of her life played in her mind. For surely he would kill her now, at this moment.

"How much, then?" he said at last.

Celia smiled at the thought of what she was about to say. It was so absurd, the sum, she almost laughed.

But what if this absurd misunderstanding with a large man could save her, save all of them?

There was nothing left to do. She would name the sum now, and risk damnation later.

"Twenty-five thousand dollars," she said coolly.

He did not miss a beat. "Fifteen."

"Twenty-five," she insisted, as if in a dream.

"Twenty, and not a penny more."

This was insane, whatever he wished her to do could not possibly be worth twenty-five thousand, or twenty for that matter. And with twenty thousand, she could almost pay off the men.

Almost. That was the key word. Almost.

With extra money they could start a new life, stop this existence of fraud. They could buy a farm, or start a dress shop, or even move to someplace where they were not known as spiritualists.

A fresh start, a new beginning.

She would stick to her price. "Twenty-five."

"Very well," he said at last.

Oh my God, she thought to herself. *Oh my . . .*

Then he reached into his cloak. This was it. He was going to kill her. Did he have a knife? A rope? She was so weak, trembling, she could do no more to defend herself than a kitten.

Folding her hands into an attitude of prayer, she began to mumble softly. "Oh, Lord, please forgive me for all of my sins."

"I have some papers for you to sign," he said as he pulled out a large document. Then he glanced at her quizzically. "Are you quite well, Miss Thomason?"

Her lips stopped moving, and slowly she let her hands fall to her waist. "Why, yes, of course."

His eyes narrowed as he again raked her over with his gaze. "Very well. Have you a pen?"

"Why, yes, of course." She all but leapt to the drawer with the ink bottle and pens and shaker, then took her place at his side.

Now, at last, she was to find out what this man was about and what was required of her.

"Can you read, Miss Thomason?"

"Why, yes, of course!" she replied indignantly.

"Are we to be limited to the same few words again?"

"Of course not."

He handed her the document, and she began to read, her eyes scanning the words, a vague frown forming on her face.

She could feel him watching her, his heated stare, and then she reread a sentence. Shaking her head, she read it again.

"You wish me to sign a document stating that I am a fraud?"

"Yes. Otherwise, I have no way of making sure you perform your duties. With this as collateral, I can be reasonably assured that you will get the job done."

"I see." She continued to stare at the document, not really seeing it, too burdened by the thoughts of what she was doing. She had to know. No matter what, she could not go further without hearing, from his own lips, what would be required of her.

She would not murder anyone. Nor would she assist in a murder. That was the only thing she could imagine to be worth twenty-five thousand dollars.

"You still have me at a disadvantage, sir. Please tell me who you are, and exactly what you wish of me."

"Haven't the spirits clued you in yet?" It was impossible to anticipate this man.

"Perhaps they have, sir. I am just asking for a second opinion."

And then he grinned. She never thought the sight of a handsome man smiling at her could be so unsettling, but it was. It didn't lighten his face, just made him appear more intense. This was not a pleasant smile.

"It's nothing, really. Nothing out of your usual realm, I'm sure."

"Please humor me and explain."

"Very well. I am Brendan O'Neal, lately of those places you mentioned earlier. And, yes, my sister recently died, here in New York. Her name was Amanda Stevens. Have you heard of her?"

"No. Is there any reason I should?"

"Well, she never did things in half measures. She was killed in an explosion. It seems the gas lighting in her new bridal home was not properly installed."

Suddenly Celia remembered. "Amanda Stevens? Yes. How awful, I do recall hearing about the tragedy. It is the very reason my aunt refuses to have the house fitted with gas. Well, that and the expense. Oh, Mr. O'Neal, please accept my condolences and . . ."

"Never mind that," he snapped. "I do not require your sympathy. What I do require is for you to convince my brother-in-law that you are genuine, and that you can bring my sister back from the grave. His name is Garrick. Garrick Stevens, and he doesn't believe in this humbug any more than I do. That is the challenge. You must make him believe you are real, that Amanda is real."

"Then what am I to do?" There must be more. There had to be more. No simple séance for twenty-five thousand dollars.

"Once you have accomplished the first deed, I will explain the rest. Is that clear enough for you?"

"Yes." She swallowed. "Yes it is."

He picked up the pen, dipped it into the ink, and

signed his name with a flourish. Dipping it once more, he handed the pen to Celia. She hesitated for an instant, realizing there was no going back once her name was on the paper. She was either starting them all onto the path of a glorious new life, or, she feared in the pit of her stomach, signing her own death warrant.

"There, there, Miss Thomason. It wasn't as bad as all that, now was it?"

Shaking sand over the damp ink, he blew on it once. Satisfied, he then folded the paper and placed it back into his cloak. "Oh, before I forget," he began, reaching into another pocket and withdrawing a leather package. "Here is five thousand dollars. I shall send Garrick round tomorrow afternoon, perhaps I will be with him. I need not tell you not to recognize me."

"Of course not." He handed her the package, and she resisted the urge to open it up and count it right there, fingering the thickness of the packet, the weight of the bills within.

Clearly he saw her movements and expression, for one of distaste covered his face. "My, aren't you a greedy little thing."

Abashed, somehow ashamed, she straightened.

"Rest assured, I am good for the rest of it, if you perform what is required."

"I know, sir," she whispered as he reached for his gloves.

"Will you do me the honor of showing me to the door?"

"Of course." Why did she feel so vile, so disgusting?

Opening the parlor door, she heard the scurrying of feet. Aunt Pru and the servants had been trying to listen, but Celia knew they could not have heard a word.

The parlor was the single room where one could not be heard, unless it was desired.

"It is a pleasure doing business with you, Miss Thomason." He extended his hand, flashing very white teeth—too white.

She had no choice but to grasp his hand in return. Even covered by the soft leather gloves, there was no mistaking the strength of his grip, the heat of his hand. Never before had a handshake felt so much like a threat.

All she could do was nod. He began to leave out of the front door, then stopped and leaned very close to her ear.

"Remember this. You are not so smart as you think, Miss Thomason."

Pulling back, she could feel his breath on her face, see once again that strange glint in his dark eyes. It was like being head-to-head with a feral beast.

"I . . . please." She tried to back away, but he gripped her hand.

"My dear Miss Thomason, I arrived here fully prepared to pay you fifty thousand dollars for your unique services, more if you wished. So you see, you bargained me down. For all of your parlor tricks, you are not so very bright at all."

And then he was gone.

Celia closed the door behind her, flicking the brass lock into place.

"My, wasn't he a handsome gentleman?" Aunt Prudence began, bustling close to her niece. "What did he want? I do hope we will see him again. Did you see the cut of his clothes? The very finest, I would say. Of first rank and . . ."

But she couldn't bear to hear any more. "I'm sorry, Aunt Pru. I have a headache. Please . . ."

Then she ran up the stairs and into her room, where she shoved the leather packet under her mattress, splashed her face with cold water from the basin, and for the first time in a very long while, she cried.

3

Celia Thomason slipped her hand between the wooden bed frame and the cotton mattress ticking. A scent of oat straw wafted up, the stuffing in the mattress, as she found the tip of the leather packet.

It was late afternoon, and still she had not counted the money. She had slept on the packet all night, walked past it as she dressed that morning, yet still she had not found time to examine the contents.

Until now.

All was set for Mr. O'Neal and his brother-in-law's visit. She had informed Aunt Prudence not to reveal that Mr. O'Neal had visited the previous evening. Patrick was already in the chimney, bellows in hand, ready to make a vase fly or the violin play a ghostly tune.

They had found out a little about the late Amanda Stevens through newspaper clippings—they had begun saving papers weeks before her death for use in their business. The details had been sketchy, she had died in a gas explosion that had been ruled accidental. She had been young, one and twenty by most accounts. And of course she had been Irish. That was all they needed to know for the initial meeting with Mr. Stevens.

And there would be Mr. O'Neal there to lend his sinister presence. Even without the strings and pulleys and the darkened room, it promised to be an unpleasant, unnatural afternoon.

The wallet felt warm and comforting, and she opened it slowly, savoring the scent of leather and the wonderful inky fragrance of fresh, crisp bills.

Maybe Mr. O'Neal was right. She *was* greedy.

But this wasn't just for her. It was for everyone in the household. She fingered the money, the bills were thick and beautifully printed and . . .

British. He had paid her in British currency.

What good was that to Celia and her aunt? Of course she could exchange the notes for American money, but that would bring them unwanted attention.

How could he have been so inconsiderate as to give her English currency?

Suddenly the oval bedroom doorknob rattled. "Celia!"

"Aunt Pru!" Celia gasped, fumbling with the wallet as she stashed it back under the mattress and replaced the coverlet.

"Is the door stuck? I can't open it . . ."

"Just a minute," she called, gently removing the chair she had propped against the knob. Uncle James had not believed in locks inside of a house, except for in his cluttered lair of an office upstairs, where it was so freezing in the winter and so blazing hot in the summer a lock was not needed to keep anyone out. Due to the lack of locks, she had learned at an early age how to wedge a chair against a door.

With one glance backward to make sure all was in place, Celia opened the door. "Yes, Aunt Pru?"

"The gentlemen are downstairs. I've been calling you, why on earth didn't you answer?"

"I was napping."

"You? Napping at midday?"

"Yes, Aunt Pru. I was tired."

The older woman gave Celia a skeptical frown, then reached up and straightened the lace on her collar. "Very well. Go on, dear. We're all ready."

Celia swept past her aunt, shaking out the skirt of her dark green dress. The household was still in half mourning because of Uncle James, and she would wear dark colors for the next few months.

She descended the staircase as gracefully as possible, wondering what the widowed groom would be like, if he would be as unpleasant as Mr. O'Neal. Perhaps he would be even worse.

The very thought almost made her slip down the last step.

Of course, the hateful Mr. O'Neal saw her stumble, a brief smirk on his face.

She entered the parlor, softly closing the door behind her. "Good afternoon, gentlemen." She inclined her head slightly. "I am Celia Thomason."

Then she saw the other man as he rose from a corner wing chair, and what she saw could not have taken her more by surprise. He was tall and slender, very gentlemanly compared to Mr. O'Neal. Mr. O'Neal began to speak. "Good afternoon, Miss Thomason. Allow me to introduce myself. I am Brendan O'Neal, and this is Garrick Stevens, my brother-in-law."

Since he addressed her first, she was forced to take

his hand. He was not wearing gloves, and his hand was large and disturbing and perfect for handling British currency.

"Mr. O'Neal," she replied briskly.

By then Garrick Stevens was before her, and she had an almost overwhelming urge to embrace him as one would a wounded child.

For that is exactly what he appeared to be, a deeply wounded boy. His hair was a light brown, already growing sparse, which added to the impression of a great expanse of very white forehead. The eyes were light blue, an innocent shade of sky, set into hollow orbs.

It was clear that Garrick Stevens had not eaten well for quite some time. His black clothing, although as beautifully tailored as Mr. O'Neal's, hung loosely on his narrow shoulders. His trousers were too large, his neck seemed to stand out like the handle in a butter churn from inside the round width of his collar.

But it was his face that was most arresting. Pale, almost waxy, with sunken temples, his thin lips colorless. He extended his hand, and it was cool and damp. Unlike Mr. O'Neal's grip, his was weak and gentle and she could feel every bone as if he had been a lifeless sparrow.

"Miss Thomason. It is indeed a pleasure to meet you." His voice was surprisingly deep, very clearly aristocratic, with none of the coarseness of Mr. O'Neal's intonations.

"Mr. Stevens." She smiled. Then she let go of his hand and straightened. "Now, gentlemen, what can I do to help you?"

"Well, Miss Thomason," O'Neal began.

With surprising agility and speed, Mr. Stevens

reached out and halted his brother-in-law. "No, Brendan. Let us see if she can determine what brings us here this afternoon."

"Am I to be tested, then?" She tried to sound imperious, but when she looked at Mr. Stevens, it was impossible.

"Not at all." He smiled tightly. "It's just that we wish"—he glanced at O'Neal, then looked down at the carpet before continuing. "What I mean to say, Miss Thomason, is that I have no hopes of ever being able to see . . ."

Then he halted, and she completed his thought. "Your wife again?"

"Indeed. I . . ." Stopping, he blinked once. "How did you know it is my wife I wish to speak to?"

Before she could answer, Mr. O'Neal rammed into the conversation with all the charm of a runaway carriage. "Come, come, Garrick." He smiled without humor. "That is the most obvious choice. I introduced you as my brother-in-law. Although I may not be the finest example of the male species at present, you, my friend, are something of a ruin."

Mr. Stevens glanced at O'Neal, and then, surprisingly, he smiled. It was a sweet, guileless expression, and Celia suddenly liked the young Mr. Stevens very much indeed.

But why was Mr. O'Neal so intent on proving her a fraud in front of his brother-in-law? It seemed to defeat the very purpose of their agreement of the previous night.

"You are *not* a ruin, Mr. Stevens. You are a young man whose wife, Amanda, was killed tragically, and you are behaving precisely as one would expect."

"How did you know her name!" Mr. Stevens cried.

O'Neal answered, "It would not have been difficult. It was in all of the papers when it occurred, along with your name, no doubt. It was quite a sensational story, I would imagine. And by now the charming Miss Thomason has concluded that you are English, and I am Irish. Our accents proclaim us as such. Just as our clothing proclaims us to be well off. And if she is a truly remarkable study, if she is very good, she has already surmised that trade brings us to the New World, and that our trade is shipping."

Now *that* was a bit of information Celia did not happen to possess.

"Let us away." O'Neal began to walk toward the door.

"Wait!" Celia almost grabbed his forearm, then stopped short as he gave her a look of such disdain, it could have shriveled an orange. She turned to the other man. "Please. I earnestly believe I can help you, Mr. Stevens."

O'Neal raised a dark eyebrow. "We are sorry to have taken so much of your time, Miss Thomason. I don't believe you can help me make sense of my sister's death, and I doubt you can help my friend here."

Both O'Neal and Celia turned to Mr. Stevens, who seemed at a loss. "I . . . well." He looked at both of them, then returned his gaze downward and mumbled, "It does seem as if it would be rude for us to leave without allowing Miss Thomason a, well . . ."

O'Neal jerked his head to the side, and Celia glanced at him, then realized he had been trying to get her attention. "Go on." His lips soundlessly formed the words.

For a moment she simply stared, confused. Then it all made sense—O'Neal had been playing a role. Of course, the role was that of himself—a mean-spirited, sarcastic beast. But in that brief instant, she had to admit he was right. Mr. Stevens no doubt knew his brother-in-law would not be enlightened enough to believe in the spiritual world.

She swallowed, remembering O'Neal was the man who had her signature on a paper swearing she was a fraud.

"Please, sir," she began, avoiding the amused glint in his eyes. "I believe I could lend comfort to both you and Mr. Stevens."

"Garrick, I repeat. Let us away."

"Well . . ." Stevens hesitated. "Maybe we should just see."

"Yes, yes!" Celia took both of their arms and led them to the tilt-topped table used for the sessions. "Please, gentlemen, have a chair while I draw the window drapes."

She took their greatcoats and stepped to the parlor door. Eileen, the newest maid, nodded and took the cloaks with a broad grin, peering into the room to catch a glimpse of the two men. Celia reminded herself to have a long conversation with Eileen about her broad grins.

The men stood around the table, Stevens, his face still cast downward, shifting his weight self-consciously as O'Neal watched Celia cross the room and close the curtains. One side caught on the rod, and she yanked once. It remained stuck, and she was thinking wildly, *This has never happened. Curtain stuck. Why now, of all times?*

She felt rather than saw him approach from behind, a looming heat that seemed to come from everywhere. Again, she tugged at the fabric, and then she felt his warm breath on her cheek.

"Amanda loved animals," he whispered. And then he reached over and, towering above her, loosened the curtain with ease.

And then he was gone, back to the table.

Celia took a few moments to compose herself, closing her eyes, pressing her cheek against the soft, heavy fabric. Then she turned her attention to her newest clients.

"Gentlemen," she said bracingly. There. That was her voice, the professional and competent tone she had heard from herself these past few months. She knew what she was doing now. This was her territory, not his.

Not theirs, she amended.

Without looking at the two men, she stepped over to the bowfront counsel where the special thick candles were placed before every session.

"It is rather chilly in this room," murmured Mr. Stevens. "Can we not produce a fire?"

"I'm afraid not, Mr. Stevens. The heat interferes with my ability to communicate with the other side."

Mr. O'Neal cleared his throat with suspicious timing. Celia ignored him as she took a candle and placed it in the center of the table, then slipped some matches from her pocket.

"Allow me." O'Neal took the match and struck it on the bottom of his boot. The wick sputtered before catching, casting all three in a flickering glow.

"Now place your hands like this," she began, her own hands, fingers splayed, resting on the table. They both followed suit. "And bring them forward," she continued, "so that our fingers are touching. Thus we create a circle."

Mr. Stevens did as he was told, glancing at his brother-in-law as if for guidance.

"I ask that you permit me a few moments to allow the spirits to find us."

"Spirits?" Stevens withdrew his hands slightly. "How many are you going to rouse?"

"Come now, Garrick." O'Neal smiled. "I am sure Miss Thomason will not call a crowd, will you, Miss Thomason?"

"Why, no, of course not."

"Brendan, this makes me most uneasy," Stevens began.

"I assure you, sir, there is nothing at all to make you uneasy." Celia used her most calming tone. "There is nothing to fear, nothing at all. It is simply that you are not accustomed to communicating with those who have passed over into the other sphere. This is a natural part of life, a continuance of the cycle."

"Of course it is," affirmed O'Neal. "Why, I'm not the least bit concerned. Indeed, I find this whole process most fascinating."

"You would," snapped Stevens. "You consider yourself a man of science. Nothing disturbs you. I am made of different stuff."

Celia gasped.

"Miss Thomason?" Stevens seemed alarmed. "Are you ill?"

She did not answer at first, but allowed her eyes to flutter half-closed.

"Good God, Brendan! She seems to be having some sort of fit!"

"Oh," she moaned. Then, with a dramatic sigh, her head dropped forward.

"Should we get her something?"

"I wouldn't concern yourself, Garrick," O'Neal said blandly. "This is part of the show. One must get one's money's worth."

Celia then began to roll her head side to side, moaning softly with every swing.

"This makes me most uneasy," Stevens whispered. "This is quite unseemly, is it not?"

"It is indeed."

Then she gasped once more, and looked up, her eyes wide and unblinking.

"Hello!" Stevens blurted.

Celia gave no indication she heard him. "I am your guide," she said in a strange, metallic voice. "We are in luck, the spirits are with us this day. With whom do you wish to speak?"

Stevens turned to O'Neal. "Good Lord, Brendan. Do you think we can really speak to Amanda?"

"I have my doubts," O'Neal replied, watching Celia's glazed expression.

"I say there," Stevens began. "Would you happen to know my wife, Amanda?"

"Amanda. Amanda . . . is Amanda ready to speak?" Celia paused, then nodded, as if responding to an unheard voice. "Very well . . . Yes . . . Yes, I will inform them."

"I suppose they must take a number and wait to be called," muttered O'Neal. Celia ignored him.

Then she turned in Stevens's direction, although her vacant stare gave the impression of sightlessness. "Your wife will speak through me."

"She will?" Stevens turned even more pale. "Amanda, dearest?"

"I can see her now. She is beside you, Mr. Stevens."

"Is she?"

"Yes." Celia smiled just slightly. "She loves animals."

"Did you hear that, Brendan?" Then Stevens turned back to Celia. "Yes, she adored animals."

"The, eh, spirits must have very reliable sources," O'Neal said.

"And music," Celia ventured. "She loved music."

"She did!" Stevens agreed.

"And . . . and she loves music," Celia said in a slightly louder voice.

"Well, yes. She did," Stevens repeated.

The violin on the wing chair rose slightly. Stevens looked over his shoulder when he heard the sound of the bow against the strings. "Good Lord," he said softly.

The violin continued to rise, the bow scratching out an uncertain tune. "Can't make out the song." O'Neal shrugged.

"Nor can I. But still," Stevens ventured. "It's just rather surprising."

Celia maintained her blank expression. "The spirits wish to know why should it be surprising that Amanda loved music?"

"It is just that, well. She did not enjoy the sound of a violin."

"She did not?"

"No. In fact, she abhorred the violin."

"Abhorred the violin?" Celia blinked just once before continuing in the flat mechanical voice. "Perhaps you did not understand her meaning. Perhaps she only disliked certain songs. The spirits wish to know how could anyone abhor the violin? It's the very sound of merriment and of celebration and dance. Even the spirits dance to a violin well played."

"That's just it." O'Neal kept watching the violin, his eyes traveling to the ceiling, obviously looking for wires. "My sister was lame in her left leg. She was unable to dance."

The violin hovered precariously, the bow swinging free in the air, clinking against the body of the instrument before returning to the chair. The violin followed, skipping against the arm of the chair, hollow echoes of the chords still hanging in the air.

"That is the beauty of the spirit world. All souls are whole and free of pain," Celia intoned. "The blind can see and the lame can dance."

Just then the vase on the mantelpiece began to rock back and forth. Stevens stiffened. "Brendan, look! Something is happening. Amanda, what are you trying to say?"

The two men continued to watch the vase as Celia stared blankly. O'Neal's expression remained passive, as Garrick's shifted to stunned amazement.

"She says . . ." Celia began. "She has a message."

"For me?" Stevens cried.

"For both of you. The message is . . . English currency is of no use here."

Both men were silent for a few moments, and Stevens spoke first. "I appologize. I have no idea what she means. Do you, Brendan?"

"I am not sure. Could you please clarify?"

"Miss Thomason is merely the vessel of the spirits. And they wish you to understand that English currency is of no use in New York."

"I believe I understand," Stevens said in soft wonder. "Amanda is trying to tell us that we must adapt to the ways of the Americans here. We are no longer in London, Brendan. Thus, all of our preconceived notions, our prejudices and British beliefs, are useless in this new world." His voice picked up speed and ardor as his face flushed. "By God, this is something Amanda would have said, is it not?"

"Absolutely, Garrick. I would recognize those words anywhere."

"Is there another message? Please! Let me know, dearest Amanda!"

"The spirits must leave now, but will return. Will return. Will return," her voice faded out. Then Celia's head fell forward, bobbed several times before she looked back at the men, clear-eyed. "Gentlemen. What transpired?"

"I wish I knew," O'Neal said, glancing at his brother-in-law. "Garrick, what do you think?"

"It was miraculous! I spoke to my dear Amanda, did I not, Brendan?"

"That must have been a comfort." Celia smiled slightly, and patted Stevens's hand.

"It was!" he cried, his face beaming.

Celia swallowed. There was something so touchingly honest about this man. How tragic that he suffered such a loss.

Of course, the brother suffered a loss, too. But that was different.

"So, friend, do you wish to . . ." O'Neal began. But a soft noise cut him off, muffled, distant. In the corner of the parlor, covered with a heavy damask cloth, was an old harp Aunt Pru used to play as a young woman. It was out of tune and had been there for decades, all but forgotten.

There was no outward indication the harp was being plucked other than the gentle sounds.

"Brendan, do you hear that?"

"Yes," he said uncomfortably. He cleared his throat, and gave a peculiar look at Celia. One of his hands was clenched in a fist atop the table.

"That was her song." Stevens continued staring at the concealed harp. "Since she couldn't dance, she played the harp."

Celia stood up abruptly and went to the windows, throwing open the drapes and letting the outside light brighten the room. She then lit several oil lamps, although they were not needed with the curtains open, and turned back to the men.

"Excuse me, gentlemen. On occasion when I contact the spirits, I am left fatigued, as I am now. Although I would love to prolong this visit . . ."

"Of course, Miss Thomason. Please forgive us—we have trespassed on your time and good nature too long as it is." Stevens rose to his feet, then looked at O'Neal, who with an ungracious shrug also stood.

"So, Garrick, what think you of Miss Thomason?" O'Neal asked.

"I . . . well. I think you are most gifted and extraordinary, Miss Thomason. And I would be most honored if we could arrange another visit. I need to think, but there is so much I need to ask of Amanda, so much I did not have time to say."

He smiled sadly, helplessly, and Celia felt her heart turn over.

"I will be more than happy to help in any way," she said warmly, her hands folded by her waist.

"I thank you most sincerely," Stevens returned. "Brendan, when shall we schedule another visit?"

"Well, Garrick. I will leave this to you and Miss Thomason. I fear I am something of a skeptic, and do not wish to impinge on your beliefs."

"So you did not believe this?" Stevens was incredulous. "My God, Brendan, what more proof do you need? It was Amanda, I felt it!"

"Then I am happy for you, Garrick. But please, respect my desire not to attend these sessions, just as I will respect your desire to believe in all this."

Stevens shook his head. "I feel sorry for you. You have just dismissed something marvelous."

"Indeed he has, Mr. Stevens." Celia nodded primly. "But that cannot be helped. One can only lead a horse to water, after all."

"How right you are, Miss Thomason." O'Neal bowed slightly. "So please forgive me if I wish to avoid your trough at all costs."

Celia was about to reply, when she paused and glared at him. Stevens, too, cast an uncertain look at his brother-in-law, who was still in a gallant bow.

O'Neal straightened, then reached into his breast pocket and withdrew a wallet. Opening it, he smiled. "It seems, Miss Thomason, I have only English currency at present."

Stevens, who had been staring at the harp, jolted. "Only English currency? My God, Brendan! Amanda warned us about English currency!"

O'Neal held his hand up. "Yes, well. You see, Miss Thomason, I have not been in this country as long as my brother-in-law, and have not had an opportunity to exchange my money. So, Garrick, if you do not mind? I can promise you I am good for it, and will repay you this evening."

Stevens, his mouth slightly agape and eyes flashing with excitement, pulled out his own wallet and handed it to O'Neal. "Um, I will retrieve our cloaks. Of course you may take whatever you need. Anything." He reached out and shook Celia's hand. "Thank you. I thank you most heartily. Oh, and when shall I return?"

"You are welcome at any time, Mr. Stevens." One pointed look at O'Neal, and she repeated, "Yes, indeed, *you* are most welcome at any time at all."

"I thank you, dear lady. I . . . I do need some air. I believe I am overcome with . . ."

"Go on, Garrick. I will be with you directly."

Stevens rushed from the parlor, and as he stepped over the threshold, both O'Neal and Celia could not help but notice his broad grin.

"Well, sir, it seems your gloomy friend has been transformed by what happened here."

O'Neal just stared at her. "You are very good indeed, madam." He plucked two ten-dollar bills from the wallet. "Will this do?"

"Very nicely," she replied as she took the bills.

He gave her a wry smile and began to leave. "Miss Thomason, tell me, how did you know about the harp?"

"As you said yourself, sir, I am very good."

"Yes. It seems you are. Good day, Miss Thomason. We will advise you as to when Mr. Stevens wishes to meet again."

She nodded once, a tight smile still on her lips.

Then he left, with one glance back at the covered harp. Celia stood in the parlor and took a deep breath.

He had been testing her! She suddenly realized that

if all had not gone well, the deal with O'Neal and his brother-in-law would have been called off. He had that paper with her signature. They could have been ruined, publicly humiliated.

That had been close, she thought with a sigh, listening for the men to leave.

"Well?" Aunt Pru stepped through the panel. "What was the take?"

Aunt Pru occasionally enjoyed speaking like a cutthroat from a poorly produced stage play.

"Twenty dollars." Celia smiled, holding up the bills.

"How wonderful!"

Then came the familiar scuffle in the chimney. Next the feet emerged, first one, then the other, and finally the rest of Patrick.

"Whish! I thought we were in for a rough one there, Miss!"

"I did too, Patrick." Celia felt as if she could finally relax. "And thanks to you, I believe he will become a regular client."

"Ah, wasn't nothing." Patrick looked down, clearly pleased with the praise.

"But it was, most assuredly." She turned back to the harp. "When did you rig it?"

Patrick straightened. "Miss?"

"The harp. When did you rig it to play?"

"Why, I didn't."

Celia looked at Aunt Pru, who also seemed perplexed.

"I don't understand." Celia went over to the harp and pulled back the cover. "Let's see." She dragged it forward, looking for the hidden strings attached to the wall. But there were none. She turned it over, tipped it on its side, shook out the cover, all to no avail. And when she touched the strings, the sour notes of an out-of-tune harp wafted throughout the room.

"How dreadful! We must get it tuned," Aunt Pru concluded.

"I'll bet it was a draft," said Patrick.

"Excuse me?" Celia looked up.

"It's close to the window, and this being November and all, I'll bet it was a draft made that sound."

"Yes." Celia bit her lower lip and pushed the harp back into place, draping the cover back over the instrument. "Yes. I'm sure you're right. A draft."

With a shrug Patrick left the parlor.

"Yes," she repeated to herself. "That must be it. A draft."

The harp remained silent, a covered lump in the corner. "Yes. A draft."

4

$\mathcal{G}$arrick Stevens sat alone in his study and stared gloomily into the fire.

He had done it all for Amanda.

Nobody would see that now, of course. It all looked different, suspicious somehow.

He had joined the secret society to impress her, to show her how very seriously he would take her concerns, her desires. When they had first approached him on the street, one of the many rough characters in this strange city, he had been frightened. That evening, after yet another strained dinner with nothing to say, he had mentioned the encounter.

"I say, Amanda," he had said. From the long end of the table, the silver candelabra lighting her delicate features—how beautiful she was!—she glanced up at him. Although the house was fully equipped with gas, she did not trust it, preferring instead the old-fashioned candles.

"Yes, Garrick." Her voice was dull now, not the laughing music that had so enchanted him in London.

"You will find this most amusing," he began, hoping she would. For it had been months since she had cast a smile in his direction. Of course there was the sad fact that her father had passed away, and that her brother had been forced to journey back to London to settle matters. That would make any woman, especially a new bride, sad indeed.

But there was more than that. Garrick suspected he had been the source of her disenchantment. Before, in London, she had listened to his every word, reacting with delight when he would recite an anecdote from his youth, especially the ones that involved Brendan.

All of that had changed. He found himself repeating the tales she used to find so engaging, only to have her listen politely and then return to her own moody thoughts.

He most certainly hoped she would find his next bit of conversation amusing.

"Yes, well," he began, noting that she had returned to pushing a bit of fricassee about on her plate. "A gentleman approached me on the street before the office. Well, I say a gentleman, but he was really nothing of the sort, nor could he ever be considered a gentleman."

The fricassee was now circling the sweet peas.

"He asked me if I happened to be connected with O'Neal Shipping."

She looked up at him then. Was that mild interest?

"And not knowing his purpose, perhaps I would have to deal with him in some sort of professional capacity, I replied in the affirmative. And do you know what he asked?"

She shook her head slightly.

"He inquired if I would be interested in joining the

United Irish Brotherhood! He must have assumed I was Brendan, for my obvious British accent did not seem to make a mark."

"The United Irish Brotherhood?" Amanda asked. "Are they the ones attempting to raise money for famine relief?"

"Why, yes. I believe so."

She was responding. At last, he had found a way to make her respond.

"Oh, Garrick, you must join them! The suffering at home is simply unbearable, even around Castle Sitric. And no one is doing anything to help, especially in England. Please, please join them! We can send them money, help whatever way we can."

This is not what he had expected. The man who had approached him was more than rough—indeed, at first Garrick had taken him for a cutthroat bound on thievery.

"When is the next meeting?" The fork was at last put down, and her eyes—those captivating blue eyes, orbs of cobalt—were dancing.

"Well, I think it is sometime this week. At least I would imagine so." He touched his lower lip with the edge of the linen napkin. "I did not listen very closely."

"Oh, may I go, too? Please, Garrick! Let me help."

He hesitated and took a sip of claret.

"Now, Amanda. I do not think it would be a good idea to become friendly with people such as this man. It simply will not do. We have too much to lose . . ."

"No, no, Garrick! Please listen to me. We have too much, period. Look at this meal, prepared by servants. We'll throw half of it away. The wine cellar—is that necessary? Of course not. But we could do some good, some genuine good. Perhaps not only furnish them with funds, but seek ways to raise even more."

"Amanda, these people are not our sort, not in the least. Indeed, they are . . ."

"Irish?" she said with her head cocked, her eyes blazing. Her features were set tightly, her lips pressed together in a humorless grin.

"No, no. Of course that is not what I meant."

"Yes it is. May I ask you a simple question?"

"Certainly," he replied automatically, although he very much dreaded what she would have to say.

"If the famine happened to be occurring in England rather than Ireland, would you not do anything in your power to help your country?"

"A famine in England?" He couldn't help but smile at the thought. "Why, what a very absurd notion! That could never happen now, in these modern times, since we . . ."

Her eyes had narrowed, a flickering there. And he realized how very wrong—at least to her ears—his words had just been.

"Precisely my point," she whispered, so low he could barely hear.

"It is not that simple." He used his most avuncular voice of reason. "There are complex economics at play here, far beyond your fair grasp."

"It seems simple to me. There has been a dreadful famine in Ireland these past few years. Entire families have perished, children and women lie by the side of the road with their lips parched green from eating grass. And from the docks they can see Irish cattle, fattened and being loaded upon ships to England, where they will be slaughtered and served with Yorkshire pudding.

I've even read editorials in the papers implying, or even stating outright, that the Irish famine is an Irish problem. It has not affected the English one jot, except to lower the price of Irish corn and butter and even lace."

When had she been reading? Where did she have access to such information?

Then he came upon the most logical answer. "Very well. So the situation is indeed dire. Why doesn't your brother help the cause?"

"He does," she replied. "He's done everything he possibly can—from not accepting rent from his tenants to slaughtering cattle from our own stock to distribute to all who are in need. But as long as we are under the yoke of British imperialism, those are only temporary aids. He's tried, Garrick, to change government policy, but he's too much of an outsider."

The way she said his name just then, it had been with something he had not heard from her for a while. Warmth? Perhaps even affection?

"But here, in this country," she continued, excitement making her even more animated, "we can really help. Just think, if Ireland was not considered part of England, and an inferior part at that, we could help ourselves! It's the absentee landlords who have so greatly contributed to this disaster, causing the poor to become the impoverished."

"Amanda," he said with some alarm. "You are advocating revolution, not simply feeding the hungry."

"It all goes together, don't you see?"

He was genuinely shocked. "You have never expressed interest in the subject of Home Rule before."

"Because I'm not interested in Home Rule. We don't need a Parliament in London to dictate our actions. We need absolute freedom."

"But you are free!"

"No. I am in another country, under the mantle of an English name, protected by money. Take me home, take away the money, and I am very much a slave of the Empire. Every bit as much a slave as those poor souls here are."

"Now that is none of our business, Amanda. If they choose to continue the institution of slavery, that is their right . . ."

"No one has a right! Not over another human being, be they Irish or African or even English."

He stared at his bride with a feeling that he never really knew her. Who was this woman?

"Well." He looked over at the rolls, longing to take one but realizing that the gesture would be perceived as callous. Still, they were probably still warm, and the sweet butter pat would melt on it.

"Please, Garrick. Promise me you will at least attend the meeting. See if I can attend the next time."

And then she had smiled at him, directly at him, for the first time in months. He felt his heart begin to pound.

"Yes, then," he said, his voice strained. "If it means that much to you."

Before he had finished speaking she had jumped from her chair and run the entire length of the table. Then she threw her arms around his neck and kissed him hard, her hair tumbling over his cheeks.

She smelled of lilacs and springtime, her own perfume. And he had forgotten all about the rolls by then.

So he had done it all for her. Everything that had happened, the events that followed, had all been born from his simple desire to please Amanda.

*   *   *

In the quiet of his rooms, Brendan O'Neal could at last be alone.

Garrick had procured a luxurious suite for Brendan at the Astor House hotel, just down the hall from his own lodgings. But Brendan never felt comfortable in sumptuous hotels, never enjoyed the impersonality of three hundred rooms, no matter how elegant the service. So Brendan had found a boardinghouse nearby, still within an easy stroll of the banking district and their rather appalling offices.

As always, Brendan did not feel at ease until his door was locked, his greatcoat and jacket were secured in the wardrobe, and his collar loosened.

Brendan settled into a plush yet curiously uncomfortable upholstered chair and looked at the stack of books he had purchased that day at a cheerful shop on Nassau Street. One of the owners, a surprisingly erudite gentleman named Charles Scribner, had an easy job of selling him an assortment of peculiar American novels, some recent scientific publications, an oversized literary magazine called *The Knickerbocker Review*, and the most recent *Scientific American*.

They were piled neatly on a small table, and for not the first time, he wondered when he would get a chance to even crack open the spines and turn a few pages. They would eventually join the other books, hundreds of them, some still in their crates in London, some under dust cloths in Ireland. A few on ships yet circling the globe.

They were every bit as rootless as he had become, mere cargo.

What had happened during the past few years?

With exhaustion that had become so familiar, he

closed his eyes, hoping to block out the memories. But they would not be blocked. It was as if they had a life of their own.

Home. It was there in his mind's eye, a place he had not seen in actuality for years now. But it would always be with him, the fresh green countryside, the rough gray stone fences glinting after a soft rain, the scent of earth. Within the household there was the constant bustling of the servants, the starched white and crisp black of their uniforms, the way Kenney, the butler, would spend his off-hours showing Brendan the best spots in the stream to catch trout. He had been the only child in a land of grown-ups, and as such he had been doted upon and cherished.

As a child he hadn't understood what a privileged world he had inhabited.

It had indeed been magical, those earliest years. His lips formed an unaccustomed, gentle smile at the thoughts, his face softening at his private memories, recollections he alone held close to his soul. They came to him as flashes, like lanterns swinging in the distance.

There was the house, his home, Castle Sitric. It had been in his father's family for several generations, and before that it had been part of Ireland's history, the ancient core the house had been built around. He used to peer out of his window at night and stare down at the peculiar structure in the courtyard. It wasn't quite a house, for that was added later. Most assumed it had been some sort of pagan temple. The entire house, all sixty-six rooms, was built around those carefully arranged stones, erected in prehistoric times by a people long vanished.

The servants had always been frightened by the ruin

that so dominated Castle Sitric, averting their eyes, scurrying past the center windows as they crossed themselves against the threat of heathen dead who walked their old paths, swirling in the mist. Once, when he was about ten, he fancied he saw some hooded figures marching in a line. That evening at dinner he had told his parents what he had seen.

"Oh, Brendan." His mother had smiled, her beautiful features illuminated by candle glow. Everything seemed to glow that night, all reflecting off the silver, the mirrors and the gleaming surface of the long, long table. "You have such an imagination!"

"But I do not." He had frowned, his lower lip jutting out. It had been the last of his childish habits, the pout.

"Son." His father had looked at his mother, and he thought he saw a wink. "You do have a bit of an imagination. Remember what you told us last month about the fairy rings?"

"I heard about them from Emily. She's nearly thirteen and Emily told me about how the fairies come and sometimes they leave little shoes . . ."

"Emily?" his father had asked.

"The undergardener's daughter, dear."

"Good God." His father laughed. "Can she be thirteen? It seems to me she was christened but a fortnight ago!"

"Well, there will be another christening soon enough."

There had been a strange hum between his parents then, and Brendan had watched them, uncertain of the meaning.

And then, after a change or two of season, the meaning became clear. His mother was going to have another child.

Brendan would no longer be the focus of their undivided attention. Their eyes would no longer light on him alone during mealtimes or when he showed them his newest experiments, or how well he rode a horse or his skill at archery.

He had never had cause for hatred in his life before the notion of a new child was presented. But now he hated his new brother or sister more than he had believed possible. At night he hoped terrible things would happen to it, the intruder, as he had come to think of the thing to come. Sometimes he even called upon the hooded figures in the courtyard to do mischief.

Just about that time, Brendan was beginning to realize his father was something of a powerful man. It came upon him slowly, this new knowledge, in bits and pieces that had always been there but that he had failed to recognize.

For one, important people came to see his father at Castle Sitric. The Lord Mayor of Dublin, members of the government, people with Lords and Sirs before their names, would attend his very own father in one of the drawing rooms. Rarely did his father have to go to Dublin, and when he did it was to see to the shipping concerns or to view the progress of new vessels.

That knowledge gave Brendan a sense of his own importance. One day he would receive these men. They would come at his beckoning. No matter what, he would always be the firstborn. That somewhat abated his hatred of the new sibling.

Indeed, as the time drew near he began to think it would be quite nice to have someone to lord over. Now there would be someone to fetch his shoes and tidy up his room.

Perhaps it wouldn't be so bad after all.

And then the day came. Brendan was sent to Cook's house just within the castle walls, where he was given biscuits and tea and cocoa and even some candied pineapple.

It seemed he had been there for a very long time, and he fell asleep, waiting to hear if he had a brother or a sister. At last someone from the main house came to the door, and there was whispering and he was given even more to eat.

That was when he realized there was something very wrong.

They wouldn't let him see his mother.

Cook threw on a shawl and stepped away, and when she returned her eyes and nose were red, but she smiled and told him he had a lovely new sister named Amanda. His mother, he was told, was very tired, and since she needed to sleep, he would stay with Cook for a few days.

That was all he was told, until the middle of the next week. Finally he was sent to the main house, his home, and there was black bunting and a wreath on the door. Brendan knew his mother was dead well before he was told.

Nothing was ever the same. His father grew distant and cold. His sister, Amanda—who had been born with a twisted left foot—cried day and night. There were physicians and surgeons who hovered with the baby, attempting to straighten her foot with splints and counterweights. One doctor employed a boxlike device and clamped it on her tiny leg. But nothing seemed to work. His father remained distant. The little baby cried, perhaps out of pain, perhaps because she somehow knew she was alone. After just a few months Brendan was sent to school in England.

The child who had seemed too young for his years now grew up too quickly. He did not come home during his first three years at school, spending the brief holidays with distant relations in London, sometimes with friends from school. When he did return, his father stayed locked in his study, and little Amanda followed him about, her solemn eyes wide and blue, her awkward gait causing her to shift from side to side with every step.

It sickened him, the changes at Sitric Castle. The home that had once been so filled with joy and laughter was now a dire, silent place.

Deep down, Brendan had blamed himself for the changes. It was he, years earlier, who had so fervently prayed for something bad to happen to the baby, and it had. Not that he believed himself to have superhuman powers. It was the magic of the house, of the stones in the courtyard. It was the magic of Sitric.

When he returned to England, he confessed his beliefs to one of his tutors. Instead of laughing, the tutor led him to books, to ideas professed by great men that were now proven false through modern science. They, too, had been led to believe in things that were not real.

"Use reason, Mr. O'Neal, good, solid reason! Use what we, as men of science, know as truths."

And so he had employed reason ever since. He even began writing in a book of blank pages, listing his thoughts under the headings of "Things I know" and "Things I do not know." The lists were usually lopsided at first, with the column of what he knew being almost blank. But that would change, little by little, as he discovered the good solid reasons behind why the tides rise and fall as they do, why the stars seem to shift. He was able to explain the inexplicable to his own satisfaction.

When he was almost fifteen he met the boy who was to become his closest friend, Garrick Stevens. Garrick was not as athletic as Brendan, nor was he glib or popular with the other boys. But he was a brilliant scholar. And when Brendan asked him a question about the Greek philosophers, Garrick answered him without having to look in the books. That impressed Brendan, and soon he learned that Garrick could be kind as well as clever. When Brendan came down with chicken pox, Garrick sat by his bed and helped him keep up with his studies. And Garrick understood how it felt to have lost a parent, for his father had died several years earlier.

It only seemed natural that when the next school holiday arrived, Brendan accepted Garrick's offer to come home with him.

Perhaps what surprised Brendan the most was that the Stevenses, illustrious family that they were, seemed to live in somewhat diminished circumstances. He was worldly enough by then to understand the basic economics of running a large estate. And although the Stevens place, called by the somewhat unimaginative name of Stevens Court, was not nearly the size of Sitric Castle, they seemed to speak of it in almost reverential terms, as a sacred and noble trust.

And it was at Stevens Court that Brendan first felt the full thrust of his Irishness. Of course there had been moments at school when his heritage had been an issue, usually on the sports pitch or in the heat of after-hours roughhousing, but at Stevens Court it became clear to him that to be Irish was considered a character flaw. The very first morning, while Garrick's mother supervised breakfast, he heard her mumble something about hiring Irish help.

"In future, I'll have to remember the limitations of the Irish mind," she had said with a shake of her elegant head.

He had felt his color rise in embarrassment, and saw Garrick's chagrined expression, but his mother gave the topic no further attention.

But he was on alert from then on, and noticed comments and open references as to the substandard nature of the Irish in general. He assumed Garrick's mother did not realize he was from Ireland; perhaps she had not caught his full name or heard Garrick mention Sitric Castle outside of Dublin.

On their last evening before going back to school, Garrick's mother invited some of their neighbors over for dinner. The boys sat quietly through the meal, speaking only when questions were directed toward them, listening politely when an elderly gentleman named Lord Warfield gave them long accounts of his glorious sports achievements at Eaton when men wore powdered wigs and silk hose.

Although none of the guests said anything disagreeable or behaved unkindly, Brendan could not help but notice the raised eyebrows when he was introduced, the sideways glances exchanged. At one point a lady with a silk turban began a discourse concerning Home Rule, but she was discreetly hushed before he could hear precisely what she was saying. No one was overtly unkind, but it was impossible not to notice the difference.

He was different from them. Yes, his manners were as

polished as theirs, he knew which fork to use and how to carry on a polite conversation with an utter stranger. He was fully aware that he was every bit as presentable as they were, and more presentable than a few. His clothing was more than adequate, his face and hands clean. Still, he was different.

The simple fact that he was born and raised on the other side of the Irish Sea eliminated the simple fact that his father was wealthy and a very powerful man. It didn't matter, for his father's wealth and power lay in Dublin, not London. And that geographic difference would forever set him apart from the people gathered around that dinner table.

It was a lesson he never forgot. And years later, when Brendan took over the daily operation of O'Neal Shipping, one of his first acts was to establish a large office in London. Soon O'Neal Shipping dwarfed most of the established English companies, and Brendan O'Neal was recognized as one of the wealthiest men in London as well as Dublin.

Still, he was different. He felt it keenly whenever at one of the clubs, or when dining with members of Parliament or at a private home. There was always the same reaction, the raised eyebrows and the inevitable hushing of a less-discreet guest. He was a curiosity, despite his smooth manners and elegant clothing.

So when Garrick Stevens, scion of a fine English family, met, fell in love with, and married Amanda O'Neal, there was much excitement on both sides of the sea. The day he caught his first glimpse of Amanda as she stepped into a carriage in London, he had been in love. In England there were barbed comments as to the wild Irish girl invading London society. Some who had never seen her claimed she walked about barefoot and ate with her hands. No one mentioned that the O'Neal fortune would restore Stevens Court to its former splendor. Nor did anyone mention that Garrick Stevens had not been a success at any of his halfhearted attempts at employment. He shouldn't have to work, his mother agreed. No decent woman of his background would have him, and in his mind a decent woman meant a woman in possession of a decent dowry.

On the other side of the Irish Sea there was lamentation that the lovely Amanda would no longer grace the parlors and ballrooms of Dublin. More than one young Irishman, and a few who had not been considered young since the last century, complained they had not a chance at securing Amanda O'Neal's affection.

But it had mattered not at all, for she had only lived a few months after the wedding.

In the end there was left only Brendan to learn precisely what had happened to Amanda in those months while he was in London. Something had been going on in Amanda's life—he was sure of it. Garrick had been of no help, so addled by his own loss he had become almost useless as a source of information, and less than useless as a business partner.

So now, alone in his boardinghouse, he pulled out the one book he had entered Mr. Scribner's store to buy—the one with blank sheets. He wrote his two column headings, the words unchanged since he was a schoolboy.

"What I know," and "What I do not know."

Brendan would not find any measure of peace until he discovered the truth about Amanda's last days. There was every possibility that the knowledge he gained would prevent him from ever finding a measure of peace, but it was a risk he knew he must assume. Perhaps he had not been there while she was growing up, and in later years he had barely recognized the comely, graceful young woman he saw in London as Amanda. But in death he had vowed not to fail her.

He had already failed the rest of his family, his mother, his father.

It was too late to help solve her life, but he would not fail Amanda in death.

Celia opened the parlor window just a crack, no more than the width of her thumb. With steady hands she raised the cover of the harp in the corner more than the previous time. And then she waited.

Nothing happened. Although there was a wind that afternoon, and a fierce chill coming from the empty fireplace as well as the opened window, no chords— sour or heavenly—sounded from the harp.

"Well," she said aloud, stepping to the center of the room, waiting for something, anything, to happen. There had to be some explanation for the sounds that had come from the harp when Stevens and O'Neal were there.

Staring at the mute instrument as if it would suddenly confess all, she went over all of the possibilities in her mind. Perhaps a heavy carriage had rolled by on West Fourth Street, vibrating the harp. Or the house was settling, as houses tend to do.

There were sometimes disturbances from the old Minetta Brook, long since drained but still flooding the occasional cellar. It may have rumbled below, thus causing the strings to stir. Maybe a small animal slipped through the front door.

Yes, she thought to herself. *A small animal with a remarkable talent for playing the harp with its paws. It happened all the time.*

There was a sharp rap on the door. "Come in," she said distractedly, inching closer to the harp. Another thought crossed her mind—perhaps someone was walking heavily nearby. Not near enough for them to have heard the actual stomp, just near enough to jiggle the harp and make it play.

Inching closer to the harp, she stomped her right foot. Nothing. One little step closer, and she stomped once more. Then again.

She heard the door open but, still appraising the harp, did not immediately turn around. Another stomp, this one with both elbows bent, to get more of a thud.

"Miss Thomason?"

"Mr. O'Neal!" Celia all but shrieked. In a more quiet voice, she continued, "Forgive me, I was just . . ."

"Good Lord, is that how American women dance? Remind me to steer clear of ballrooms."

"No, you see . . ." Then she realized he was smiling at her, not unpleasantly, and she returned the smile.

"I assume you are trying to find new ways to produce a sound from the harp." He nodded toward the instrument. "I must compliment you, Miss. Your ingenuity is most impressive."

"Oh." She swept a thatch of hair back from her eyes. "Yes. Thank you, sir. It did work . . ." she chose her words carefully, "surprisingly well."

"It did." He had brought with him a crisp scent of outdoors in the folds of his cloak, of cool air and trees.

Again she was struck by his sheer size, but also by the color of his eyes. They were a rich brown, deep and bright. She hadn't really noticed his eyes before.

"I came to compliment you," he said with a small, rigid bow. "You understand why I could not do so when I saw you earlier, or in the form of a note. In case I have failed to mention it, we must avoid written communication at all costs."

"Of course."

He nodded, then glanced around the room. "Do you have any further tricks planned for Garrick?"

Celia stiffened at his tone. "Sir, you make me sound like a court jester."

"That is certainly not my intention. Nor is it my intention to simply frighten Garrick out of his wits."

"I would not do that even if it was your intention, sir," she snapped, her hands clenched. Then she remembered who had the rest of the money she so desperately needed. In a calmer voice, her composure regained, she asked him, "Then what *is* your purpose?"

He took a deep breath. "My primary concern is to comfort him. Since Amanda's death he has not been himself. I have tried everything possible to coax him from his lethargy, but nothing works. When he believed you had communicated with her, when he thought it was possible to reach her, well. That is the first time since the accident he has seemed like himself, the old Garrick. And also." He hesitated for a moment.

"Please continue."

"I believe he knows more than he has revealed about the accident."

"Why would he wish to keep anything from you?"

"I'm not sure. But I do not believe he is intentionally

misleading me. I just believe the shock of the accident may have erased some of the finer details from his memory."

"Yes. I have heard of that happening in some cases." Her brows drew together briefly, and then it passed.

His full attention was focused on her. "Do you have knowledge of such memory lapses?"

"Well." She wondered if she should continue, and decided she should. It could prove helpful, and the more effectively she could assist O'Neal, the more rapidly she would be paid in full. And if it could aid Mr. Stevens, well, that would be most worthwhile. "I . . ."

This was more difficult than she had thought it would be, and she realized she had never told anyone before about what had happened when she was a child. Not even Aunt Prudence or Uncle James.

"Please," he urged, his eyes suddenly bright. His studied expression of perpetual calm was gone, and there was a fascinating animation to his features. It lent him a compelling, almost sympathetic air.

"Yes, well." She closed her eyes briefly, then opened them before continuing. Yet she could not speak with him watching her face. It was too intimate somehow, too disturbing. Slowly, she paced to the far window, placing her hand against the cool pane of glass before she began.

"When I was eight years old, my parents embarked on a journey to Italy. It was to be the wedding trip they never took, for my father had been unable to leave his business at the time of their marriage. He was a broker of fire insurance, you see. Always very busy, because there were always a lot of fires. That's what he told me." She traced the painted wood of the window with a finger. "So I was sent here, to Uncle James and Aunt Pru's house, for the duration of four months. And just when that time was to be concluded, when they were to arrive home, we got word they had been killed. It was in the form of a letter carried here on the very ship they were to take home."

Her throat began to tighten, and she felt the stirrings of anguish in the pit of her stomach, harsh and bitter and for so long carefully ignored. The words were so simple, so very cold. "It wasn't even a ship accident. They were on a lake in a little boat. It seems they went out too far, too far. There was a sudden storm, not a ferocious storm. No other damage seems to have been inflicted. Even the little boat came back to the shore. But not my parents. My father never did learn to swim. They perished."

"How terrible," he said softly. "How very difficult that must have been for you."

"Yes, well." She cleared her throat and then turned to face him. His expression was soft, giving the illusion that he was almost experiencing the same emotions she had recalled. "The point is that I can recall little of the weeks following the arrival of the news. I must have seemed quite normal to all who observed me, for no one addressed me about my feelings. Indeed, after the funeral there seemed to be an understanding that no one was to speak of my parents or the accident. All of their mementos vanished, the letters they had written to me during their trip. It was as if they had never existed, and I went along with everyone else. I must have thought that was my only choice. I recall being afraid that if I cried, or made an unpleasant scene, I would be sent away. I don't know where. So I went about my days and weeks as usual, celebrated birthdays and holidays. Yet all that time I was not quite in a conscious state. And only years later, quite recently, in fact, did I find dozens of sketches I drew during that time."

"Sketches?"

"Yes. I used to draw, I was drawing before I learned to write. My parents, my mother especially, encouraged me, furnished me with charcoals and crayons and paper. The odd thing is that I remember the drawings, what it was like that day in the sun, or on a certain picnic by the East River. And then I found sketches dated the weeks after my parents died."

"And yet you have no memory of executing the drawings you found?"

"None at all. At first I couldn't even fathom where they came from. They were behind a drawer in my room, and I only found the papers because a glove had slipped back. I had to remove the next drawer in order to retrieve it."

"Fascinating. And may I ask about the nature of the drawings?" A gentle smile touched his lips. "Were they little-girl fancies?"

"No. They were nightmarish, scenes of death and shipwrecks. Monsters. Sea creatures. But they were so intricately rendered that had I been in my right mind, I most certainly would have recalled them."

"And have you continued to draw in that fashion?"

"No. I have not sketched a single line since then. I had assumed I just lost interest, but when I found those drawings I realized the real reason why. I had poured all of my anguish into those sketches. Every page vibrates with pain and sorrow. So drawing had lost all joy for me."

"I am sorry to hear that," he said. "And I thank you for telling me about your experience. Like you, I feel that Garrick is still greatly affected by Amanda's death, and may not be in his proper mind even now. Again, thank you."

"You are welcome." It was awkward, yet somehow a relief, to have told someone of the drawings, to have spoken the truth. And for some reason, Celia felt as if Mr. O'Neal not only sympathized with her experience, but understood.

"Sir," she said briskly, regaining her composure. "I do need to know more about your sister if I am to convince Mr. Stevens she is indeed here with us."

"Yes, yes, of course." His eyes remained fixed on her, unsettling and unblinking. "Well, in all honesty I did not know her very well. We were so far apart in age, over a decade. My mother died after bringing her into the world. I was sent to England to school, and then she married Garrick."

"I see. Well then, what did she look like, her physical attributes?"

"She was a strange little girl, at least I thought so, limping after me when she was a child. But then she grew into a rather enchanting young woman. Her limp by then was barely noticeable, although she felt its presence keenly. But she had long strawberry blond hair and beautiful blue eyes. I have a miniature of her I shall bring next time, quite a good likeness, and Garrick has a daguerreotype taken last year."

"It was a love match then, your sister and Mr. Stevens."

"Yes, it seems it was, although . . ." His voice faded, and he closed his eyes for a moment. "At times I had my doubts, and even now I do wonder if I should have been more mindful of Amanda. There was one conversation we had on the ship."

"When you came to America?"

"Yes. She was barely into her first season in London when she met Garrick. I believe he was the first man to see her as a woman, for I am ashamed to say I did not. I was too busy, too preoccupied. They met and he courted her almost under my nose, yet I did not see."

"You must have been very pleased indeed to have your only sister marry your close friend." Celia smiled at the thought, but O'Neal did not smile back.

"No. I was not pleased."

"Whyever not?" She could not hide her surprise.

"Because I knew that in London, as an Irish woman, she would suffer. Every characteristic that would be overlooked or even praised in an Englishwoman would be held up for ridicule—her hair, her manner of dress, her accent. Even her exuberance and vivacity would be reckoned a fault. And with her slight limp, well. I just pictured a life of misery."

"And you didn't feel Garrick could protect her?"

"Garrick?" He gave a short bark of a laugh. "Garrick couldn't protect me, and I was a man. I saw what it was like in London, even amongst the best of people of the highest rank. No, Garrick wouldn't have protected her. And he was without the means to do so."

"Without the means? I am perplexed, sir."

"You see, Miss Thomason, the Stevens name may be vaunted for its past glory, but at the present time that glory is without a financial base."

"In other words, the family wallet is flattened."

"Precisely."

"But that is hardly Mr. Stevens's fault."

"I did not mean to imply that, Miss Thomason. I am just stating that in his financial position, he had no means of protecting Amanda, of shielding her from society's prejudices. So when they became engaged, it was determined that Garrick would join me in O'Neal Shipping, become my second-in-command."

"And who determined this should be the case, sir?"

"Ah, now that is a most fascinating part of the story. At first Garrick's mother refused to entertain the notion of his marrying Amanda. Poor Amanda had several things against her, mainly being Irish and having a father and brother engaged in working for a living."

"Horrendous, most horrendous." Celia smiled, and O'Neal paused, watching her for an instant before he continued.

"Indeed, Mrs. Stevens pronounced those exact words, or something to the effect in any case. But when Garrick told her about our arrangement, and of the financial gain to be had by the Stevens family, well. She swallowed her distaste, at least she pretended to. Our compromise was that Garrick would take his new bride to America to run the company here."

"How did you feel about this arrangement, sir?"

"Well, fine. It was just . . ." Then he stopped. "No. I am not being honest. It was demeaning to me, to Amanda. To our Irish heritage. Thank God she never knew the real reason Garrick was to come to the States."

"Are you certain?"

"Yes. Fairly certain, at least. Although on the ship coming here, she did make a few strange comments."

"Such as?"

"Every bride probably has doubts and fears. She simply stated that perhaps she should not have married Garrick so quickly. Perhaps she should have waited, seen more of the world, observed men. She was almost a child in some ways. That was part of her charm."

The clock on the mantelpiece began to strike.

"I should be going," he said. "When should Garrick return? I was thinking that perhaps . . ."

"Yes?"

He seemed distracted, looking around the room.

"Mr. O'Neal, what should I say or do with your brother-in-law? Shall I ask something particular? Is there any path you wish me to take, any specific questions to answer?" Deep lines creased his brow and he looked over his shoulder, then at the harp.

"Sir?"

"Yes. I almost forgot what I was here for." He continued his visual search for something.

"What would your brother-in-law like to hear? Are there tender words that would comfort him?"

"Oh, yes. Of course. Well, at this time I would indeed like him to feel comforted somehow. But I wish also to know if she told him anything, if she confided in him." He raked his hand through his thick hair. "I need to know what she was feeling before she died, if Garrick got the sense she loved him. She was very open about her feelings. Too open. She was not one to keep her emotions in check. So I wondered if she had been unhappy. I have a fear that the accident was deliberate on her part, a way to escape unhappiness."

"Sir, surely you do not suspect she took her own life."

"I-I know not. It has crossed my mind. Our father died, that's why I was not here. I had to return to London to rectify some legal matters. I was gone for six months and, well. I know nothing of her mental state at that time, nothing of the emotions she may have been feeling. The circumstances surrounding the accident are vague. There are some letters she sent. I will give them to you. Anything you can discover from Garrick would be most helpful. And I would . . . I would be most eager to know . . ."

"If she loved you."

"That matters not." A muscle in his jaw tensed.

"If at all possible, I'll find it out for you," she concluded.

"No. I'll tell you what I wish to know. As I said, I want to know if she really loved him, loved Garrick. Whether her death was really an accident. That should be simple enough for you to learn. You must have your tricks you employ to discover such things. We'll go from there."

Celia ignored the disdain in his voice, not allowing herself to be hurt. This was purely a business matter. "But sir, what else? Do you want to know her wishes, her dreams? I'm sure she told her husband."

"Perhaps," he said crisply.

"I can find out. Trust me, I can discover more than you . . ." Then she saw his face, the loathing there. Of course. She was a fraud. Anything she could learn was learned through subterfuge and deceit. Anything she could tell him, no matter how valid or real, would of course be obtained through those means.

There was no use telling him anything else. There was no use attempting any other relationship with this man besides business. She needed his money. He wanted her to find out information about his sister and his brother-in-law, nothing more.

And again, that hurt.

"Would you care for some tea, sir?"

She had changed the topic. Still she could feel the tension between then, the constant electricity they seemed to produce wordlessly. She waited for him to speak. Did he feel it too? Had he experienced the strange tension?

"What is that?" O'Neal was standing very still, his head tilted slightly to the side. All of his energy seemed to be coiled tightly, as if ready to spring.

Had he read her mind? Did he know her thoughts?

Then she heard the mechanical winding of the mantel clock. "The clock? It is merely announcing the hour of five."

"Not the clock! Damn it all, not the clock!" he snapped. "Can you smell it?"

At first she wasn't sure what he was talking about. She didn't know this man. Perhaps he was mad, or altered after his sister's tragic death. "Sir, would you rather have a brandy?"

"Can you not smell it!"

"But I have not poured the brandy yet. Please, Mr. O'Neal . . ."

And then she smelled it, an unfamiliar scent. It was floral, a woman's perfume, but unlike any she had ever encountered. It was fresh and green, an aroma both light and potent.

"What is it?" she whispered.

"You can smell it?"

"Yes. I can now."

He was about to continue when he straightened. "Very good, Miss Thomason. Again, I must compliment you on your ingenuity. Tell me, how did you find out?"

"I am at a loss, Mr. O'Neal. What are you asking me?"

"This scent. It was Amanda's, my father had it mixed specially for her in Paris. But what I do not understand is how you were able to obtain a sample. The last bottles were destroyed in the explosion. How did you know this was Amanda's scent?"

"I . . . well, I honestly . . . I do not know."

"Well then, keep your secrets." His fury was barely contained. "But remember, I am paying you to convince Garrick, not me. This was a wasted effort. You will never make me believe you are anything but a charlatan, a master—or should I say mistress—in the art of humbug. Good day, Miss Thomason."

With long strides he left the room, not looking back.

"Please, sir. This is just a coincidence, whatever scent you detected. I had no idea . . ."

Just beyond the threshold he paused for a moment. He seemed about to turn to face her, but then with renewed energy he continued, slamming the door behind him.

Celia simply stood in the empty parlor for a moment, her emotions running riot within her.

What was happening to her? How could this man twist her so? How could she continue working with him without losing her very soul? For there was something about him, something dangerous and dark. Yet she also sensed another side.

Her hand reached up and she touched her own face, feeling the heat of her flushed cheeks.

Then she stopped.

Someone was behind her. She could feel it, the sense of being watched very closely. The downy hair at the nape of her neck seemed to tingle. Slowly, without removing her hand from her face, she turned around.

At first she saw nothing. The parlor was empty, the late-afternoon light casting familiar shadows.

Then, between the two windows was a swirling mass, faint at first. The movement quickened, faster and faster, and soon formed a vague outline of a woman.

Celia knew immediately who was in the room with her.

"Hello, Amanda."

5

For all the times she had imagined such an encounter, envisioned a moment when something otherworldly would accept the frequently issued invitations, she had never really thought about what she would actually do in such a situation.

But at that precise moment, alone with the spirit of a very dead person, Celia—the well-known medium—was absolutely paralyzed with fear. It was an all-consuming terror, and she could barely articulate a thought in her own mind.

She watched, detached, as the form took on a more definite shape. Details came into focus, the distinct outline of a female figure was emerging from the shadowy silhouette. The chair behind her became less distinct as the swirls began to form a dressing gown, and the delicate quilting of the fabric became apparent. The satin sash about her waist began to glint in the light. Then one finger moved, a simple gesture, and the buffed nails were clear, then a ring—a wedding ring.

Amanda stood motionless, yet was the very embodiment of movement as she took on a solid-looking form, twisting and churning into reality. Next was her hair, as rich handfuls of silken hair cascaded down one shoulder.

Celia wanted to run, to flee, to get as far away as possible from this thing. Yet her feet remained immobile, as if she had taken root there.

The door behind the panel opened, and Celia could tell by the footsteps that it was Patrick.

"Miss, I just . . ."

Celia refused to allow her eyes to leave Amanda, not turning around to see Patrick. Just then Patrick's familiar footsteps echoed a skid and a halt. "Jaysus!"

"Please stand back, Patrick. There is nothing to fear."

"Jaysus!" he repeated in a slightly louder pitch.

Amanda blinked once, then turned slowly toward Patrick. It was a strange motion, almost as if she was underwater, as if fighting some unseen force for the ability to move. And her hair remained in one piece, as if the usual laws of physics did not apply to her.

It was then Celia was given the first clear sight of her eyes. Two bright black orbs that seemed to burn from within her indistinct, delicate features. It was as if some inner cord compelled her to maintain visual contact. It was impossible to look away.

The eyes were at once not human, yet so utterly so it was wrenching to see. The entire scope of a life seemed to be reflected from those two eyes. It was a distillation of the human experience, intensified and potent. Everything was there—pain and suffering, agony and fear. Yet along with those dreadful emotions were the glorious ones, the parallel echoes of love, dreams, triumph, and above all, hope.

It was the feral nature of man through a gauzy mist of humanity. It was both terrifying and exquisite.

The other parlor door opened. "Celia, dear, did you see where the . . ." Aunt Pru began. And then a simple "Good Lord!"

The sound of a glass dropping shattered the silence in the room. And then there was the thicker, heavier thud of a body hitting the carpet.

Celia gathered the strength to speak. "Patrick, please see to my aunt. I believe she has fainted."

"No," her aunt replied. "That was Patrick. He's out cold. Tell me. This is a real manifestation, is it not?"

"Yes, Aunt Pru," she barely breathed.

Aunt Prudence remained in awed silence, transfixed by the sight. Finally she whispered, "Who is she?"

Celia, about to reply, then stopped herself, making a swift decision to keep the spirit's identity to herself. It seemed a private, intimate piece of information for her to reveal about Amanda at that moment, like sharing the innermost secrets of someone without permission. It simply did not feel right.

"I do not know who she is, Aunt Pru." In a way it was true, for Celia really knew very little about the woman Amanda had been, or what she had become.

The ghost seemed to comprehend the exchange, and a small hint of a smile formed on the blurry lips. That simple gesture had the power to knock the breath from Celia, for it was a connection with the dead. Now Celia and Amanda were somehow linked, somehow they understood something on a very primitive level. Then Amanda tilted her head slightly and shook her head in silent inquiry, the hair again remaining strangely immobile.

"I am Celia Thomason," Celia said in a firm voice, uncertain of what else to do or say. Her voice was stronger than she had imagined possible.

Amanda's smile dissolved into a neutral, blank expression. Yet her body began to move strangely, twisting and coiling as if in some discomfort, even pain. Her hands reached out, fingers stiffened, clawlike, as if gripping something.

"What is that scent?" Aunt Prudence whispered. Celia had ceased to heed the numbing fragrance of the perfume. Yet it hung in the air, a thick, boundless swath. "It smells like a thousand flowers."

The ghost opened her mouth as if to speak, but no sound issued forth, and the agitated movement of her body continued.

From outside the parlor they heard the sound of someone entering the house, being let in by Eileen the maid. Amanda seemed puzzled, her hands still outstretched in an empty, frozen grasp.

As startling as her eyes had been before, they now danced with a new light, animated and alive and imploring something of Celia.

"What is it?" Celia asked. The eyes intensified, churning with molten fire that reached almost beyond Celia's ability to tolerate it any further. "Please, what can I do to help you?"

Amanda's lips moved, but again there were no words.

There was one knock on the parlor door, and Eileen entered. "Miss Thomason, you have a gentleman . . ." The sharp gasp was followed by footsteps, thicker, heavier steps than Eileen's had been.

By the expression on the ghost's face, Celia suddenly knew who was about to enter. Amanda's mouth formed a silent "o," and one of her hands—still bent in a claw—reached her temple.

"Miss Thomason," Garrick Stevens began. "Good day to you. I do hope I am not . . ."

His footsteps halted, and Celia had an urge to look at his face, to see what expression was revealed there. But she was unable to pull away from Amanda's features, as if some unseen force held her to the ghost.

"My God." Stevens's voice was a hush.

The spirit backed away, away, fading into the wall. And then she was gone. The only thing that remained of Amanda Stevens was the fleshy, almost sickening scent of her perfume.

Now Celia did face the others. Aunt Pru, although pale, was still standing upright. Eileen had her eyes closed, hands clenched before her, mumbling silent prayers and crossing herself. Patrick was still facedown on the floor, and Celia thought distractedly that when he awoke, he would find himself with a broken nose.

Stevens was absolutely white, even his lips, where a sheen of perspiration glistened in spite of the chill in the room. He backed out of the room, eyes still wide, knocking over a small table. Without pausing to right it, he went directly to the front door, which he opened with such force it slammed against the wall.

Celia began to follow him, rushing to the door and pulling her warmest shawl off the cloak tree.

"Celia, no!" Aunt Pru called. "Please, you must stay!"

The composure Aunt Prudence had demonstrated earlier had vanished. Suddenly she seemed frail and more than a little frightened. "What was that? Who was she, that woman?"

"Just a moment, Aunt Pru. I must follow Mr. Stevens to see if . . ."

"No! Please!" Aunt Pru clenched her hands together. "Please do not leave, Celia. He'll come back again, I am sure."

There was a sharpness to her voice, an edge Celia had not heard before.

Patrick, facedown on the floor, began to moan, then opened his eyes. "What happened?"

Eileen began to sob quietly, and Hannah came in from the kitchen, hands on hips.

"What is going on, ma'am? All the slamming and . . . Eileen? Why are you crying?" Then she looked to her left. "Patrick!"

Celia took one more look at Aunt Prudence and realized she couldn't follow Stevens. Her aunt was right, he would return. But she had so much to ask, so much she needed to know, not only for Mr. O'Neal.

Now Celia had been pulled in. After staring into Amanda's eyes, Celia would not rest until she knew what had happened to Amanda Stevens. Why she had chosen to appear from beyond the grave.

And why was Garrick Stevens so afraid of her?

From the window she could see him pushing his way past a clump of pedestrians, elbowing a woman as he gained speed and only narrowly escaping the wheels of a carriage. The driver raised his crop in surprise, and she heard him shout an oath as Stevens continued his reckless dash.

Whatever she had just witnessed between Amanda and Garrick, it most certainly was not a happy reunion between two people in love.

*   *   *

The ledgers were in a shambles.

Brendan rubbed his eyes and turned up the wick of the oil lamp. He paused just as he was about to pick up the pen, observing his hand as if it belonged to another person.

It was trembling. The more he willed it to stop the more violent the tremors became.

"Stop," he ordered from between clenched teeth. But it continued.

He would ignore it, he decided.

Glancing around the office, located in an old, rickety building on Water Street, within view of the South Street Seaport, it was difficult to realize this was the same room he had left in such logical and careful order over a half year before.

Of course the location—one of the most notorious streets in the city—was worse than he had imagined when he so hastily signed the lease the previous year. He had been so pressed to find space that he ignored the advice of his acquaintances simply because the building was so close to the ships themselves. Instead of the staid financial district, he was in a street filled with taverns, houses of ill repute, and murky characters.

He had intended to relocate, when he received the news of his father's death. Hadn't he instructed Garrick to move to a more reasonable part of town?

He was sure he had, even in the confusion of his hasty departure. But Garrick must have been unwilling, or even unable, to perform that task.

And if the evidence in the office itself could be read, it seemed there was very little Garrick had been up to completing. It seemed impossible that such utter chaos could have prevailed in such a short time, that years of meticulous organization, the carefully arranged system he developed for O'Neal Shipping that he had reconstructed in the new location, could be turned into such complete confusion in a few months. Had someone deliberately attempted to sabotage the ledgers, they could hardly have done a better job.

Even the room itself was a mess. Brendan had tossed the half-eaten bits of bread and sour meats away before starting to work, rinsed the cups that had once held—if his sense of smell was correct—rum with sandy water from a chipped pitcher. Yet in spite of his attempts to clean, he had already seen two mice. Two very well fed mice.

It was getting dark, but he had to continue going through the books Garrick had kept during the time he was away. And from what he had seen so far, he knew it would take more than one night to make sense of the scribbling, the lopsided columns of indecipherable numbers. It would take days, if not weeks, to determine the meaning of Garrick's scrawls. Even the occasional word he could read made little sense.

Nothing did. None of his instructions had been followed. If Brendan didn't know better, he would have assumed that Garrick had not expected him to return.

Wearily, he looked back down, his eyes widening in an attempt to keep himself awake. They stung with fatigue. The lack of sleep. He squinted at a word, a smudge of ink and a swirl and . . .

"Horses?" he said aloud. Tossing the pen down, the ink sprinkling on his cuffs, he shook his head in confusion.

Garrick had been shipping horses to America from Ireland? What on earth for? They were not accustomed to transporting the delicate thoroughbreds across the ocean. Surely most of the animals would perish during the journey, making the venture inhumane as well as financially irresponsible. He could not make out the names of the individuals who had requested the horses, but that was almost beside the point.

What had Garrick been doing while Brendan was in London? What had his reasoning been? Months before Amanda's death Garrick had clearly been in over his head. Perhaps it hadn't been the explosion and the loss of his wife that had altered the smart, meticulous Garrick he had known at university.

There must have been something else, another event that triggered the change. Perhaps his little spiritualist—the paid spiritualist—could discover the truth. She most certainly had her ways. Any woman who could discover the very scent of an individual, and then replicate that scent, could ascertain anything.

Reaching for the pitcher of water on the corner of the desk, he noticed that although his hand was still trembling slightly, he was calmer than before.

Maybe Miss Thomason could even discover what was wrong with him, why his hand would shudder like that of a frightened schoolgirl. It had started only in the past few days, this trembling. No one else had seen it. For now, it was his secret—one he intended to keep for as long as the nuisance continued.

How had she been able to find Amanda's perfume?

A peculiar woman, Miss Thomason. She was admittedly attractive, although not in a manner all men would universally appreciate. Her figure was slight, without the curves that seemed to be considered stylish. The clothing she wore was plain but well made, perhaps not the height of fashion, but elegant. Her hair was a rich brown chestnut. Undoubtedly soft, for he saw it shine even when the parlor lights were dull. He wondered about the length, for there seemed to be a great deal of it twisted in the back. Was it curly or straight?

It mattered not. All he needed was to secure her services. That was the only vital fact he would concern himself with. That was all that was necessary.

And her features, they were rather pointed. He smiled at the thought of her chin, which was sharp without being severe. Pronounced, with a hint of a cleft. Pert might be a better word, he amended, with a mouth that was red without the use of artifice. She revealed small white teeth as she spoke her clipped words when she was so clearly annoyed with him. She didn't seem to smile much, but her eyes, large and dark, were compelling, and conveyed more than her facial expressions did. Probably a great deal more than she intended.

The question was, could Miss Thomason genuinely help Garrick?

He looked down again at the tangled mess before him. Then he realized something. He had neglected to give Miss Thomason the American currency she had requested. She had gone to the absurd length of having the request be announced at the fraudulent séance. It had gone right past Garrick, just as she had intended.

He had the currency in the safe. If she was to continue performing at her very best, he would need to keep her satisfied. It was only prudent that he would return to her home and deliver the next installment to her directly.

As he stood and stepped over to the safe, he failed to notice that his hand had stopped trembling.

Celia and Aunt Pru did their best to calm the household. It was an impossible task, given what both Eileen and Patrick had seen and the rattled state of everyone's nerves, including Celia herself. Making the situation even more difficult was the simple truth that even Celia had no idea what had really transpired. Instead of discussing it immediately, they busied themselves with the more practical matters of seeing to Patrick's bleeding nose, and the scorched bread for that evening's supper.

Celia removed the bread, checked the range, and opening the hot latch with her apron as a pot holder, added another scoop of coal to the fire. Then, she opened up the other door and pulled out the roast. "A spoon, please." She reached behind and was handed the requested spoon, and began to baste the roast.

"Miss Thomason, do you think it was an angel?" Eileen, who had said very little for the first hour, spoke in a hush.

"I . . . I don't know, really," Celia replied honestly, wiping her hands on her apron. "But I believe we should keep this to ourselves."

"Nonsense," exclaimed Aunt Pru, who had slowly recovered after several cups of tea, lightly spiked with brandy by a concerned Hannah Egan. "We'll do nothing of the sort! Tell everyone, Eileen. You too, Patrick. Let the whole world know that Miss Celia Thomason can summon angels. Think of the fortune we can make! Why, we may very well be forced to move into larger quarters to accommodate our improved situation."

"But I don't know how it happened. There is absolutely no guarantee that I'll ever be able to replicate the event again. This just happened, Aunt Prudence. I had nothing to do with it. Nor did you. It occurred, and we were here. That is all."

"Again, nonsense. You did something, Celia. There was something in your actions, or your thoughts. Perhaps you did something a little differently, altered our set pattern just a little bit. Whatever it was, it was not just chance. It was you, Celia. Something came from you, and that something caused the angel to visit our parlor." She paused, placing a hand against her round cheek. "Do you suppose it is too late to notify the papers today?" With a sad sigh she shook her head, the iron gray ringlets dancing girlishly as she did. "Never mind, there is time for that tomorrow."

"Please," Celia said firmly. "This is wrong. We should not make money from . . . from other people's misfortune."

There was an uncomfortable silence in the kitchen for a few moments. Patrick looked down at his boots. Eileen flushed. Finally Aunt Prudence let out a laugh, but not her usual cheerful laugh. "My dear, just what do you think we've been doing these last months if not gaining income from other people's losses?"

It was as if Celia had been struck in the middle. Never had they articulated what they were doing aloud, uttered the words that they were, indeed, frauds and charlatans of the worst sort. Now it was out. Aunt Pru had spoken the truth out loud.

"I . . . but . . ." Celia began.

"Perhaps you were helping people in earnest. And you did help a great many people, I am sure. You made them feel special, important. And you made them feel as if they could speak to their loved ones now dead. Already you have blessed every one of your clients with a gift. Yet don't you realize that what happened today simply proves that you were not all humbug after all? That you were, and are, really able to rouse something mysterious from beyond?"

Celia was about to deny what was just said, when there was a thunderous knock on the door.

"That must be Mr. O'Neal," Celia said, suddenly rushing to the door. No one else could pound the door so. It was both an attempt to escape the conversation, and an absurd desire to see Mr. O'Neal, perhaps to tell him what had happened. This changed the entire complexion of their deal. The sight of the real Amanda altered everything.

Straightening, she turned the large brass knob and pulled the door open.

"Miss Thomason," said the middle of the three men on the front steps.

But it was not Mr. O'Neal. It was the men coming to collect Uncle James's debt.

6

"Miss Thomason," said the largest man, still holding his place in the middle as he had a half year earlier, still possessing a hideous mottled onion bulb for a nose. "I see you are yet in mourning for your late uncle. A pity, really. A pretty girl like you shouldn't wear such dreary, dismal gowns. A shame, those dresses. Right, boys? Wouldn't you suggest something a little more, how shall I say it, friendly? Festive?"

The other two men grinned and nudged each other.

Celia swallowed. They couldn't possibly harm her physically, not steps away from the rest of the household. She needed to concentrate on the business aspect, not be frightened by their bullying ways.

Surely she had three more weeks in which to repay the debt.

"Good evening, gentlemen." She gripped the doorknob behind her and closed the door. The last thing she wanted was to have another member of the household see her with these men, to ask questions that would be too difficult to answer. "I do believe our arrangement requires further attention three weeks in the future. Not now. So if you will please excuse me, I need to . . ."

"Come, come," tsked the bulb nose. His clothing appeared exactly as it had the previous spring, a checkered vest, a burgundy-colored tie, a strangely formal stovepipe hat, and a rather shabby overcoat. The points of his collar were rimmed with grime. The other two were similarly, if somewhat less grandly, attired. "There is no reason to be unfriendly, Miss Thomason. No reason at all."

"I beg your forgiveness, sir," Celia replied. One of her neighbors, Mrs. Billingston, looked at the men as she scurried into her own house. The unmistakable sound of heavy locks tumbling into place seemed to strike the smallest man as humorous, and his narrow shoulders shook as he laughed quietly to himself.

"I will be honest, Miss Thomason," began the center man. "Times have been hard for us. Isn't that right, boys?"

"I am sorry to hear that, gentlemen." Her mind raced. What could she do? What were her choices? There was nowhere to run, no place to hide.

"How kind of you, Miss Thomason, to be so very concerned with our welfare. But you see, we were hoping you could assist us."

She did not reply.

"We were hoping to procure a small, how shall I phrase it? A small sum of money in advance of our final arrangement."

Panic gripped her middle, but she tried to remain calm. "I am very sorry, gentlemen, but I am afraid I cannot assist you."

The demeanor of the three men shifted so very

slightly, only someone who was accustomed to watching people cautiously, observing each small nuance, would have noticed. Celia noticed. The two side men let their grins drop. Both glanced at the center man. He took his time in responding, examining his fingernails, straightening his grayish cuffs.

"We have been instructed to retrieve five thousand dollars," he said in a deceptively casual voice.

Her knees buckled slightly, and she reached out to grip the iron banister.

"I believe I do have that amount, but it is unavailable at the moment."

He glanced up at her, then twisted his head as if ridding himself of a crick in his neck. "That is a shame, is it not, boys?"

The two men remained motionless, other than their eyes, which looked warily at the man in the center. They were afraid of him, she realized.

"Come closer, Miss Thomason. No need to be a stranger. We're all friends. And I have a feeling we're about to become even better friends. Isn't that so, boys?"

Instinctively she drew back.

"I said closer." With a single swipe he grasped her skirt, and only her hold on the banister prevented her from tumbling down the steps.

One thought kept coursing through her mind . . . *Why is this happening to me? Please make this stop* . . .

"I have funds in foreign currency," she whispered, the stirrings of desperation clenching within.

"Funds in foreign currency? What good would that do us!"

She reached down to push his hand away, but he

merely held tighter. His breath was hot and thick on her hand, and she pulled back.

"Well, boys. What should we do?"

"I promise, the money is good. All you need to do is . . ."

"Miss Thomason." The deep baritone rose above her panic. Wildly, frantically, she turned to the voice. There, solid and large—very large—stood Brendan O'Neal.

The two side men stepped away, leaving the onion-nosed one holding Celia's skirt. "Leave us, sir," he said over his shoulder, not looking at the source of the voice. "We have no quarrel with you."

"I am afraid you are mistaken," O'Neal said. His eyes flashed to Celia's, one brow raised, questioning.

It was as if a warm blanket had been wrapped around her shuddering shoulders. She was no longer alone. In all of the emotional turmoil, in the utter fear she had experienced that day, she suddenly felt safe, cared for.

She didn't have to be strong all alone.

Nodding at him, she tried to smile. Then something extraordinary happened. His fierce, strong features—the sharp nose, the aristocratic expression of disdain—softened. For a brief moment she felt him, his soul, his heart.

For that brief moment he touched her.

Then he grinned and gave her a fleeting wink that was gone before she could respond. And he again returned to his most intimidating self.

"I repeat, you are mistaken. I do have a quarrel with you."

The onion-nosed man finally looked over at O'Neal. His grip loosened on Celia's skirt as he took in the size of the other man, the obvious strength. Then he stood and glanced at his two cronies, who were attempting to surreptitiously creep away.

"Well, I am sure we can clear up this misunderstanding." He nodded, then removed his top hat. "Sir," he added.

"I am sure we can," O'Neal replied. "Now leave Miss Thomason alone."

"Sir. Our dealings with Miss Thomason are a most urgent financial matter. A business matter."

"Very well. Then I suggest you conduct your business matters during proper business hours." He slowly reached into his inside pocket and Celia held her breath. What would emerge—a weapon?

The three men clearly had the same impression. Bravado rushed from them like water in a sieve. O'Neal calmly produced a pocket watch, snapped open the cover, then flipped it shut and returned it with leisurely aplomb.

"I believe the customary business hours conclude at five, do they not?"

"But of course! Yes indeed . . ." He bowed to Celia, then to O'Neal. "We had no idea the hour was so late, did we, gentlemen?"

The other two nodded with eager sincerity, their heads bobbing in unison. "We was here on a matter of business, you see. Yes. Well, good day to you both." He tipped his hat, bowing slightly as he all but bounded off the steps to join his companions.

The three men left almost as one solid unit, shoulder to shoulder, winding through the square and only barely avoiding a tree.

"Miss Thomason?" O'Neal was at her side in two

strides up the steps. His hand cupped her elbow, and she felt warmth sear through the black wool of her sleeve.

"I . . . thank you." She realized how close she had come to disaster. In her will to protect the household, she would have done almost anything to prevent them from entering.

What would have happened to her, to Aunt Pru?

"What sort of business did you have with those men?"

She hesitated before speaking. "While I appreciate your concern, I do not believe you need to know."

"I heard part of your exchange with them. They were moneylenders, were they not?"

"Again, I do not believe . . ."

"How could you be so naive as to get involved with men of their quality? Surely you must know there are more appropriate ways to procure funds. There are proper channels, institutions called banks, in case you have not heard . . ."

The last thing she needed was a lecture.

"Yes, I am aware of that, Mr. O'Neal." Suddenly she was more exhausted than she had been in her entire life. Her very bones seemed weary, as if weighted down by lead.

"Are you ill, Miss Thomason?" His tone was no longer a verbal challenge, and he peered down at her almost as if he was concerned.

Avoiding his gaze, she looked down at the hem of her skirt, the marks of the onion-nosed man still visible. "No, Mr. O'Neal. I'm not ill, just fatigued."

"Have you had tea yet, or supper?"

"No. We were just preparing supper when those three charming gentlemen arrived."

"And you failed to invite them to join you? Where were your manners, Miss Thomason?"

In her exhaustion, she almost turned to ask if he was mad. Then she saw his expression, a slight smile there, and she grinned. "I have no clue, sir. I am most certain they think me very ill mannered indeed, especially when held against their own stellar behavior."

"They were shocked, Miss Thomason, judging by their hasty exit. But tell me, since you have been outside entertaining your various gentlemen callers, is it possible you have missed your own supper?"

"Not only is it possible," she said, realizing how chilly the night air was, then how very hungry she had become. When was the last time she had eaten? At breakfast. "It is entirely probable that I have missed supper."

"Well, Miss Thomason, I too have come here on matters of business. But first, perhaps we can discuss the issues over a meal at the Astor House?"

"The Astor House!" Celia repeated, stunned. Everyone knew that the two most elegant—and expensive—dining establishments in all of New York, perhaps all of the United States, were Delmonico's and the Astor House. Uncle James claimed he had been there when Davy Crockett signed the registry. But she never quite believed him.

Celia Thomason, dining at the Astor House?

"Do you not approve of the Astor?" O'Neal asked with all sincerity. "I was led to believe that it's a respectable establishment."

"Oh, it is, sir. I have not been there since . . ." The truth was, never. She had only walked by, or seen it passing from a carriage window, the beautifully dressed men and women who seemed to have stepped straight from *Godey's Lady's Book* as they stood elegantly before the massive structure.

And it was a well-known fact that regular citizens, even regular citizens who lived just off Washington Square, could not simply waltz through the Astor's blue granite facade unless they were guests of the hotel, or with a guest. All of her acquaintances naturally lived in the city, and thus had no reason to maintain rooms at the Astor House.

Yet she didn't want him to know she had never been there. She was well bred. To all appearances she was comfortably maintained, residing just off fashionable Washington Square—if only for the near future. No, there was no need for him to know the absolute truth.

"You have not been there since when, Miss Thomason?" he urged.

"Since my uncle passed away," she said almost truthfully. It was an accurate statement, perhaps leading the listener to mistakenly assume she had frequented the place like a mad creature with exotic out-of-town guests until the unfortunate death of her uncle forced her into mourning. Well, that was his misunderstanding, strictly speaking. She stiffened, as if insulted by the very notion that Celia Thomason had never been to the Astor House.

"Of course." He bowed. "I apologize. My brother-in-law has secured rooms there, and I presume he will be dining there this evening. And I have not yet canceled my own suite there. Thus I was hoping we could pass a meal in an atmosphere that is more comfortable to him. It is vital that you gain his complete trust for our plan to succeed."

"Yes, yes, of course."

"So while I apologize for the short notice, would you please accompany me to supper at the Astor House?"

"I . . . yes. Certainly." She glanced down at her plain dress, with neither lace nor trim, and realized she had nothing appropriate to wear to such a grand meal. The best she could do would be to freshen herself up and wrap herself in her best cloak, which wasn't nearly splendid enough for the occasion.

"If you wish, I will wait here for you."

"Oh, forgive me! Please, come into the parlor."

She opened the front door, and immediately the household, who had been gathered on the other side— including Aunt Prudence—scattered in all directions. Recovering, Aunt Prudence deliberately turned and faced them.

"Oh! Mr. O'Neal! What a very pleasant surprise."

Both Brendan and Celia were staring at the glass in her hands, the glass that had moments before been placed between her ear and the front door to provide enhanced sound quality. "Good evening, sir." She smiled guiltily and made a delicate coughing sound. "Celia, dear, you'd best get ready. You can wear my best capuchin, the dark green silk one with the hood. As for your hair, perhaps Eileen can help dress it more suitably for the occasion. I believe supper is served at nine o'clock promptly at . . ." Her round cheeks flushed as she almost revealed her eavesdropping.

"Mrs. Cooper," Brendan said with polite ease. "I do hope it does not inconvenience you in any way, but I would be delighted if your niece could accompany me to supper at the . . . hum . . ." Rubbing his chin, he turned to Celia. "Where did we agree to dine?"

"I don't recall." Celia tilted her head. "Was it Sullivan's Oyster Emporium on Canal Street?"

"Is that the cellar with the sawdust and the six-cent plan?"

"Indeed it is," Celia encouraged.

"No, that was not it. Was it that tavern run by the notorious Mrs. . . ."

"Good heavens, no, Mr. O'Neal," Celia exclaimed.

"Forgive me, then, Miss Thomason. I seem to have forgotten where we had decided to take our supper."

"The Astor House!" Aunt Prudence finally cried, unable to bear the tension for another moment. "I believe I heard you refer to the Astor House as you were speaking loudly and walking through the front door. I distinctly heard you say the Astor House. Upon my word, I did."

"Indeed?" He raised an eyebrow. "Well, in that case, Miss Thomason, would the Astor House suffice?"

"Well, I suppose it will just have to do, although I confess to a longing for oysters tonight."

"But rest assured, the Astor House can provide you with a dozen oyster dishes, can they not, Mr. O'Neal?" Aunt Prudence was growing alarmed. "More than a dozen, I would judge, and of a far higher quality than Sullivan's Oyster Emporium. Now you go upstairs with Eileen, while I entertain Mr. O'Neal. And Eileen, use my comb box—I believe there is a turtle-shell comb that would be lovely on Celia."

"Mr. O'Neal," Celia began, "I'll be with you in a moment . . ."

But she did not have a chance to conclude. Aunt Pru, suddenly a giddy young thing once more, reached up and slipped her arm through his. "Now, Mr. O'Neal, come with me and have a glass of brandy. Speaking of my turtle comb reminds me, have you ever enjoyed the pleasure of a truly magnificent turtle soup?"

With a helpless glance at Celia, he looked down at a beaming Prudence Cooper, who had not stopped talking. "Well, I met my own dear husband James at a turtle feast many years ago. Indeed it was . . . well. Many years ago. It was at Bayard's Tavern. They had a three-hundred-pound turtle from the West Indies, and my, the soup they made! They served it up from one in the afternoon until ten in the evening, and I believe I had five bowls before Mr. Cooper finally noticed me. There has never been a turtle soup the likes of Bayard's. It was more of a chowder, with plenty of calipash."

"Calipash?" Celia heard him ask politely as they entered the parlor.

"Why, yes! That is much like a . . ." Aunt Pru's voice faded, and Celia paused for just a moment before she climbed the stairs, her smooth forehead creased with two light lines.

Within a span of less than thirty minutes, he had demonstrated an ability to bully the most aggressive of bullies, look at her with a startling degree of gentleness, make her smile, loudly berate her business acumen, and then charm her often trying aunt with sweet patience and humor.

So far she had been both intimidated and enchanted by this man, infuriated and captivated. So, what sort of man was Mr. Brendan O'Neal? It was a question she longed to have answered, yet it was also a question she feared. For once she knew more about him, she had a peculiar, uncomfortable feeling she would never be free of him. And no matter what happened, she knew already that just meeting a man such as Brendan O'Neal had changed her forever.

Celia had never been a woman to consider her appearance very carefully. Not that she did not care—she did. She simply did not wish to go to the ridiculous lengths of other women in order to secure a man. For that was the ultimate goal, real or implied, in attending to physical beauty. And Aunt Prudence, by her constant harping on Celia's hopelessly tall and slender frame, had reinforced the notion that nothing but heroic measures would alter the outcome. As a result, Celia had always been neat and well groomed, but always in the most simple and unobtrusive way.

She had intended to wash her face and hands, perhaps slip into one of her best plain gowns and maybe brush and repin her hair—all of those steps being her usual pre-anything routine. But as promised, or threatened, by Aunt Pru, Eileen followed her into her room.

"Really, Eileen. Thank you, but I can manage on my own."

"No, Miss. Mrs. Cooper insisted I come up with you. And besides, my fingers have been itching to get at you!"

"Pardon me?"

"Miss Celia, do you not know how lovely you could be? Oh, please, please let me help you!"

Eileen's tone was so sincere, her hands clasped before her, that Celia gave in. It was easier than attempting to get rid of her.

And seeing Eileen in that pose, hands together as if in prayer, reminded Celia of earlier in the day, when the ghost had come. Suddenly, the thought of physical help was welcome.

As Eileen worked, Celia thought about the day, about the ghost, Garrick's exit, the three men and Brendan O'Neal, and finally, about the Astor House. There was a dreamlike quality to the past ten hours, it seemed as if breakfast had been a lifetime ago.

"Here we go, Miss Celia. Raise your arms. Grand!"

She submitted to the pinches and the pulls of her best corset and chemise, to the tug of the hairbrush and the sharp jabs of pins. Finally Eileen tied a velvet ribbon around Celia's neck, much like a noose, Celia thought.

"Oh, Miss Celia," whispered Eileen, stepping back and observing her own handiwork. "You look beautiful, just like a fairy!"

"A very tall fairy who . . ." Celia began. Then she saw herself in the full-length oval mirror as Eileen tilted it forward.

Of all the strange events of the day, perhaps this was the strangest of all. Celia slowly raised her hand to her cheek, as if to make sure the reflection was really hers. For in truth, she hardly recognized the image.

It was a Celia Thomason she had never before seen, never even imagined. The dress, one of her plain and functional deep maroon taffeta gowns, had been altered just slightly by the addition of a creamy rose sash, softening the entire gown. And Eileen had somehow fastened lace at the cuffs and bordering the neckline, making the transition from prim afternoon dress to a rather elegant dinner dress.

"Eileen, you are a marvel!"

Her hair was braided on both sides, fastened with

two of Aunt Pru's combs, but otherwise much the same as her usual style. Those minor changes, however, made an astonishing difference, from plain to elegant. And the black ribbon on her neck, the only extra adornment, lent her skin a luminous quality. Even her eyes seemed brighter, her lips full and red.

"Eileen," she said in wonder. "You made me look pretty."

"No I didn't, Miss Celia." Eileen placed her hands on Celia's shoulders. "You have always been pretty. I just added a few bits here and there to make you sparkle. Your beauty has always been there—you just couldn't see it before."

Taking a deep breath, she hugged Eileen and descended the stairs, wondering what kind of reaction she would receive, if any at all. The moment she stepped into the parlor, Aunt Pru gasped, and Brendan jumped to his feet. An expression of astonishment crossed his face, and then he smiled, slowly, with warmth and genuine pleasure that caused the corners of his eyes to crinkle.

"Miss Thomason, shall we?" He crossed the room and crooked his arm. It felt so right, her hand on his. She felt giddy, like singing and laughing and crying all at once. Aunt Pru handed her the silk cape as promised, but unfortunately—because of the vast difference in the two women's height—the hem of the cloak came just slightly below her knees.

"Oh dear," sighed Aunt Prudence as she handed Celia the kid gloves.

"Why, Miss Thomason," he said softly. "I believe you will start a new fashion. By next week it will be all the rage."

"Thank you, sir. This is such a very new style, they have yet to even dream of it in Paris."

She left her home with him by her side, solid and real and so very alive it was difficult to see beyond his potent existence. But she did, savoring every moment, the way he hailed a cab—as audacious as any New Yorker, stepping into the middle of the street and whistling—his hand on the small of her back as he guided her into the coach.

"The Astor House," he said crisply to the driver, who nodded with respect and pride—not every day did a fare ask to go to such a lofty destination.

They drove down Broadway, that glorious bustling street, the gas lamps just lit, the glow from shop windows and homes bathing the avenue in warmth. A.T. Stewart's Marble Palace was the anchor of the great shopping stretch, taking up more than an entire block and housing separate departments for clothing and food and dry goods. Mr. Stewart called it a "department store," and it was nothing short of magnificent.

Everything in the world could be had on Broadway, tea and silk from China, skins and ivory from Africa. There was a store for everything imaginable, and much that was not. Some shops were already preparing for the Christmas and New Year's holidays.

"They seem to dress earlier every year," she commented.

He said nothing, but smiled and looked at the gentle slope of her throat, the soft white of her hands.

She pointed out the spot where the Astor Place Opera House riot had spilled over in May, explaining the frenzy over who was a better Shakespearean actor, the British-born William Macready or the younger

American Edwin Forrest. Twenty-three people had lost their lives, mostly young men, mostly over a misplaced patriotic belief that watching an Englishman perform *Macbeth* was denying the basics of Jacksonian democracy.

"The Bowery B'hoys take offense at brocade waistcoats," she explained, watching the sights from the window as they passed an omnibus. "They thought the opera house and its patrons too grand for America. Poor Mayor Woodhull was at wit's end, and thought he was doing the best thing by calling for two divisions of the Seventh Regiment to assist. And so they arrived with their musketry, lined up in their military rows before the crowds. And somehow, they began firing—matching stones with rifle volley. Twenty-three perished, none of the soldiers of course. But in the end the real tragedy wasn't *Macbeth*, but Americans firing upon Americans. That had never happened before, and God willing, it will never happen again."

"It will."

She turned to him. "Excuse me?"

"I said it will. I'm from Ireland, and I've lived in England. Yours is a new nation. But I'm afraid it will happen again on a far greater field, American against American."

He watched her reaction in the flickering lights. Instead of arguing, she swallowed and glanced out of the window once more. "Yes," she said softly.

Then she continued speaking of the formal gardens left over from the last century, with names like Vauxhall and Mount Vernon and Washington, where all of the fine people would gather to hear music and see entertainment of all sorts. There were roses and white

fences and climbing trellises and swings where even
adults could fly to the clouds. Of the times she went to
Niblo's gardens with her parents and had real French
ice cream and lemonade, of the impromptu great
horseraces down Broadway. Over there, she said, were
all new buildings, everything had been destroyed in
the Great Fire of 1835. Down that little alley was a
small cemetery with headstones dating back to the
seventeenth century.

And as she spoke he watched her, not following her
pointed finger as she described locations and events
from her childhood, or from New York's past. He just
watched her.

A strange emotion knotted in his throat. What
spell had she cast over him, this perplexing American? He was not unfamiliar with women—on the
contrary, he was considered something of a rake by
more than a few in England. But this one was fresh
and vivid, somehow unspoiled, although she should
have been lavished with praise by the men of New
York. If she ever stepped foot in London, she would
be a sensation.

How he would like to be with her then.

"Here we are!" Her eyes widened at the sight of the
Astor House, five floors of pure splendor, with running
water and every room lit with gas. Imposing marble
columns framed the wide entrance, with the most luxurious of stores on the ground floor. Leary and Co. Hat-
ters were just to the left, where Uncle James had bought
his last top hat.

The carriage pulled up, and the driver hopped
down to hold the door for Brendan. Brendan in turn
helped Celia to the street, to the carriage block on the

curb just so her feet would not touch the muck of the pavement.

She felt dizzy with excitement, and clutched his arm as they ascended the small white steps.

"Tell me, Miss Thomason. Have you ever enjoyed champagne?"

She smiled, wondering what to say. Of course he would think her a provincial dunce if she admitted she had never even tasted it. This wasn't a lie, she rationalized to herself. This was simply a way to make Mr. O'Neal feel more comfortable in a new country with unfamiliar surroundings. It would be positively inhospitable to deny the man the drinks he was accustomed to, and should she confess to never having drunk champagne, well, he would certainly abstain himself out of politeness.

Besides, she had always longed to taste champagne.

"Oh, yes." She leaned toward him. "There is nothing I enjoy quite as much as champagne."

He smiled, and they entered the massive lobby.

And that was the last perfectly clear moment of the evening.

7

$\mathcal{J}$ohn Jacob Astor, whose wealth had originated from a spectacularly successful fur-trading business, decided that among his many possessions there should be a hotel. So with the impatience and audacity that only a great deal of money could provide, he got one, and in the process redefined the very meaning of the word luxury.

Designed by Isaiah Rogers, the celebrated architect, it was a massive structure of almost four hundred rooms built around an airy courtyard. Besides plumbing and gas lighting, each room featured a unique, elaborate in-house bell system with the futuristic name of the "announciator." There were curiosities galore in every corner of the place, from the remarkable notion of separate keys for each guest room to stiffly uniformed bellboys performing every task requested, through the usual means as well as through the announciator.

Each room was embellished with lavish furniture, mostly heavy black walnut, resting on the finest and, some complained, most garish carpet imaginable. John

Jacob Astor was intent on proving his spectacular wealth, not necessarily his taste. He firmly believed that guests who were able to pay such astronomical rates should be rewarded with whatever eye-popping novelty or luxury he could buy.

"Just think," Brendan murmured as he lifted Celia's cloak from her shoulders. "All this from the skins of wild animals."

"And still, no one seems able to hit the spittoon," she replied, carefully stepping over a puddle of tobacco juice. Several young boys clad in red jackets scurried about the lobby mopping the spills with discreet brooms and sponges.

"Mr. O'Neal, sir," intoned a somber-looking gentleman who appeared from nowhere, and seemed to be dressed like an officer of a small European army, with gold epaulettes squaring his shoulders and gleaming brass buttons. "How delighted we are to have you return. Your rooms are in excellent order." He then turned to Celia, his eyes taking in her attire and demeanor to ascertain, she suspected, if she was worthy enough to enter the Astor House.

Apparently she passed inspection. "Ma'am." He bowed. "Allow me to take your wraps. Refreshments are being served in the lounges."

Brendan glanced around the lobby, oblivious to the lavish wealth displayed with such abandon. He scanned the room for Garrick, who should be comfortably settled into the Gentlemen's Lounge, or perhaps relaxing at the bar. But he was nowhere to be found, at least not then.

The decor was all but overshadowed by the sumptuous fashions of the other patrons. The men's brightly colored waistcoats flashed from the folds of their coats, boots shimmered from under the gaslighting, watch fobs jangled. These were the most splendid of the splendid, pound per pound the wealthiest and most powerful gentlemen in the world. For these were not, for the most part, New Yorkers. This was a truly international multitude, and if one listened carefully one could detect accents of all kinds, watch the polished manners of European counts and men of note.

But it was the women who glittered with the most brilliance, with the sheen of their gowns in every shade of the rainbow, with their glistening hair and, of course, the jewels about their arms and throats and even braided into their hair, ribbons of diamonds and gold.

The women regarded each other with cool, yet white-hot, interest, sliding glances from behind feathered fans or elegantly gloved and bejeweled hands. The newest fashions from France were on display, well before the swiftest publications could print the patterns. And sharp-eyed matrons of all ages quickly determined just which fabric would suit their figures, and which styles would be most likely to conceal their flaws.

All of this Celia watched and noted from the safety of Brendan's side.

"Have you seen my brother-in-law?" Brendan asked the attendant.

"Ah, Mr. Stevens. He has not yet appeared for supper, although I suspect he will arrive shortly. Shall I inform him of your presence, sir?"

"Yes, please do." Brendan nodded, dismissing the man as he held his arm for Celia. "Champagne, Miss Thomason?"

She nodded as if, of course, it was time for champagne, just as the afternoon signaled teatime and the sound of a rooster meant the break of day.

They strolled through the lobby slowly, and Brendan repressed an urge to smile. For him, it was a pure delight to be with her, to watch her attempt to remain calm and composed even as her eyes sparkled more brightly than any gem in the room. And while he enjoyed her company, he was also aware that somehow, her behavior moved him. He was touched by her, not that there was anything pitiful about Celia Thomason. Yet there was a winsome quality to her that he found difficult to dismiss.

She was the only woman in the lobby without jewels. Her plain black ribbon was her only adornment, yet still she seemed to shine above the rest.

They entered the lounge, silver trays being held aloft by steady-footed waiters. He caught the eye of a server who paused and handed them each a flute of champagne.

"Oh, it's so cold," she commented. Then she flushed and took a sip. Her eyes widened and she smiled. "Oh!"

"Is the champagne to your liking, Miss Thomason?"

With unfettered delight she took another sip. "Yes, it's wonderful!"

It was a joy to witness her pleasure, such a simple and pure happiness. "Now be careful, my dear. Champagne has a way of creeping up on you."

"Well, Mr. O'Neal, I can't imagine anything I'd rather have creep up on me than this!"

He laughed, and she paused, watching his brown-black eyes glisten in the orangish light. The champagne tickled her lips as she watched him drink from his own glass, and she suddenly wondered very much what his lips would feel like against hers, and if . . .

Stop this, she told herself.

"Mr. O'Neal." She tried to keep her voice even and businesslike, but it was most difficult with the general air of gaiety swirling through the room. The women all seemed so beautiful, the men all so handsome—none, of course, more handsome than Mr. O'Neal. Other women took note of him surreptitiously, glancing from behind silk fans or under long lashes as they passed.

He was, she concluded, the most dashing man in the room, perhaps in the entire hotel. Maybe even in all of the city.

No, she decided. He was nothing less than the most dashing man in the world.

And the second glass of champagne sprinkled her nose with pin-sized bubbles.

"Yes, Miss Thomason?" He leaned toward her, as if she had been speaking.

Oh, yes, she thought. She *had* been speaking.

"Mr. O'Neal," she repeated. It was such a wonderful name, Brendan O'Neal. It was warm yet dignified, elegant yet somehow approachable.

"Miss Thomason?"

What was she about to say to him? Then she remembered. "Yes, Mr. O'Neal. I was just wondering, does your brother-in-law come to supper often?" There. She had said it. That called for another sample of this remarkable champagne.

"Indeed he does," he confirmed. "He seems to have supper on a regular basis." He gestured to another server. "Miss Thomason, may I suggest a cup of punch? It's quite refreshing."

"No thank you. This is quite refreshing enough."

He gave her a look she couldn't precisely read as she

reached for a glass of champagne for herself from a passing tray. She was only being polite, she reasoned. The poor waiter was so busy, she couldn't possibly bother him when it would be only too easy for her to help herself.

"Miss Thomason, I really believe you should . . ."

Odd, she thought, how she could hear his voice so clearly, yet the words were supercilious.

Supercilious. Now wasn't that a funny word? Whoever thought of it?

He had such beautiful hands. Long fingers, strength there; neat, square nails. Such beautiful hands.

"Miss Thomason?"

And teeth. Very white teeth, not too big, not too small. Sometimes people, even the best of people, had terrible teeth. There was Mr. Ludlow, for instance. A man with everything—his own carriage, or did he have two? A large brick house on the square. A lovely wife. Well, perhaps lovely was too strong a word. Lovely. That wasn't it.

"Supercilious," Celia proclaimed.

"Excuse me?"

Brendan O'Neal was very handsome indeed. By far the most handsome man in the room. A woman passed, her gaze resting for an instant on Brendan O'Neal.

"He is, isn't he?" Celia confirmed, sipping her champagne.

"Who is?" he asked.

But of course he knew. He knew exactly what she meant.

And then he took the champagne from her hand.

"What are you doing?" she asked, her voice high-pitched as she attempted to reclaim her glass. But he stacked it onto a tray, and then it was gone.

"Miss Thomason, I believe . . ."

And then there was the loudest sound she had ever heard.

Did she scream?

Without thinking, she threw herself against Brendan O'Neal for safety. Surely the walls were about to tumble in on everyone. She clamped her hands over her ears, closed her eyes, and waited for the end to come.

Nothing happened.

Slowly she opened her eyes. A column of men in white uniforms with white gloves entered the room, marching in unison.

No one else seemed the least bit frightened, although a few people smiled at her and whispered behind their gloved hands.

"My dear," O'Neal said, gently removing her hands from her ears. "That was the dinner gong. I was trying to warn you—it tends to alarm the unsuspecting diners."

"I . . . I . . . of course." She straightened. "I knew that. I was just seeing if you knew. Did you know? You did, didn't you?"

She missed the grin on his face.

"Now we follow these gentlemen into the dining room," he explained.

In pairs, couples filed into the adjoining room, accompanied by the rigid waiters, who marched with absolute solemnity.

"When do we get our blindfolds?" She had meant to whisper, but somehow her voice carried. Several men and a few women smiled, but the waiters ignored her.

Then they were led to long tables. The waiters suddenly had white aprons tied about their waists. Where had those come from?

And then he entered, the grand headwaiter. He stood in the center of the dining room, glaring at his men with a glacierlike stare. He, too, was in crisp white, but without the apron. Across his chest were badges, and she wondered what they were for, for triumphs of dinners and luncheons past?

Without warning, he turned on his heels and struck a mighty gong. And the waiters marched into the kitchen, returning in an instant with massive silver tureens with ornate lids, and rested them on the tables.

By then the diners had been settled into their seats. With the second clang the waiters lifted the lids of the tureens like cymbals in an orchestra, steam rushing into the air, and as one they slammed the lids down.

"Ha," she said to Brendan. "They thought they had me! I was expecting that!"

In a whirl the servers ladled out the soup without spilling a single drop. Oddly, they held the lids in their left hand as they served with their right, giving the impression of medieval knights with their mighty shields.

When everyone was served, there was a split-second pause. Almost imperceptibly, the grand headwaiter nodded—not a nod, really, more of a slight bob of his great head. And the waiters clanged down their lids once, returned them to the now-empty tureens. Raising their burden high over their heads, they trotted back into the kitchen for the next course.

"We must tell your aunt that we dined on turtle soup," she heard him say.

Dinner passed in a blur of clangs and gongs, punctu-

ated by clattering plates and wineglasses being filled
and refilled with each course. Silverware clanked and
conversation wafted in and out of her mind.

There was game, from black ducks to plover and
short-neck snipe and quail. There were elaborately
dressed game pies and molded pâtés and forcemeats.
There were dozens of beef dishes, with olives and
mushrooms and tomatoes and goose liver and beef
pies, all with vines or artfully pressed bits of pastry.
Each spectacular dish was a still life, the work of a
master. And each platter vied for attention, clamored
for the ultimate compliment of being broken and cut
and consumed.

Then came fish, some with their eyes embellished
with tiny onions glowing like pearls, and oyster pies layered with truffles, and snails slipped back into their polished shells. The food seemed to never end. There were
ices in silver cups and cakes of infinite flavor and fashion, from butter cream iced cakes to a six-layer orange
confection decorated with delicate flowers made of colored sugar.

It was the most, and the most marvelous, food she
had ever seen.

One man at her table took a single slice of goose, and
then it was gone—his goose, one slice. It was whisked
away with the other finished or nearly finished or un-
touched dishes, piled high and covered and taken away.

She wondered where Mr. Stevens was; and when Mr.
O'Neal started talking, she listened, but really she was
taking in the sights and sounds and everything else
about dinner.

After that things became very peculiar. She was
aware that he was helping her to her feet, and then

there was a whirl and then she was in a wonderful, soft bed.

And that was all she could remember.

Celia sighed, inhaling the fragrance of the pillow. Whatever soap the girls had been using on the laundry, she had to remember to tell them how very fresh and crisp it made the linens smell.

Her head ached.

"Would you like some water?" the man asked.

The man!

With a gasp she sat bolt upright. She was in a room she had never seen before in her entire life, ensconced in a massive bed she had never before been in. And at the foot of that massive black walnut bed was Mr. Brendan O'Neal, fully clothed, seated in a rocking chair. Back and forth he went. Suddenly, Celia had an awful feeling she was going to become ill.

"A touch of mal de mer, Miss Thomason?"

She threw her back against the fortress of pillows behind her and clutched the sheets and coverlets under her chin.

"I . . . how . . ." she began.

"Do you happen to have a friend by the name of Mary?" he inquired languidly, examining his fingernails, then returning his gaze to hers. Again he rocked back and forth in the great chair.

"I . . . no. I do not have a friend named Mary," she rasped.

"That's a pity, because you're visiting her."

"What?"

"I sent word last night to your Aunt Prudence that you had met your old friend Mary, and were going to visit with her and return this morning. So if I were you, I'd make all attempts to recall a friend named Mary from your youth. It will make your entrance into Washington Square much more pleasant."

"I . . ." She swallowed, breathing hard. "Mary?"

"No. You Celia. I came up with the name Mary simply because everyone, at some point in their life, can lay claim to at least one acquaintance by the name of Mary. Which is precisely why I did not use a more problematic name such as Bertha or Madeline."

And he rocked some more.

"Oh," she said at last, closing her eyes.

What had she done last night?

Clenching the sheets in her fists, she tried to remember, but the pounding headache prevented any rational thought.

Had she . . . with him?

Brendan O'Neal?

"Are you quite well?"

Finally she opened her eyes. "Could you please stop rocking?"

"Yes. Certainly. Forgive me."

There was an uncomfortable silence, and then he started rocking again.

"If I may say so, I do believe you should have had the punch when it was offered, Miss Thomason."

She did not reply. All of her efforts were centered on recalling the events of the previous night.

"And may I also add something else?" he said.

Last night, she was thinking. *What had happened last night?*

"I believe we should get married as soon as possible."

"Oh, Lord."

"Is that a yes?"

"I . . ." She had to think of something, anything. What on earth had happened last night? Was it possible that they . . . No. That was impossible. She would feel different, there would be a vast change. Keeping her voice conversational, she said as casually as possible, "Is Mr. Stevens here?"

"Don't you remember?"

"Of course I do." She thought there was a very good chance she might be ill. "I was just wondering if the situation is, um. Well. I was just curious. What I mean, is that, well. Is the situation precisely as it was last night?"

"It is."

"Well, that's . . . good."

"No, I fear it is not good, Celia. Do you mind if I call you Celia? We are, after all, betrothed."

"No we aren't!"

"May I call you Celia, my dear?"

"Yes, but no, we are not betrothed!"

"I believe we should leave as soon as possible. Immediately after the ceremony."

"Excuse me?"

"To find Garrick."

"To find . . . well. Of course we should. But I do not believe getting married is necessary."

Languidly, he again examined his fingernails. "After last night, I fear it is. And the sooner we complete the details, the sooner we can try to find Garrick."

"After last night?" This was impossible, she thought frantically. Wouldn't she remember something as monumental as *that*? Surely she would! Why, she couldn't even recall kissing him.

"You *do* remember last night, Celia. Don't you?"

And she didn't feel any different than she had the day before. Wasn't this supposed to be a life-changing experience?

She nodded, hoping to change the topic. "About Garrick . . . has anything changed since last night?"

"Again, no," he replied. "At the risk of repeating myself, do you have any idea why he may have left town? When I asked you last evening, you seemed to find the whole thing quite amusing. Then you said that you knew exactly why he fled, but you refused to tell me."

"Well . . ." she began, feeling a new wave of nausea wash over her. "I believe your sister actually appeared to me yesterday afternoon. He seemed quite upset, and he ran out of the house before I could stop him."

"Interesting. But as I have said before, I am not paying you to fool me. While I respect your professional consistency, and agree in principle that you should pretend at all times to be the genuine article, I am paying you to convince Garrick that you have the ability to summon Amanda. And as I have also stated, I do not wish to have him frightened out of his senses. On the contrary, I want him to regain those lost senses. Now why don't you rise. I'll have some coffee and toast brought up. Do you happen to have a gown that would be appropriate for a wedding?"

"I don't wish to offend you, sir, but neither do I want to marry you. But thank you very much for the offer. Oh, and thank you for last night."

A dark eyebrow arched.

"I mean, for the dinner! It was quite lovely." At least, she thought it had been. The details were rather vague.

"I am delighted you were so pleased with your meal. But aside from that, I do fear we must marry."

"But, sir, I . . ."

"You may call me Brendan."

"Yes, sir. But I have no desire to marry. Not you, not anyone. This is no reflection on you. I have just seen so many truly miserable marriages, the whole notion does not appeal to me. But rest assured, we will locate your brother-in-law, I will perform the duties for which you contracted me, and once I am paid I can return to a more normal life."

"And what if there is a child?"

She felt as if a fist had slammed into her middle. "A child?" she gasped.

"Yes." How could he be so cool, so unemotional?

"I . . . well . . . I didn't . . . did I . . ."

"As you know, I am the only remaining O'Neal. While I had thought of marrying one day, I believe doing so at this point would be advantageous to both of us."

"I . . ." There was nothing she could think of to say. "Well, as you know, I . . . oh my God." She clamped her hand over her mouth. She wasn't sure if she was going to scream or become ill. Then, glancing down, she realized she was wearing some sort of nightgown with long lacy sleeves. It was exquisite, the loveliest thing she had ever seen, much less worn.

And then she realized it was torn. A great jagged rip had split the delicate fabric over her left shoulder.

"You tore your gown." He nodded toward the tear. "We will marry before the end of the day."

"No. No," she whispered. How could she possibly marry a stranger, and a stranger who had clearly attacked her? Granted, she could feel no bruises, could detect no signs of violence other than the torn nightgown. But she would never marry, certainly not Mr. O'Neal. Not anyone.

"You have no choice, I'm afraid. Now those three gentlemen from yesterday. They seemed quite insistent."

"As soon as you pay me, after I have completed the task you wish me to fulfill, I will deal with them. So you see . . ."

"I do not intend to pay you, Celia."

"What!" she shouted, and she didn't care.

"Why should I pay you when you have made the situation with Garrick worse, not better? He's terrified and he has vanished. I could have accomplished those two deeds without your help, Celia."

"But that makes you a cheat."

"No it does not. And besides, coming from a professional fraud, your insult does not hit its mark."

"I will not marry you."

"Yes you will. Think of the absolute disgrace when the newspapers see your signed admission of being a fraudulent spiritualist? Or how Aunt Prudence would feel to know her dear late husband had left you both in debt? Yes, I know all about your Uncle James's debts. If you believe those three men will go away on their own, you are very much mistaken. The only change will be that they will pursue your aunt rather than you. And where will your aunt live? Not to mention the servants, of which there are already too many for any practical purpose."

This was impossible, it couldn't be happening. How could her world have turned so utterly wretched in a matter of minutes?

Now she had no future. Absolutely none. She would be tied to this man for the rest of her life.

"Tell me," she said at last. "How could you possibly marry someone who does not wish to marry you?"

He flinched almost imperceptibly, but she had seen it. Then he rose to his full height, and again she was reminded of his colossal size. At times she had forgotten his vastness, since his movements were graceful enough to not call attention to it. But now, alone with this man—this very large man—it was impossible not to feel like an insignificant speck lying at the foot of the mightiest of trees.

Looming above, he spoke as if she had not uttered even the mildest of protests. "I will have your clothes sent up, as they were pressed this morning. And then we will go to Washington Square and share the good news with your aunt. Good morning, Celia."

Stiffly, he walked from the room, closing the door gently behind him.

Staring at the closed door, hearing his footsteps retreat, she had an overwhelming sense of fear and loneliness.

And then Celia began to cry.

Why was he doing this?

He stood in front of his mirror, the rooms that had been Garrick's. Of course Brendan had slept there the night before, after having seen Celia was settled in his own abandoned rooms. He'd never seen someone have such a reaction to two glasses of champagne. She had been giddy and enchanting, twirling around the room in the nightgown that would have been Amanda's. He had found it in Garrick's trunk.

And then she had tripped on the hem, tearing the gown just before she fell asleep. And she snored.

Why did he want to marry her, this peculiar American woman?

Because something deep within him told him he would never be lonely with Celia.

But now, of course, she hated him.

Yet if he did not marry her, he knew he would never see her again. He would go after Garrick, she would remain in Washington Square, and that would be that.

Still, how on earth had he come up with the insanely illogical plan to marry her? He had been almost as startled as she had been when he heard the words coming from his mouth.

He let her believe that she had been compromised. That, and the signed document and his knowledge of James Cooper's business dealings, were all he had.

And what a charming bit of work he had performed.

He wouldn't be surprised if she hated him forever. It was certainly what he deserved.

He finished knotting his cravat. It was perfect, the knot. And that was good. Details such as the perfectly knotted tie were part of what identified him. He left the room wondering how Celia would react, if this would turn out to be the biggest mistake of his life, or the best thing that had ever happened to him. No longer did he feel as if he was on the edge of a cliff about to be pushed. Instead he was on the edge of a cliff waiting and fully expecting to jump.

He failed to notice the vague scent of perfume that had enveloped the room. He was too preoccupied to realize the familiar, unique fragrance had somehow made its way to the Astor House. No, he did not stop to ponder the perfume.

After all, it was his wedding day.

8

*C*elia said nothing as the carriage rattled its way to Washington Square. Still feeling wretched, she sat stiffly against the opposite side of the carriage so she would not have to touch Brendan O'Neal, would not so much as brush against his arm.

The same sights that had so delighted her on their way to the Astor House now meant nothing. The glorious stretch of Broadway, with the magnificent emporiums, the crowds of people of every variety and nationality, the vendors and the sheer vibrancy of the city, passed by her weary eyes without the merest flicker of interest. She was too absorbed in her own misery. For it had been her own naive stupidity that brought her to this terrible point in her life.

Had she only thought, had she only realized what her foolish trust of this man would bring her, she would have slammed the door on him the very first time he knocked.

That's what she should have done. But she hadn't, and now her life was ruined.

O'Neal, by contrast, was infuriatingly sanguine. Cheerful even. His dastardly deed of the night before seemed to trouble him not at all. Her gaze slid to him surreptitiously, without turning her head, so he would not notice her stare.

Her sly glance was met with a grin.

Quickly, she returned her attention to the window.

She had no choice but to marry him. That was obvious not only for the monetary reasons, but because as much as she abhorred the mere thought of having a child with this man, she supposed there was a very real possibility that a child was already on its way.

Now she would be no better than a servant. Her dreams of an independent life had been dashed. No freedom of either mind or spirit or body, no life beyond the whims of this man who had already taken so much from her. Taken all, without asking.

This had always been her nightmare, a personal vision of torment that cast her in the role of the helpless, powerless victim. And her nightmare had all come true in a matter of hours, accompanied by a champagne supper.

"Are you feeling better, my dear?" O'Neal asked.

How could I feel better? She longed to scream. Only a beast would have taken advantage of such a situation. Only a beast of the most criminal, wretched sort would have committed such a vicious deed.

A dastard. That was what he was—nothing but a dastard straight from an afternoon matinee.

Shifting in the seat, she again tried to recall what exactly had happened the previous night. Well, she assumed what had happened. Her nightgown had been torn. But since she couldn't remember the precise details, she thought it best not to speak the words that were on her mind.

Instead of telling him exactly how she felt, she replied by keeping her voice as even as possible. "Tolerable, sir. I am feeling tolerable."

Maybe she could kill him in his sleep. That's what she could do! She'd wait until she'd played the role of the obedient little wife, lulling him into a sense of complacency. She'd smile, be docile. Submit to his animal whims. After all, there was an element of curiosity that had not yet been satisfied. It would be gratifying to experience the event at least once in her lifetime, or at least once in her memory. And then, after he had abused her for the last time, for the final time, she would smother him with a fluffy down pillow.

That thought made her smile.

He was staring at her. "Please don't do that, Celia."

"Do what?"

"Sneer in such a fashion. The glint in your eyes makes me nervous."

"I wonder that anything in this world could make you nervous," she said primly, smoothing her skirt.

"I could wonder the same thing about you, my sweet."

She felt her cheeks flame and pretended she was elsewhere. Anywhere. With anyone but this robber of virture, this killer of hopes.

"I do hope the minister arrives at your home shortly," he said as casually as asking her to pass the saltcellar.

"Yes. He is always prepared to tend to the sick of spirit, the needy and the depraved." Then she looked at him. "The deprived. I imagine he will."

She did not see his smile.

"And I presume your aunt will adjust from having

you visit your dear, fictitious friend Mary to having a wedding this afternoon?"

"I imagine she will. The shock may very well kill her, but I imagine she will."

"I see we have reverted to repetitive lines."

"I imagine we have."

They took a sharp turn toward Fifth Avenue, the carriage tilting, and Celia did all she could to avoid physical contact with him. And she was almost successful. But her grip on the looped leather strap beside the door slipped and she slammed into his left side. For a moment her arms flayed against him as she slid to the floor of the carriage.

With the remains of her dignity she raised herself back into the seat. The hood of the green cape had twisted, and her face was flattened against an expanse of fabric. Attempting to remain calm, she pushed the hood back so she could again see. "Excuse me, sir," she mumbled, her cheeks reddening.

"Now, Celia. We will be man and wife very shortly. I do not believe you need to behave like a blushing schoolgirl, charming as your blushes are. Indeed, you were certainly not schoolgirlish last evening. Not in the least. Had I not been there and . . ."

She clenched her teeth. Again she slid a glance at his face. He was smiling! He seemed pleased by her predicament!

Brendan turned his own attention straight ahead, and slowly his smile faded.

It occurred to him then, the question he had yet to answer for himself.

What on earth was he doing?

He had always reveled in his solitude, in his ability

to survive on his own. Unlike so many others, he needed no one, relying only on himself. So why was he allowing—no, he revised—forcing this woman into his life? He was an honest person, yet he was gaining her as his wife under the most duplicitous of circumstances.

"Why?" he said aloud, closing his hand into a fist.

"Excuse me?" she asked. For a moment the hostility was gone from her eyes, the darkness he had seen since early that morning.

And in that moment he saw her as the woman from last night, the easy laughter, her hand on his arm, the pure joy she took in the most common of things, from a pretty silver spoon to a stiffly unsmiling waiter.

"Nothing," he replied, lingering on her features before returning his gaze to the nothingness straight ahead.

As they turned the final corner to her home, he wondered if he would ruin both of their lives, if he was a selfish being, if . . .

Her gasp interrupted his thoughts.

"What is . . ." he began, then saw the crowds of people spilling into the street. As they inched closer, it became apparent that Celia Thomason's house was the center of attention.

"What happened?" Her voice was a bare whisper as she began to open the carriage door.

"Wait a moment," he snapped, pulling her toward him.

"What if there's been an accident, if someone's been hurt. What if . . ."

"Shush," he soothed, his arm around her. And for some reason she relaxed against him, even as her eyes remained wide with alarm and confusion.

He rapped in the carriage hatch, and the driver opened it immediately.

"Driver, can you see what the commotion is about?"

"Yes, sir."

They could hear him asking questions of the pedestrians, but the replies were muffled. He opened the hatch and leaned down into the cab.

"Sir, it seems this all has something to do with a Miss Celia Thomason who resides at this address."

"How does it concern Miss Thomason?"

"Well, the word has spread that she can really summon spirits. The servants, it seems, all saw a ghost. Of course that seems to be a common enough thing these days, sir, but then the family tried to quell the rumors. You know how things like that go. It's closing the barn door after the animals have already gone. Word spread through their ranks, the servants told one another from house to house."

"So those are servants?" Brendan asked. "How could they all get the day off?"

"No. Those are also the employers of the servants who wish to see the lady, and those men over there?"

Celia and Brendan both peered in the direction he pointed from above.

"They are all . . ."

"Reporters," Celia said before the driver could answer. "I recognize them. That one in the scarlet waistcoat works for Mr. Greeley."

Then Celia caught a glimpse of her aunt. She stood before the closed front door, her face beaming, nodding excitedly and speaking to the crowd.

"What should I do?" She turned to Brendan. Then she stiffened and shrugged away from his grasp. "I'm getting out."

"No." His strong arm clamped her by his side. "They

mean no harm, Celia, I am sure. But it is dangerous, you may be mobbed."

She hated to admit he was right, but in truth there was probably a good chance that she would, indeed, be mobbed, overtaken by the unruly masses. In the distance she could see the arrival of members of the new police force, identified by their metal star-shaped badges. But they seemed as confused as the rest of the crowd.

"Let us drive away from this," O'Neal proclaimed. "Then I will determine the best course." He spoke with maddening authority.

Suddenly her perplexed bafflement gave way to a wave of fury. His voice had offered no choice in the matter. He would dictate her movements, and later, of course, her thoughts.

It was beginning already. The end of her life as a free woman.

With a suddenness that took them both by surprise, in one swift movement she jerked away from him and slipped out of the carriage.

"Celia!"

Her feet hit the packed dirt of the street, and she focused her attention above the stovepipe hats and bonnets that surrounded her home. Over those heads she saw Aunt Prudence, those incongruously youthful curls. That was her goal, the only thing of which she was certain at that moment. She wanted to reach Aunt Prudence.

She wanted to leave Brendan O'Neal behind.

Elbows nudged her, bodies radiating heat even in the chilly November air. There was a foul stench of unwashed wool, the peculiar smells of humanity that one never notices except in such unnaturally close quarters.

Forward, she kept moving forward, but her progress was slowed to almost no movement at all, pressed to immobility.

Where was Aunt Prudence? She lost her bearings, surrounded on all sides by strangers pushing and shoving. Even the sky above seemed to be eliminated by the throng. Someone was stepping on the hem of her skirt, and then another foot trod further up the skirt, causing her to be pulled down, further down. With all of her might she tugged to free herself, but only succeeded in ripping the skirt from the bodice of her very best gown.

"No," she heard herself moan.

How could this be happening, a mere few yards from her own front steps?

Out. She had to get out, but didn't know which direction would lead her to safety. The deeper into the crowd she sank, the more she felt as if she were drowning.

Someone hit the side of her head with an umbrella or a walking stick, either accidentally or on purpose, she didn't know, but her ears were ringing and she began to fear she would not escape.

What a ridiculous way to die, she thought to herself.

Then powerful arms clamped around her waist. She tried to push away, her back toward her captor, but he was too large, too strong.

"Of all the stupid, idiotic, insane stunts . . ." her captor growled into her ear, his accent and voice blessedly familiar.

"Brendan," she breathed, knowing he could not hear her.

"Lunatic," he answered.

Her feet were not even touching the ground, and she went limp in his grasp, his large hand shielding her face.

He propelled them forward with his sure, powerful strides, forging a path through the thick wall of humanity.

And suddenly she heard Aunt Prudence's voice.

"This way! This way, sir!"

Someone in the crowd shouted, "There she is! That's her, Celia Thomason!"

There was a hush, then the frenzy seemed to build. And then, somehow, she was in the front hall of the house, the door bolted against the press outside.

For a moment Brendan kept her in his grasp, holding her tightly against his chest as if unwilling to release her. All she could hear was the thundering of his heart against her ear, his heavy breathing.

He looked down at her, the fist clutching the lapel of his coat, her head still down and pressed against him. Gently he loosened his hold, yet for a moment she clung to him. Just for the barest of moments.

Aunt Prudence was speaking, and through the ringing in her ears she heard the words as if from a great distance.

"Celia! My, what excitement! The Reverend Hallem is in the parlor, awaiting your arrival. Oh, dear me, Celia. What excitement! And the crowds, they all wish to see you, to pay us vast sums of money. Patrick and I have determined that we will rent a large hall for a great assembly, and then . . ."

It was too much. Celia felt the unfamiliar dizziness. Yet another person was determining her life. Aunt Prudence. Even Patrick had it all planned. No matter what, she was no longer in charge of her own destiny.

Had she ever been?

Brendan glanced down and saw the pallor of her

complexion. His arm again braced her as he addressed Aunt Prudence.

"Mrs. Cooper." He bowed his head slightly. "I must apologize on two counts."

Aunt Prudence stopped her chatter and looked up at Brendan O'Neal, puzzled. "Sir?"

"I should have taken much more time courting your lovely niece. But in truth, I was so immediately taken with her charms that I could not rest until she became my wife."

"Oh, Mr. O'Neal." Aunt Prudence blushed fetchingly.

Brendan was laying his own charm on with a trowel, Celia thought.

"Secondly, I most certainly should have come to you first, Mrs. Cooper. For that, too, I most humbly apologize."

"Nonsense, sir! I am just delighted that my dear Celia has won the heart of a man with so many stellar attributes."

In other words, thought Celia, *a man with that most lovely of all stellar attributes, a substantial bank account.*

All she wanted to do was sleep, to sleep and forget the previous few days, from the awful men demanding payment for Uncle James's debts to Brendan O'Neal and his vanishing brother-in-law, and the surging crowd outside. And of course Amanda. Now she was doubting she had ever really seen the apparition at all. There was another explanation. Certainly there was.

"Now, dear," said Aunt Prudence. "Let's go upstairs and get you freshened up for your wedding."

Her wedding. Above all, she wished she could forget the terrible fact that in a matter of minutes, she would be married to Brendan O'Neal. Escape was impossible—even if she climbed out of the window, she would merely fall into the hands of the rabble.

There was no convincing Aunt Prudence that she did not wish to marry, for Aunt Prudence had always assumed she secretly longed to wed, but her lack of dowry and opportunity made her feign distaste for the wedded state.

Wearily, she climbed the stairs to her room—a long, gallows-like ascent—where Eileen waited to assist her into whatever dress was the least funereal to don on this, her most festive day.

9

*S*omehow, Brendan O'Neal had managed to secure a wedding dress for Celia. In a matter of hours he had not only procured the gown, complete with matching silk slippers and half-long white kid gloves trimmed with tulle ruche. There it was, laid out in all its perfect splendor on her bed.

"Isn't it lovely, Miss Thomason?" Eileen whispered, as if speaking too loudly would cause the gown to turn black and wither.

Indeed, it would have been far more appropriate had the dress turned black, for Brendan O'Neal had gifted her a most unusual wedding costume. She touched the fabric, fine tulle over white satin. There was no doubt it was nothing short of exquisite.

It was also in the worst possible taste, considering the recent events that had brought them to this moment. For one, it was white. While the new fashion of wearing white had been embraced by some brides, they were usually of the very young and deeply blushing ilk, not by spinsters firmly on the shelf—as Aunt Prudence had proclaimed her on some of her more exasperated when-will-you-get-married speeches.

Not only was white more of a girlish shade for a bride, it was certainly not the most proper shade for any woman, bride or not, who should be in at least half mourning. Uncle James had not yet been dead a full year. And there it was, a startling white gown trimmed with roses of puffed gauze. The corsage was pointed, the lightest of fabrics lined the daringly low neckline. Even laid out on her bed, she could estimate the bodice would plunge dangerously close to the tight waist.

Maybe that was also a statement, referring to her unmaidenly behavior of the evening before.

"Lands sake." She sighed. "I suppose I have no choice but to wear it."

"Miss Thomason! I would give anything to put on something as grand as this!"

"Well then go ahead. Maybe he won't know the difference."

Eileen smiled uncertainly. "He's desperately handsome, Mr. O'Neal is. Why," she continued, helping Celia out of her torn dress, "I believe he is the most handsome man I have ever seen. Ginny in the kitchen says she almost died when he brushed against her yesterday."

"So did I," she responded between clenched teeth.

"His eyes, Miss. There is something about them, something almost sad."

"Perhaps," Celia murmured. She, too, had seen that, a darkness there.

Then she straightened as Eileen held up delicate garments that had been tucked beneath the gown. "Unmentionables! He sent me unmentionables along with the dress!"

"Yes, Miss. I think it was romantic of him. And practical as well, for your regular unmentionables would not go with the dress."

"Of course not. My regular clothes actually cover my body."

Eileen giggled as they removed the last of her own clothing, and then slipped on the new undergarments.

As much as Celia hated to admit it, she had never felt such fabric against her skin. The chemise was spun of a fine silk, and seemed to caress her shoulders. "Oh," she breathed, almost involuntarily.

The corset was smaller than she ever believed possible, but Eileen laced it and it fit her as if it had been made to her precise measurements.

Then came the petticoats, several stiff and lovely and blindingly beautiful things that tied onto the corset, which had special silk loops. There were white silk stockings, several pair, in case one should be ruined. And the slippers, of the same shade of satin as the dress. They would not be practical, she thought, trying to invent a reason not to delight in the way they encased her feet. Why, one good stomp in the mud and they would be absolutely ruined.

And then Eileen helped her on with the dress.

Celia was unable to breathe for a moment. Was this what it was supposed to feel like to be a bride? No, this was better. It had to be better. For she suddenly felt as if she had stepped out of a fairy tale, a gossamer creature not of this earth.

"Well," she said softly as Eileen worked to fasten the delicate silk-covered hooks and ties. It didn't seem real. It didn't seem possible.

"Oh, Miss." Eileen stepped back. Then she straightened. "Now your hair. There is a headdress here, more tulle and roses and . . ."

Celia barely heard the rest as she was led to her dressing table and Eileen began to unpin her hair, brush and comb and braid and repin. She toiled in uncharacteristic silence as Celia stared ahead.

What a very strange day it had turned out to be.

At last Eileen stepped away. "Oh, Miss," she said in an almost reverential hush.

She stepped over to the full mirror and tilted it for Celia to view herself.

It wasn't Celia. That reflection could not possibly be her, just as she could not possibly be getting married in a matter of moments.

She looked as if she had stepped out of an oil painting, something in a fantasy of silk and cream and flowers. Eileen pulled on the kid gloves as Celia thought, *This is not me. This is someone else, not the solid, sensible Celia, but some candy-wit, some bit of richly wrapped fluff.*

"Well, well," she said to her reflection. "Who are you?"

"A princess," exclaimed Eileen. "A royal princess!"

"A royal princess in someone else's spring gown." Celia finally smiled. It was absurd. "I wonder whatever happened to the woman for whom the dress was made?"

Then a terrible thought crossed her mind. Was this something from his dead sister? Could this have been Amanda's wedding gown?

But almost as swiftly the thought vanished. No. Amanda was much smaller, inches shorter than Celia.

There was a knock on the door. "Celia?" Aunt Prudence poked her head into the room. "Dear, are you . . . My! Oh, heavens me!"

Eileen and Aunt Pru exchanged excited babble about Celia, about the fine quality of her groom, about other topics Celia simply refused to hear. Eileen ran down first to alert the minister and the groom of Celia's impending arrival. And then came Celia.

The guests, such as they were, had gathered in the parlor. In their best clothes stood the servants, Patrick in a stiff, uncomfortable-looking collar, Eileen, grinning as if the entire production had been her own. Ginny, Patrick's younger sister, just come from Ireland, a frantic Hannah—a clean apron her concession to the occasion. The austere Reverend Hallem straightened and nodded in wordless approval.

Celia recalled at that moment, somewhat incongruously, that once the British-born reverend had told her (in confidence, of course) that the moment he opened his mouth, his aristocratic accent and bearing proclaimed him as, he modestly admitted, "a god."

If that had always been the case, it was no longer so. For without a single word being uttered by anyone, it was Brendan O'Neal who dominated the room. Even with his back turned, staring out of the window through the lace panels, O'Neal was overwhelming.

His broad shoulders seemed to strain the fabric of the formal frock coat. She took a deep breath before entering.

One step over the threshold, and slowly he faced her. And that single shallow breath caught in her throat.

Eileen was right. Brendan O'Neal was nothing short of magnificent.

"Celia." Her name had never been spoken that way before, as both a warning and a promise.

"Mr. O'Neal," she replied primly.

He smiled. "It seems the dress fits you well, suits you well."

"Yes. I must thank you." She stepped toward him, stopping just short of the center of the parlor. "How did you procure one at such short notice?"

The others exchanged perplexed glances, for never had they seen a bride and groom engage in a bit of informal chatter even as the guests and priest awaited.

Brendan replied, "From a seamstress at the Astor House, the shop next to the milliner."

"Oh, yes. I believe I have seen that shop. And how was it ready and altered so quickly?"

"A lucky happenstance. It appears that you are the exact size of an unfortunate bride whose groom bolted sometime last April."

"Ah. That explains the rite of spring quality to the gown."

The reverend cleared his throat. "Well, ladies and gentlemen . . ."

The parlor door opened, and Aunt Prudence, wearing a gown that must have been fetching decades earlier, before the rich tea cakes and sweetmeats took their toll, bustled into the room. And the ceremony began.

To Celia, it all seemed to move so slowly, as if in a dream. The reverend's voice sounded strange and distorted. The noises outside seemed to have abated, the normal sounds of carriages and voices had replaced the crowds who had been there just a while earlier. The new police must be doing their jobs well, she thought distractedly.

The reverend continued speaking.

Brendan listened to the familiar words being read,

the same phrases he had heard over and over, but never about himself, never concerning his own life. And not for the first time that day, especially as this moment drew closer, he wondered what in the name of all that was sane was he doing?

He glanced down at Celia, and she, too, seemed stunned. Naturally she would, the way he had bamboozled her into this wedding. In all probability he was ruining both of their lives on an irrational whim.

Should he stop it now?

The servants were all smiling, Aunt Prudence seemed pleased beyond all reason. Everyone was beaming, with the notable exception of the bride and groom.

He heard himself speaking the words required, heard Celia speaking her part, hesitant and grave. She looked miserable in spite of her luminous beauty.

Automatically he reached into his pocket for the ring. It had been his mother's ring, and he had found it with his father's papers when he had straightened out the estate.

His parents.

From what he could recall, theirs had been a true love match. Although it was difficult to recall his mother without the continuous ache that had been his life without her, he had vivid images of her face, the way she would soften when she looked at him, her only son. And the way those same fine eyes would sparkle like diamonds when she turned toward his father.

He wanted that. He longed to have a woman of gentle beauty sparkle at him. Fanciful thought.

Was that it? He wondered if the reason he felt so compelled to have her, to possess this woman, was because there was something about her that reminded him of his mother. Yes, she was a virtual stranger. But he sensed her spirit, her soul.

He helped her pull off her left glove and slipped the ring onto her finger. It was a tight fit. He hadn't thought of that, the possibility of the ring being too small.

There was no denying her beauty. Perhaps that was his goal, to have a lovely woman on his arm when it suited him. If that was the case, then she would join the other possessions he acquired and then promptly forgot—the magnificently bound books, the artwork by masters, the unpacked cargo he'd bought on momentary fancies.

And then he noticed the scent.

His bland expression darkened as he looked around the trim parlor. It was Amanda's perfume. Even now, during the wedding ceremony, Celia was bent on trickery.

He wasn't himself. Since returning to America, he had been altered somehow.

Was it possible that Celia and her aunt had drugged him?

Celia, too, caught the now familiar fragrance. Hesitantly, she looked up at Brendan. His jaw was working as if exercising great control over his anger.

The reverend's voice rang out in triumph. "I now pronounce you man and wife!"

And then she appeared.

Celia saw her first. The movement caught her attention, and her eyes immediately focused on the corner just behind the servants. Slowly, as before, the form began to take shape. Someone was speaking to Celia, but she did not respond. The emerging entity was too engrossing.

Brendan, in his irritation, hands clenched, finally looked at his bride, then followed the path of her sight. He, too, saw it.

"What the . . ."

The others in the room exchanged bewildered glances. Then the reverend saw the shape. His mouth formed an almost comical "o" as his eyes widened, as the Book of Common Prayer slipped from his long thin fingers to the carpet.

Her eyes were the first distinct feature to emerge, bright and shimmering. Brenden marveled—those were Amanda's eyes! How could Celia and her fellow tricksters have known the exact shade, the peculiar dark blue, the brightness in his sister's eyes?

Had he shown her the photograph yet? It mattered not, for even if he had, it did not explain the coloring, even the dark flaxen of her hair.

Gradually her facial features took shape, the brow, the nose, the rather full lips. As she became more distinct he saw the small scar under her left eye, the one that happened when she tried to follow him over a stone fence once.

He must have mentioned the scar to Celia, he thought distractedly. It was invisible in the daguerreotype or in any painting of Amanda. No artist would risk losing the commission by offending the subject or her family by including any scar.

He concentrated on the mundane, on the down-to-earth realities of the situation. For Brendan O'Neal was no fool. He would not be duped by anyone, never.

Especially not any woman. Especially not Celia.

The floral scent was overpowering now, and the servants and Aunt Pru stiffened, recognizing the perfume from the last time the phantom appeared. One by one they moved from the corner where she was, shuffling shoulder to shoulder. Yet no one left the room. They all remained, not so much afraid as warily curious, feeling great comfort in sheer numbers, for the living far outnumbered the nonliving.

Patrick pulled out a handkerchief and held it against his nose. The perfume was becoming almost sickening. One by one the others placed their hands or the ends of their aprons over their faces against the increasing stench.

The spirit seemed to concentrate intently on Brendan, only Brendan. A smile turned up the corners of her mouth even as the rest of her figure contorted in the eerie, underwater-like gyrations.

A sense of wonder breathed within Brendan in spite of his intellectual uncertainty.

This was impossible. Absolutely impossible.

"Amanda," he uttered, almost against his will.

Then she seemed upset, her unnatural eyes turning to Celia, then back to Brendan.

And as everyone watched—from Reverend Hallem to Aunt Prudence to the servants and, of course, Celia and Brendan, Amanda's mouth opened in a silent, piercing cry. It was distorted, freakish. It was horrible, an expression of pure anguish.

She began to fade then, a clawlike hand drawing to the exaggerated, twisted lips.

The scent lingered after the specter had vanished.

There was a strained silence in the parlor.

Reverend Hallem cleared a dry throat. "As I said . . ." he began in a high, warbly voice. He swallowed audibly, then continued. "You are now man and wife."

Celia turned to Brendan.

He looked down at her with such hatred and contempt, she thought she would die.

"How dare you," he growled like a wild animal in a trap.

And then, without looking at Aunt Prudence or the reverend or the servants, he slammed out of the parlor, and then out of the house.

The wedding reception was something of a disappointment, given the unexpected departure of the groom and the equally unexpected appearance of his late sister in the middle of the ceremony.

Hannah brought out a beautifully iced cake on the family's prize silver cake plate, the tray rattling precariously with the cook's frayed nerves. Until late that afternoon it had been an ordinary spice cake, but the announcement of the impromptu festivities inspired her to great feats of decorating.

"Oh, Hannah," said the groomless bride attempting to sound as if this were the most common of events. "What a lovely cake!"

Aunt Prudence uncorked some of Uncle James's finest brandy, taking a hefty swig for herself before pouring minute drops into the best glasses. The reverend drained two before she relented and gave him a full serving.

And there was Virginia punch and tea and coffee, which were not nearly as popular as the brandy, and a strained atmosphere that could be easily cut with the cake knife.

"Well." Celia smiled, the smile wavering. "The beauty of this particular arrangement is that there is no need to impress the groom. It is just us, old friends all."

She held up a cup of punch and they toasted themselves.

But the image that had been emblazoned on everyone's mind was that of Amanda. There was no doubt she had been seen, her scent most vividly heeded by all.

"Best wishes, my dear," said a still-shaken Reverend Hallem. "This has most certainly been a . . . of all the . . . well, of course one must indeed say . . ." he stammered, his God-like command of the language failing him when he needed it the most. Finally he straightened. "I must be off for Evensong."

"Of course. Thank you, Father Hallem."

"Should you require further services, please feel free to contact me," he said over his shoulder as he bounded from the room, then the house.

He seemed delighted to leave.

Celia saw him galloping down the street. He had neglected to collect his coat, his hat or gloves . . . and the payment for performing the ceremony.

The few remaining pedestrians lingering before the house were astonished then intrigued to see a priest flee the house and dash into the night.

Once he was gone, Aunt Prudence recorked the brandy and Celia's shoulders slumped.

"What on earth happened?" Prudence said aloud.

"I don't think it was of this earth, ma'am," said Patrick. "That was genuine. I'd been having doubts about what we saw the other day. Wondering if maybe we had all been fooled somehow. But that was a real spirit, a genuine thing."

"I don't mean that," snapped Aunt Prudence. "Although that will require some attention. I am referring to Mr. O'Neal's abrupt exit."

"Oh, Aunt Pru." Celia sighed. "He thinks we tricked him, that we are frauds. Cruel frauds."

"Well, of course we *were* frauds, but not anymore."

"Mr. O'Neal thinks we did this?" Patrick said incredulously. "He thinks we are that good?"

"Not necessarily that good," Celia corrected. "That cold-blooded and calculating. He thinks we are nothing but . . ."

"What do you think she was trying to say?" Eileen, who had been thus far silent, suddenly spoke.

There was no need to ask who she was talking about.

"I don't know," Celia admitted.

"I thought it was a warning of some kind," said Hannah. "She seemed frightened by something."

"Us, probably." Patrick smiled. "She scared the wigs off of us, and we in turn probably scared her to death. I mean, well. Sorry. You know what I mean. But she can't harm us, not anymore. She can't harm a hair on any of our heads. She was just a picture, like a picture."

"She did seem frightened." Aunt Prudence uncorked the brandy once more and poured herself another hefty portion. "But not of us. At least not right away."

"You're right, Aunt Pru. At first she seemed pleased to see Brendan, I mean, Mr. O'Neal. Only after that did she seem to be frightened, or at least very unhappy."

"She looked at you, Miss," Eileen said. "She looked at you, and then she went from being beautiful to being, well, horrible."

They were all quiet for a few moments, each wondering what her appearance could have meant. The clock ticked loudly, keeping hollow time.

"Do you think," Celia began quietly, then stopped.

"Do you think perhaps she was trying to warn Brendan against marrying me?"

"Why do you say that, my dear?"

"Oh, Aunt Pru, because . . ." She halted. There was no possible way she could ever explain the true reason for the hasty marriage, that spinster Celia had behaved like a wanton strumpet.

How Brendan must loathe her. And how Amanda must share in that contempt—for her abhorrence had been powerful enough to bring her back from the Other Side.

Did they all know over there? Were her parents and Uncle James shocked?

Before Celia could continue her thoughts, or determine what next to say, there was a mighty knock on the door. Eileen curtsied and stepped away to answer. In a moment she returned with a cream-colored note sealed with red wax.

"It's for you, Miss." She glanced down. "I mean, Mrs. O'Neal."

It was from Brendan. She started to loosen the wax with her thumb, then stopped.

"If you will all please excuse me," she murmured, then left the parlor and fled up the stairs to her own room.

The note was simple, just a few lines.

Madam,
    Our original arrangement still exists. The farce of a ceremony, accompanied by your clever entertainment, changes nothing, other than my willingness to indulge your professional chicanery. If you are to receive any of your much-needed funds, you

must fulfill your obligation to me. Garrick is still missing. I am going to find him and bring him back, at which point you will receive the remainder of your payment. That is, upon your successful restoration of his wits and emotions. After today, I have no doubt you can convince him. Following that, I will return to London. Alone. For, Madam, I have no desire to ever see you again, other than in your considerable professional capacity. Once in London I will obtain a swift annulment to our unfortunate situation, and send you the papers directly.

                                B. O'Neal.

Celia felt sick for a moment, grasping the corner of the dresser that had been hers since childhood. Then she took a deep breath.

Although she wasn't exactly sure how she would accomplish the task, she knew exactly what she needed to do. And nothing could stop her.

Not this time.

10

For all the care Eileen had taken with her hair, for all the delicate lacing and fluffing that had been required to transform Celia into a bride straight from a tinted fashion plate, she stripped herself of the sumptuous attire without a second glance at the satin and tulle pile left behind.

The single thought racing through her mind was that she had to find Brendan, to speak to him, to tell him that the vision he had witnessed had not been a product of the Thomason trickery. Everyone else had been stunned by the apparition.

Why had she allowed him to leave? She should have grabbed his arm and held him, she should have pounced on him like a cat on a mouse. Or more accurately, like a mouse on a very large cat.

But she had been so very stunned by the entire day. The cumulative effect of the strange and startling moments had rendered her limp. Had she managed to think of stopping him from leaving, she would not have been physically capable.

She grabbed a black and plaid dress from her wardrobe, long sleeved with plain white ruffles at the wrists and throat. It was a vast change from the cream satin gown she had worn moments earlier. It was plain and humble and rough.

Cinderella was most definitely home from the ball.

With hard strokes she brushed her hair and repinned it in the back, plucking out the bits of flowers, leftovers from the wedding.

The wedding. She was married now, Celia Thomason O'Neal.

And the wedding night had, apparently, been passed the night before. A wedding night she could not remember. Then immediately following the ceremony, the groom preferred to bound from the house rather than pass another minute, not to mention another night, with the bride.

All in all, it had not been one of the better episodes in her life.

"Celia O'Neal," she muttered out loud. It sounded strange on her tongue, the name of someone else.

None of that mattered.

She kicked off the delicate satin slippers and silk stockings and pulled on her usual sturdy, no-nonsense black hose and ankle boots. They felt thick and heavy. It was as if she had exchanged a delicate rose for a thorny, knotted stick.

Yes indeed, Cinderella was once again in the ash bin.

Celia straightened. Did she appear any different than the Celia she had known all her life? No. There was no difference there. She looked down at her left hand, at the simple gold ring whose appearance had so surprised her during the wedding ceremony.

It was old, she realized. Used and discarded by someone else, perhaps by a cousin of the unfortunate spring bride who unintentionally donated the wedding gown to the seamstress on Broadway. A matching set, secondhand dress and used ring. She tried to yank it off to see if there was an inscription, but stopped. She couldn't bear it if the inscription was something romantic and wonderful, speaking of true love and timeless passion. Nor did she wish to see a cynical inscription, a cold set of dates or, worse still, nothing at all.

No. She would leave it on, at least for the time being.

Dressed and ready, she went downstairs, where the others were still enjoying tea and cake and for the moment pretending the best they could that they had not witnessed a ghost.

"Celia, my dear." Aunt Prudence smiled. Then she realized Celia was preparing to leave. "What in heaven's name are you doing?"

"I am going to try to find my husband," she said, tying the ribbons of the black bonnet under her chin.

"No. You mustn't chase after a man, not ever."

"But he's my husband and . . ."

"Especially if he's your husband. No. Let him find you. That is what the male animal most enjoys, the thrill of the chase."

"Aunt Pru, thank you for your advice. Now I am going to step outside, fetch myself a cab, and find him."

"He will find you, my dear. And then all will be well. Come, have some cake. It is quite delicious."

She stared at her aunt, this woman she had been losing sleep over, the fragile creature she had been trying to protect. And she realized that maybe she had been wrong. Perhaps sweet Aunt Prudence was made more of metal than of delicate old lace.

"I have to find Brendan."

Aunt Prudence nodded at Hannah, who was slicing some more cake. Then she pulled Celia into the foyer with more force than she had imagined possible.

"You must wait him out," Aunt Prudence said. "And when he returns, you will do whatever it takes to make your marriage work."

There was no trace of a smile on her face. Celia, stunned, blinked. When had she ever seen sweet Aunt Prudence without her vague, endearing smile? She was now entirely serious.

"Forgive me, Aunt Prudence. You must be overwrought." And, Celia suspected, perhaps she had overindulged in the brandy.

"I am not overwrought. I am trying to make you do the sensible thing." She waved her plump hand in the air.

"I don't know what to say," Celia stammered. "Aunt Pru, you have me astonished."

Her aunt spoke in a low, calm voice. "I went along with James when he insisted we take you in after your parents were careless enough to go and drown. I felt we couldn't afford to keep you—I wanted to send you someplace else. But James didn't feel right about you going to the foundling hospital or the orphans' asylum. He was right, of course, the neighbors would have talked. And so we kept you—treated you like our own daughter, all the while draining every penny from us, everything that my dear James had worked so hard to gain. I wore gowns from ten seasons earlier, while you were always in the newest fashion. The tutors. Do you know how expensive your education was? My dear James spent a fortune on you. I longed for you to marry, to make a match that would free us from our present situation. But you never did. And then James died. So, now it is your turn to sacrifice. When your husband returns, you will do everything in your power to make things right."

Celia felt as if she couldn't breathe. "I . . ." she stammered. "I never knew you felt this way about me."

"Finally you are able to help bring money into the house. And now, when a wealthy gentleman appears and suddenly offers to marry you, and paying clients are lining up to see you, you decide to end your career as a spiritualist. We cannot afford this. You must make things right. You will stay with Mr. O'Neal."

Aunt Prudence squinted, took a deep breath, and smiled at Celia. "There, my dear. Do we understand one another? So come on inside, back to the celebration. For indeed, we have much to celebrate. Do we not, dear Celia?"

Celia was unable to speak. The sounds of conversation and laughter wafted into the hallway she knew so well. Before her stood the aunt she had known so well. And suddenly, she did not know either the house or the aunt in the least.

Aunt Prudence cocked her head slightly, a gesture of gentle befuddlement. Then she smiled again and went back into the parlor.

"The bride will join us in a moment," she announced. "She simply needs to go upstairs and remove her bonnet and cloak. Then we can toast her properly."

Very softly Celia closed the parlor door, leaning her cheek against the cool wood for just a moment. Then she swallowed, and without looking back, she left the house just off Washington Square. And even though her drawstring purse was empty, she vowed to herself that she would never return.

Not ever.

She was at the Astor House, staring at the two large glass orbs that illuminated the entire stretch of Broadway with their orange flame.

The carriages rolled by, and the ones that stopped carried the privileged ladies who were then tenderly assisted to the pavement by their husbands.

How long had the walk taken her? Perhaps hours. She was uncertain of everything now. All except for one single thing.

She had to find Brendan.

Not to attempt anything ridiculous, for she had already made herself ridiculous in her own eyes. As she had walked to this place in the evening air, her breath puffing before her, passers-by staring at the lone young woman stumbling through the streets, she realized that Brendan was somewhere in this city, and whatever he was doing, he thought dreadful things about her.

That was what she needed to rectify before she could ever consider what she could possibly do with the rest of her life. Brendan thought ill of her, and that was more intolerable than anything else.

She took a deep breath and climbed the steps to the entrance. The doorman eyed her with suspicion, as well he should. It was after dark, and she was unaccompanied. And she was most certainly not dressed as the other women milling about the lobby. Of course she had not been dressed as the other women were the previous night, but then she had been with Brendan. Doors that had opened wide for her the night before were now slammed.

Holding her head erect, she walked straight to the long, marble-topped desk. The uniformed clerk looked up.

"Yes, Miss."

"Good evening," she said. "I would like to see my husband, Mr. Brendan O'Neal."

"I am afraid your husband," the clerk emphasized the word *husband* rather unnecessarily, "has checked out of the hotel."

"Oh, has he? Very well."

The clerk returned to a large ledger he had been examining. Celia remained at the desk, thinking about what to do next.

"Yes, Miss?" The clerk was watching her.

The use of the appellation "Miss" had not been lost on Celia.

"Please refresh my memory. Where did Mr. O'Neal go?"

"To his home, Miss."

"His home?"

"Yes. Now if you will please forgive me, I must finish my work." Again, he looked down at the ledger.

She cleared her throat.

Grudgingly he raised his head.

"My good man," she began. That should flatter him—he could not have been more than twenty. "Which house did he go to? You see, we have so very many homes in and about the city, I tend to lose track of him occasionally. Was it the house in the country? Or the dear little town house we keep on, um, one of the more charming lanes downtown?"

"I was instructed not to reveal his location."

"I see." Then an idea struck her. "Very good, dear fellow. Excellent work. I will personally commend you to him when I see my husband. But I have in my possession something he requires."

Now that most certainly did not come out right, but she held her head high and waited for the answer.

"You may leave the item, whatever it is, with us, and we will send a boy to deliver the item. Good evening, Miss."

Celia flushed slightly, but then another idea came to her. "May I please have a quill and ink and paper?"

The clerk seemed surprised that she might possibly know how to write. "There is a writing stand over on the far wall, next to the plants. Everything you require is there for your convenience, Miss."

She nodded, ever the gracious lady, and walked over to the desk. On a piece of paper she wrote, "Brendan O'Neal, Astor House. To be delivered immediately."

Then, as casually as possible, she attempted to blend in with the other guests. Gliding from cluster to cluster, she moved on the moment a gentleman appeared to be on the verge of speaking to her, or when a lady began to eye her with suspicion. All the while she watched the desk, waiting for the clerk to leave.

At last he did, and another clerk appeared.

Now was her chance.

She walked again to the desk.

"Yes, Miss," the clerk said.

"This is an urgent letter for Mr. Brendan O'Neal."

He glanced at the paper. "Thank you," he said.

"Wait a moment! If you please, where is he?"

"I will send a boy with it directly."

"But I had hoped to give it to Mr. O'Neal in person."

"I am sorry, Miss. Strict instructions."

There was nothing left for her to do but leave now, and hope to catch the boy on his way to deliver the note. Then she could follow him, and . . .

She waited by the side of the building, away from the glow of the gaslights.

This was insane, she thought, rubbing her hands together. She had forgotten to take her gloves when she left. This was absolutely insane, mad.

But she had to try to see him, just one more time. If nothing else, she wanted to restore a small bit of whatever it was that they had shared. There had been something, she had felt it.

What had he felt for her? Respect, perhaps? Enjoyment of her company?

She blew on her hands to warm them up. Several delivery boys had bustled into the night, none of them with her letter.

Maybe it hadn't been respect, but she knew—now, in hindsight—that something else had been blossoming. Friendship, maybe. A friendship that might have grown into something else, if only things had not happened as they did.

Stamping her feet, she realized her toes were growing numb. She was still wearing the sheer unmentionables from the wedding, and she most certainly wished she had changed into some of her more . . .

"There he is!" she whispered to herself.

A small boy scurried from the Astor House, a leather satchel over one shoulder, the letter in his hand.

She followed him up Broadway, where he delivered a package from the satchel. She hid whenever he looked back, whenever he sensed he was not alone. There were staircases and bare trees and once she ducked behind a frozen water trough.

They went to Jane Street, and down Mott, and roamed on Charles where he delivered several notes from the leather sack.

And now, Celia didn't really care anymore. Her nose was running. Her hands were frozen blocks of ice. Her ears felt as if they would break off, in spite of the bonnet covering them.

Finally they were on King Street.

He couldn't possibly live here, she thought. Modest boardinghouses, nice and respectable enough but certainly not up to the standards of someone who was used to rooms at the Astor House.

Then she saw the boy hand her letter over to a portly woman in gray taffeta. She examined the note, checking the other side, then closed the door.

This was it. This was where he lived.

She was beyond caring what anyone thought of her now. The steps to the front door seemed to loom before her as she climbed up and up. Her hands fumbled with the brass knocker, and then she banged it once, twice.

The door opened, and the portly woman stared at Celia.

"Yes?"

Celia attempted to straighten, but she was too cold. "Brendan O'Neal," she rasped, her voice raw from the frigid air. "Please."

"Miss, I happen to run an establishment with the very best quality of people . . ."

"Brendan!" Celia shouted. "Brendan, please . . ."

But her voice was too soft.

"Miss! Would you please leave immediately, before I am forced to . . ."

"Brendan!"

She was well beyond manners now. The portly woman looked at her as if she was an enormous bug.

"Well, I have never!" The woman began to close the door.

"No, please listen to me." Celia realized she was crying.

The door was closing, the little sliver of warmth and light was narrowing to a thin line and soon it would be gone.

Suddenly the door opened, and there stood Brendan O'Neal.

"Sir, this lady here has been making a pest of herself."

He looked down at Celia, then turned to the landlady.

"Mrs. Harris, that is no lady," he said. "That is my wife."

"Mr. O'Neal!" she exclaimed.

With what seemed to be great reluctance he picked her up in his arms.

He was warm, so very warm, Celia thought. She closed her eyes as he carried her up the steps.

So very warm.

"Mrs. Harris, may I please have some blankets and a hot water bottle?"

"Yes, indeed. Why, I never, in all my life," she muttered to herself, stepping aside for them to pass. She made some more hmmphing sounds, clicking her tongue and muttering something about decent, respectable folk and her decent, respectable house.

Brendan looked down at Celia as they reached his door. "So, is this how you have spent your wedding night?" he said. The irritation was clear in the way he pressed his lips together. He would rather not see her, not ever again. That is what he had written, and that is clearly what he had meant.

She waited for him to toss her down the steps, to dump her there and close the door.

And then she remembered nothing.

11

$\mathcal{T}$he voice was distant, as if coming from the hollow end of a long tunnel.

"This is becoming something of a habit," he said.

Celia struggled to open her eyes, to emerge from an exhaustion that seemed to envelop every particle of her body. Finally, she felt her lids open.

Yet still she could not see. There was nothing but darkness, solid and thick and unyielding.

"I'm blind!" she cried. Sheer panic swept through her, erasing all shards of fatigue. "Oh my God! I am blind!"

And then he removed the cloth from her eyes.

"Oh," she said quietly, feeling foolish.

He stepped away from the bed, his back turned to her as he looked out of a window. She could not tell if he was attempting to control his anger at her being there, or attempting to control his laughter.

"Did you not receive my letter?"

There was no laughter in his voice.

"Yes, I received your letter."

"Was it not clear enough for you to comprehend?"

"It was perfectly clear."

"Then why are you here?" Brendan turned toward her, and her breath caught like a bubble in her throat. The early-morning sun was streaming over his shoulders, haloing his hair, lending him an almost otherworldly appearance.

Why was she there?

So many thoughts came to her mind. She could say that their marriage vows forced her to come, that she fully intended to take her place by his side as his rightful wife. That her aunt didn't understand how she felt, or that everyone seemed to want something from her and she didn't feel as if she had anything left to give.

And that in spite of it all, she was tired of being alone.

Or she could tell him the truth: that she really did not know why she was there. There was some reason beyond her own understanding that compelled her to find him, to seek him out.

"I repeat. Why are you here?"

"Aunt Prudence said some unbelievable things to me," she said lamely, aware how childish she sounded even as the words came out. "She said I had been a financial burden my whole life. That I owed her for taking me in when my parents were killed."

For a few moments he said nothing. Then he spoke, not unkindly, just uninterested, as if a stranger had unburdened a list of woes at an inconvenient time.

"I am sorry your aunt is not the woman you thought she was. Now, if you will be so kind as to return to your own home, it would be most appreciated."

Fumbling for something to say, anything to engage

him, she thought of explaining that the visit from Amanda was indeed genuine. But this would not be a good time for that, not the way he was waiting for her to leave.

Then she noticed a map unfurled on a table by the window.

"What is the map for? Are you planning another voyage?"

He stared at her for a few moments, his eyes glinting. He wore a simple white linen shirt with no collar, the buttons open at the throat where she could see a glimpse of hair on his chest. Leather suspenders looped over his powerful shoulders, and even in such a casual stance he was splendid.

Suddenly he snapped up the map and rolled it into a tube, but not before she saw the familiar contours of New York.

"Are you going to look for Garrick?" she asked, sitting forward on the bed. "Is that what the map is for?"

With more force than necessary he pushed the map into a leather cylinder-shaped container.

"I will leave the room," he said. "You may get dressed. Then I will order a carriage to take you back to Washington Square."

He began to walk away.

No! He couldn't just leave her! But she couldn't blurt that out, she realized. He would have nothing but contempt for her.

She had to do something, say something. He was almost out of the room, almost out of earshot.

"No!" she blurted.

He stopped and slowly turned toward her. "No?" He was incredulous, his expression darkened with disbelief.

"Yes," she said almost primly. "I said no."

"Can you not make up your blasted mind?"

"There is no need to swear at me."

"The bloody hell there isn't!"

She remained outwardly calm, although her heart was pounding uncomfortably.

"I asked you a question, and I would like a civil answer."

He remained still, his dark gaze unwavering.

She continued in a conversational tone. "I asked if you are going to look for Garrick. Are you?"

The single nod was barely perceptible.

"Take me with you! I could help you! Once the innkeepers and anyone else you encounter hear your accent, see your clothing, they will fleece you beyond belief."

"That has already happened, it seems," he replied tersely, glaring at her.

She refused to be pulled into an argument she could not possibly win. Instead she kept to the one that gave her a chance. "I could help," she said once more. "I can be of assistance to you."

"Contrary to what you must believe, I am an astute man, madam. I am no fool."

"That was not my implication, not in the least. But I do have sources here, I know many people."

"Of course you must. Your, how shall I say it? Your 'professional ties.' "

"Some," she admitted. "There may be information in our Green Books which may prove helpful in finding Garrick's whereabouts. We have compiled an astonishing amount of material there. But besides that, I am very good at getting information from unlikely sources.

I can be of great assistance to you, sir. The choice is yours. Charge blindly into this mission, or take me as your guide."

"The woman who moments ago thought she herself was blind because I had placed a damp cloth over her eyes?"

It took every bit of her willpower not to cringe.

He continued. "Will there be an extra charge for this service?" Then he gave a pointed look at her wedding ring, and she slipped her left hand beneath the coverlet.

"No. There will be no extra charge."

"Well, then," he said crisply. "There is some truth to what you say. I do not know this city. And the sooner we locate Garrick, the sooner we can reach the conclusion of this unpleasant business."

She, of course, was the unpleasant business. The notion made her swallow.

How he loathed her.

"Good. I will allow you two hours to gather your belongings from your home. Then . . ."

"No," she said.

"No?"

"Yes. No."

An explosive sigh escaped his lips as she continued.

"I will wear the dress I came in. That is all I require."

Brendan stared at her, unblinking and so very still she too did not move.

"What about your precious Green Books? Do you not need to get them?"

"Yes, you are right. I'll send a note to Patrick and have him bring them to me." And then she spoke, almost not of her will. She needed to say one last thing.

"I did not produce the spirit at the wedding. I am not so cruel as to do something like that."

As angry as he had been before, his fury now seemed to erupt into a fierce outburst. "How dare you deny it! You are not only a phony, madam, you are a liar as well!"

"I am not!" Rising to her feet, she jumped out of bed, her fury matching his own. "How dare you, you, you . . ." Words failed her. All of the choice, most vile terms fled her mind just when she needed them the most.

"Yes?" he snarled.

"You awful person, you!"

Crossing his arms, he stared at her with a glint of infuriating amusement in his eyes.

"I did not do that." She attempted to calm herself. "I could not. How could I have known we were going to have a wedding? How could I possibly orchestrate such a thing? I was far too . . ."

"Hungover?" he offered.

"No. Distracted. Honestly, Brendan, I would never do something like that. Not to anyone. Not to you."

The vague smirk left his lips, as his gaze traveled to her shoulders, then down, down.

In her agitation she failed to realize she was wearing nothing but the sheer unmentionables from the wedding, the flimsy chemise, and nothing else.

"Then did your aunt produce the apparition of my sister?"

The question took her by surprise.

Had Aunt Prudence managed to produce such a realistic spirit? The day before she would have said no, impossible. Not Aunt Prudence. Not the woman she had known and loved and even tried to protect all of her life.

But now, after what had happened, she didn't really know her aunt at all, had no idea what went on in her head.

Her expression of confusion was all he needed to see.

"Thank you," he said softly.

"For what?"

"You just answered my question."

"No, it's just that . . ."

"Be ready in ten minutes. We will breakfast downstairs, I will alert Mrs. Harris of the additional place setting. I'll have fresh water brought up."

That was all he said. Nothing about where they were going, how they would travel.

Nothing about the very real fact they were now man and wife. And he did not mention what was to happen after they located Garrick.

The pale man in the tavern had been noticed by the others.

Furtive, hunched over his single drink, he jumped every time the door slammed shut, every time another patron erupted in a bark of laughter or arguments grew vociferous. When other men tried to engage him in conversation, as is the norm in a small tavern in a small town, he stared blankly.

They wondered if he did not speak English, although he ordered his ale in a perfectly modulated tone. Perhaps that is all he knew of the language, how to order a single drink to cup in his elegant white hands. They were not the hands of a laborer, or a farmer or even a clerk. They were the hands of a gentleman.

Which, of course, made the stranger even more fascinating to those who noticed him.

Occasionally the man pulled out a folded parchment and read it, rubbing his eyes and temple as if in exhaustion before carefully folding it and returning it to his waistcoat pocket.

Over and over he read it. The words, the terms, remained the same. It was what he had agreed to, before everything changed. Before the words came back to haunt him.

He loved her, Amanda. He loved her still. And everything he had done, misguided as it may have been, was done for Amanda, and Amanda only.

It had not been easy to please such a woman. So perhaps he had taken risks that in hindsight were less than prudent. Still, it had all been for Amanda.

And for Brendan O'Neal. He had longed to prove himself worthy of the man's trust. But like Amanda, Brendan was not easy to please.

He had hoped to win the respect of both O'Neals with the same deed. For Amanda, it would have seemed honorable, even glorious. It may have even caused her to fall in love with him as he had fallen so desperately in love with her.

And for Brendan, whom he had wished to impress, it would have meant a large sum of money.

But it had all gone so terribly wrong.

Now, with that Celia Thomason woman, the mess had become even more tangled. He'd been so startled to see the image of Amanda, to smell her scent, that he had behaved foolishly. He had been unmanly, which had been the last thing in the world he had wanted.

But now, away from the house on Washington

Square, it seemed possible that Miss Thomason had been nothing but a fraud. A clever one, admittedly, but a fraud nonetheless. She had even pretended to be convincingly alarmed to see the product of her own fakery. That had been a brilliant touch, even he was forced to admit that.

The more he turned it over in his mind, the more he realized he had been duped. As realistic as the spirit had seemed at the time, there were numerous ways she could have produced the vision, a lantern slide perhaps. Or an accomplished painting.

Indeed, there were an infinite number of ways the deception could have been created. Maybe it had even been the simplest trick of all—they had just paraded a young woman before him, and his own mind filled in the blanks, saw what he assumed he was going to see.

He had nothing to hide.

That is what he had to remember. That had not been Amanda in the parlor. She had not paid a visit six months after her untimely demise. Thus, no one knew. No one at all could inform Brendan, or Miss Thomason. Or anyone.

There. Now he felt better, so much better. He had adored Amanda, and he had nothing to hide.

He would go back to the city. He could face them, face them both, Brendan as well as Amanda.

Celia, he corrected. He could face Celia Thomason.

It had been an accident, Amanda's death. And it had been ruled as such by the authorities and, more important, by public opinion.

Yes. He would leave now, go back to face them all.

He had nothing to hide.

Brendan entered the suite with a small suitcase and hat in hand. "Our carriage is waiting. Are you ready to travel, madam?"

"I am." She sighed. "Where are we going?"

"I was hoping you could offer some suggestions." He was about to sit on the edge of the bed, then hesitated and drew a heavy chair from across the room.

It was a uniquely uncomfortable chair.

"Where do you think Garrick would go?"

"When we were younger he used to frequent a public house in a small town called Tudburry. The Swan's Back, I believe it was called. That seemed to give him some comfort when his life became too rough."

"If you believe he is at a tavern, Mr. O'Neal, we may not be able to locate him for quite some time. There are hundreds of taverns in this city, hundreds more nearby. We can't possibly attend to each one properly."

"Yes, but think of the fun we'll have trying."

"Excuse me?" She propped herself up on one elbow and faced him.

"I don't know why I just said that." There wasn't a smile on his face. "I'm not feeling very well."

Without thinking she moved over on the large bed. And without thinking, he stretched out on the bed beside her. Both fully clothed, both lying atop the coverlet.

"I haven't been myself lately," he said, staring up at the ceiling. Crossing his arms over his chest, he took a deep breath.

"You've gone through a lot. You lost your father, then your sister, in a most appalling fashion. Now Garrick is missing. You have a right to be out of sorts."

"Perhaps. But I haven't a right to torment you."

They lay together in silence, a foot of space between them.

"You haven't tormented me," she said softly.

"Yes I have. From the moment I saw you I have behaved abhorrently. In the past I have not always been, well, noble. But I have been honest and decent. But you seem to bring out the most devilish behavior in me." He turned his head on the pillow to face her, and she tilted to return the gaze. "I have not been honest with you."

Suddenly she was feeling ill, but she did not flinch. "How have you not been honest?"

"About the night at the Astor House. About . . ."

"Please." She felt the heat rise to her cheeks. "Please don't continue. I would rather not hear any more about that night."

"No, please. I must."

"Oh, lands," she whispered. "Very well, then. If you must."

This was going to be humiliating, she thought, steeling herself against the bawdy images that were sure to be evoked.

"Nothing happened," he said flatly. "I can only apologize and . . ."

At once she sat bolt upright. "What?"

"Nothing happened."

"Impossible."

"It's true."

"You didn't tear my nightgown?"

"No. You stepped on it while dancing, then stumbled against a bedpost and twirled to the ground. You said it was part of the dance."

"I was dancing? But I can't dance—I'm a terrible dancer!"

"I know."

"I ripped the gown?"

He nodded.

She fell back against the pillows. "Nothing happened?"

"The maid helped you to bed. I slept in the drawing room. I didn't see you again until the next morning."

"Then why do I *feel* so different?" She didn't want to elaborate, but indeed she had sensed a change deep within her, a physical shifting of the way she viewed everything.

She had felt more feminine, more like a woman. But now she knew it was all a jest. She was not a woman whose charms had seduced a sophisticated gentleman, had not driven him out of his wits with her divine wiles.

Instead she was a poor excuse for a dancer who became inebriated after two glasses of champagne and tumbled to the ground.

She had imagined any magic between them. And then she had been an even bigger fool, following him there to his boardinghouse, trailing after him like a wounded puppy.

Pathetic. She was nothing short of pathetic.

"Celia, are you crying?" His voice was tender, soft.

"No," she snapped, dashing away a traitorous tear with a rough slap.

With the same gesture she shoved away his hand, for he had been reaching to stroke her face.

"Then why did you let me believe that something happened between us?" She tried to keep her voice even.

"Again, I don't know."

"Was it sport?" Her breath was deep, shuddering. "Was it amusing to see me so abased?"

"No, of course not!"

"Then what other reason could you have had? What other possible reason was there to make up such a vile fiction?"

She had to leave, to escape. Pulling away from him, her feet almost touched the ground when he yanked her back. Now she was on her back, pinned down with him on top of her.

"I don't know," he almost shouted. "I don't know why I misled you . . ."

As she struggled to escape him, he stared down at her, their faces inches away from each other.

"Let me go." She clenched her hands, pushing and pulling against the weight that was pressing down on her. She felt closer than she ever had to another human being. Her legs beneath the layers of skirts were trapped, and she turned her head side to side, thrashing against the heat of his muscular body, resisting the force that held her down.

Staring down at her, breathing hard himself, he watched the spark in her eyes, the anger and hurt there, the pain he had placed within her.

And then he leaned down, slowly at first, and then with an animal speed that caught them both by surprise, he pressed his lips to hers. Gently, he forced her mouth open and swept his tongue into her mouth.

Still she struggled, more fiercely now, her entire body revolting against the assault.

And still his lips remained on hers, and then, very gently, he moved his mouth to her cheek and neck, then her ear, and without lifting his lips, down her throat. Sensual. Like nothing she had ever imagined.

Her struggle lessened.

"What are you . . ." she breathed.

She closed her eyes and took in the scent of him, a clean, spicy scent, and her fists relaxed. Then, somehow, something altered. No longer was she pushing him away, but she was pulling him closer, ever closer, as if it wasn't possible to be near enough to him.

"Celia," he rasped, and the sound of her name was so strange, so very different than she had ever heard it before.

The wool of his jacket rubbed against her cheek, and she pushed it off, hunkered it over his shoulders until there was nothing but the clean white linen shirt and the silk cravat at his throat.

Not thinking, she loosened the cravat, and tugged it off with one finger. The buttons of his shirt seemed to pop off like pearls on a broken necklace.

His skin. She needed to feel his skin, as much as possible, as quickly as possible. His hands ran along her back, and she felt hooks and ties give. It was taking too long, much too long, and just as her frustration grew he gave a mighty yank and the sound of ripping fabric rose above their breathing.

And then, at last, her breasts were free, rubbing against him, and she clutched his bare back, her mouth trailing over his shoulder and throat.

"Celia, I . . ." he began.

"Brendan, please, I want you. I've always wanted you. Touch me. Love me."

With that, he took her lips in his again, gently touching, probing, exploring.

She closed her eyes and enjoyed the sensations flowing over her. She let out a slight gasp when she felt him move over her, but then the pleasure of the feel of him tight against her made her writhe in ecstasy. She heard him moan and whisper her name against her ear, his hot breath sending shivers up her spine.

Every sensation of his hard body on hers was new. She was wet and throbbing—feeling a way she never knew was possible.

It was as if a new world was opening up, embracing her. Somehow, they both had all their clothes off, and she felt the long, hard length of him against her. Rubbing against him, feeling every hard inch of him, the sensations seemed to roll and grow. He kissed her again softly, then hungrily, as he spread her legs with his knees and nudged himself inside. Their eyes met. "Are you sure?" She couldn't speak, only nodded and bit her lip as she felt a brief burst of pain. He began moving, slowly, giving her time to adjust to his size. His eyes never left hers.

He began to move harder and faster, and she buried her head in his neck as waves of intense pleasure broke over her. Over and over he called her name, and with a shudder he collapsed against her.

They lay together, hearts racing, breathing ragged, his chin nestled against the crook of her neck.

After a while she whispered, "What was that you were saying?"

She felt him laugh, his massive shoulders quake, before he replied. But when he spoke there was no smile in his voice. "I was about to say that the reason I told you those lies was simple."

She pulled back and looked deeply into his dark eyes, questioning. He raised his head and brushed back a thatch of her hair, then ran a thumb over her eyebrows. "I said those things because I so very much wanted them to be true."

"Mrs. Harris?"

Brendan knocked on the door and entered the parlor, the landlady's lair.

Seated on a settee, she looked up with a smile. "Why, Mr. O'Neal! Your carriage has been waiting for over an hour."

She then noticed he was wearing a different set of clothes than he had at breakfast. How elegant, she thought to herself. Only the Europeans are civilized enough to change for breakfast as well as for dinner.

"Yes, well." He smiled. He *was* indeed so very charming! Mrs. Harris tilted her head to her best advantage. "I believe we may not be traveling today after all. Mrs. O'Neal is in need of some new gowns."

"Is that so?" she clicked, surmising that young Mrs. O'Neal might be in a delicate state. "That time does come more swiftly than we ladies ever suspect." She almost added that when expecting her own first child, she needed new clothing at three months. But since dear

Bertram was twenty-nine now, it was not a topic she wished to bring up.

"Is this her first time?" she asked with a smile.

Mr. O'Neal actually seemed taken aback. "Excuse me?"

"I said, is this Mrs. O'Neal's first time?" Men, thought Mrs. Harris. At times they could be thick as planks.

"Why, yes," he stammered. "I . . . well, yes."

"And how has she been so far?"

"I . . . well. So far, she seems to be . . ." Then he straightened. "I, what I mean is, is there a seamstress to come round?"

"Certainly! Just down the street there is a Madame LaFarge. Her real name is Betty Sinclair, but Madame LaFarge seems to bring in more business. Or you can go to Broadway. I believe Stewarts has seamstresses who travel."

"Very well. Thank you, Mrs. Harris."

As he was leaving, she began to chuckle. "Forgive me, Mr. O'Neal," she said. She was thinking of Joseph, her second son, now living in Boston. "Do tell Mrs. O'Neal that the second time will be a far more pleasant experience. Indeed, I nearly enjoyed my second . . ."

"Thank you! Good day!"

Strange. Mrs. Harris looked at the slammed door. He very nearly bolted from the room! She hadn't taken him for a nervous man.

"Europeans." She sighed.

On the other side of the door Brendan O'Neal paused, shaking his head. How bold these people were! Glancing up the steps, where Celia was valiantly attempting to stitch her one gown back together, he shook his head. "Americans," he mumbled as he went out of the front door.

From his position just across the street, he watched O'Neal leave the boardinghouse.

Why had he left the rooms at the Astor House to stay at a boardinghouse? Made no sense, none at all.

Nothing made sense anymore. Not O'Neal, not Amanda's death.

And now O'Neal had married Celia Thomason. Miss Thomason was now Mrs. O'Neal.

The very thought sickened him.

He should have seen it coming, should have done something, anything, to prevent it.

Celia O'Neal.

First there had been Amanda, and then suddenly there was Celia. His feelings had crept up on him like a thief, just as it had been with Amanda. When had he first noticed his passion?

In his mind he could see her in the parlor, Miss Thomason to him, to all who crossed her threshold, but Celia in his mind. His Celia.

She could never be happy with Brendan O'Neal. She was delicate and fine, he was a big Irish brute.

Later she would thank him.

Just as Amanda would have, had the accident not prevented her from speaking.

Yes indeed. He smiled. Soon Celia would thank him.

"Oh, thank you," said Celia after one of Mrs. Harris's kitchen maids brought up a sewing basket. The maid peered in curiosity at Celia before bobbing a swift curtsy. After all, she had seen Celia wearing the very dark dress she was mending earlier in the morning. Now it was in tatters.

Celia flushed, her mouth set into a small smile. How odd that her world had changed in a matter of hours. In a matter of minutes, really.

Whatever would happen to her next? To them? Would they be man and wife in earnest now?

Or did he still intend to leave her behind, to pay her off and leave her behind?

Threading a needle, she looked down at the torn fabric, frayed well beyond the seams. The dress was hopeless anyway, she thought as she held it up. But she would give it a try, see what she could repair.

Her mind wandered as she sewed. She thought about Aunt Prudence, wondered what they were doing back at the house. Then she thought of the three men who would come soon to collect the money Uncle James owed. And the crowds that had been there yesterday to see her, such sad people, who wanted nothing more than to speak to their lost loved ones.

Then she noticed the fragrance.

It was the scent she knew so well now, the scent of Amanda's perfume.

Very slowly, Celia raised her head. And there she was, Amanda, standing no more than ten feet away from her.

"Hello," Celia said softly.

The now familiar process of materialization was taking place, and Celia watched as Amanda became more solid, as she once more took shape. Her eyes, as before, were gleaming. Yet unlike the earlier appearances, Celia saw something in those eyes.

She saw kindness.

And without realizing it, she smiled at Amanda, at this young woman who would have been her sister-in-law.

Celia had a sudden thought even as the apparition stood before her: Had Amanda not been tragically killed, she never would have met Brendan O'Neal. He would not have come to her aunt's home to seek her services.

Celia's own happiness at that very moment was linked inextricably to Amanda's death.

"Oh, Amanda. I'm so sorry."

Then something extraordinary happened. Amanda smiled at her, an expression of such warmth and understanding that Celia wondered why no one had told her what a remarkable person Amanda had been.

Maybe they had never really known. Maybe even Brendan, who had seen her only as a distant little sister, had never realized what an uncommon woman that little sister had become.

Amanda shook her head gently, as if to say no, the smile still on her face.

But her features altered from serene kindness to something else.

"What's wrong?" Celia asked.

Amanda's eyes grew wide, the smile faded. And she pointed to the window.

"Is something outside?"

As if it took a moment for her words to register, Amanda's ghostly white hand kept pointing, then she started to nod as if, yes, yes, that was it.

"Is it someone, someone I know?"

The nod became more frantic, almost convulsive.

"Someone you knew, Amanda?"

Yes, yes! her expression said, but then Celia thought she heard words in a lilting accent, more pronounced than Brendan's.

Yet Amanda's lips had not formed words.

He's outside! Look, Celia, look now!

Celia jumped to her feet, the sewing tumbling to the floor, and peered through the window.

All she saw was a fleeting glimpse of someone running away. It was impossible to tell who it was, just a male form in an innocuous cap and jacket. She couldn't even judge his age or height or build, just a flash of a man fleeing on the cobblestones, ducking into an alley.

Celia turned to Amanda, who was beginning to fade.

"Please, wait," Celia began, stepping toward her. "Don't leave me. Please, tell me more . . ."

Be careful, Celia. Be careful for Brendan, for yourself. Or what happened to me will happen to you.

The words overlapped hers, not spoken, but somehow understood.

"What can I do? I do not know who to fear. Please, more, give me more information."

Stay close to him, to Brendan. Don't let him go. There will be danger, there will be . . .

The voice was gone, dwindling away as her image dissolved.

"Come back!" Celia heard herself cry. "Oh, please come back!"

There was a timid knock on the door.

It was the maid who had brought up the sewing kit earlier.

"Ma'am? Did you call for me?" She seemed nervous, her gaze darting past Celia and into the room.

"No, no. Thank you. I'm fine, just fine."

The maid again looked over Celia's shoulder. "Very well, ma'am. If you need me, please just call."

"Thank you."

Closing the door after the maid, Celia realized she was dizzy, shaky. And all she could do was stay there with her torn gown and wait for Brendan to return.

To hope that Brendan would return.

13

The first time he went to a meeting, he did not know what to expect.

Of course he had been nervous. Wary. More than a little aware that he was in an unfamiliar land and surrounded by strangers who knew what they were about.

It was in an old barn that night. The location was changed every time, the word of each site passed along in taverns and on the streets, in the docks and sometimes even on Sunday mornings after church.

He had felt awkward, out of step at first, as if there was a great secret of which he was unaware. That is precisely what the situation was, a great secrecy.

And then he heard the speakers.

The first man was unimpressive initially, stammering on about famine relief and a man's right to feed his family. He mentioned a few names, unfamiliar towns that seemed very far away. In his present comfortable circumstance it was all but impossible to envision the misery so many miles away, and he was about to leave before the hat came toward him, passed around for coins and bits of gold.

Then the speaker seemed to come to life, as if a great wind of passion had wafted through the gaping spaces in the old barn walls. Now he spoke of freedom, of liberty. Where else but America, the birthplace of such a great nation, could such men gather and discuss a method to free yet another nation?

Something within him stirred, an awakening. Thus far his life had been a fairly routine one, given his circumstances, given the times. But when he heard what he could become a part of—why, he could be a part of history! Then he was riveted, unable to tear away.

This wasn't what he had thought it would be. This was dangerous, daring, an adventure. And he would become part of it. Perhaps even a great moving force, a romantic hero such as Robert Emmett, perhaps even a legend.

But it would require great sums of money, the speakers all said. Not only to feed the hungry, but to arm the men later, to actually start a revolution. No great fight was ever won with fists, the third speaker had said.

He would do it.

It was not a legal enterprise, he knew that now. But as the third gentleman, the one with the glorious voice, had stated, the American Revolution was not a legal enterprise either.

Perhaps one day his name would go down in Irish history the way George Washington and Paul Revere were regarded in this nation! It was possible, and if he became very involved—if he were able to give them all the money he could raise—it was even probable.

Now at last he had a reason, a purpose.

And he knew one thing for certain. That one meeting had changed his life forever.

*   *   *

Brendan found it difficult not to whistle as he approached the Astor House. Amusing, he thought, since he had never been much of a whistler. Indeed, it was a habit he had previously detested in others, a vexing sound that made him long to do a minor bit of bodily damage to the offending warbler.

And now he longed to join their ranks.

That thought alone caused him to grin. Brendan O'Neal, who had also never been much of a grinner, was smiling in such a pleasant manner, other people returned the smile, friendly people all.

America was such a very amiable place; he nodded to yet another pedestrian.

The Astor House, in its pompous grandeur, amused rather than irritated him. Its fraudulent self-importance, with uniformed men posted to keep out the bulk of this democracy, struck him as delightfully ironic.

"Mr. O'Neal," intoned one of the guards.

Brendan smiled at the young man, which seemed to take him aback a great deal.

At the front desk, an equally unctuous clerk made a slight bow, as if Brendan were royalty.

"Sir. You have several messages."

"Oh, thank you," he said, glancing at the handful of notes before slipping them into his pocket. "And could you recommend a seamstress to me?"

"Do you mean a tailor, sir?"

"No, a seamstress."

"Forgive me, sir, but what about the young woman who you employed recently?"

"A young woman? I'm afraid I do not . . ." Then suddenly it all fell into place, how Celia had managed to appear at his boardinghouse the night before, with the delivery boy. Now he understood the scenario. She must have followed the boy by stealth.

He began to chuckle at the image of how she had followed him.

And he felt something else, a peculiar sensation he had never before experienced. He wanted to see Celia, right then. As soon as possible. To tell her he knew what she had done.

He walked away from the desk, leaving a perplexed clerk to ponder, not for the first time, how very different the wealthy were from the rest of the world.

It came to Celia in a flash.

If she could move very, very quickly, perhaps she could run downstairs and catch enough of a glimpse of the man who she thought murdered Amanda to identify him. He might be lurking about still, positioning himself for a better view. It was just possible.

But she must get down to the street as quickly as she could.

There was no time to think, no time to second-guess.

She opened the door just a crack. "Excuse me," she called in a voice just above conversation level. There was no response. In a slightly louder tone she repeated the words. "Excuse me."

The maid appeared one flight below. Gazing up at Celia, she adjusted her lace cap. "Yes, ma'am?"

"Oh, yes. Could you please come here?"

"Certainly, ma'am. I'll be right up as soon as I take care of the colonel's room."

"No, no, please! This is an emergency."

Puzzled, the maid paused for just a brief instant before skipping up the steps.

"Yes, ma'am," she said as she arrived before Celia's door.

Celia opened her door and ushered the maid into the room. "This is going to sound a bit strange," she said in a rush. "But do you happen to have a change of clothing here?"

"Ma'am?"

"I know this is highly unusual, but you see my gown cannot be repaired, and I need to go on a brief errand."

"Ma'am, I only have this one dress. I live out, ma'am."

"It's just a temporary loan." Celia used her most cajoling tone.

"Ma'am, I have rooms to clean. The linens need changing."

Celia smiled. "It will just take a few moments. Please. I need to see someone on most urgent business."

"Oh, ma'am. I really could not."

And then Celia tilted her head and displayed the most winning smile she was capable of, an expression of such enchanting honesty combined with warmth that the maid could not refuse.

That was exactly what Celia had hoped for. Within a very few minutes, Celia was down on the street, following the path of the man who had vanished.

Brendan saw her sitting in the chair, her head bent over something.

Funny, he mused, how very different she seemed to him now. She was a bit stockier than he had realized, and her hair had more red in it than he remembered.

He really knew so very little of her.

She hadn't heard him enter, so intent was she on her

sewing. He grinned, remaining silent as he crept closer to her. And then he reached out, his large hand closing over her soft shoulder.

And the woman jumped.

"Sir!" she shrieked.

"Who are you?" he demanded simultaneously of the stranger who was wearing his wife's tattered gown.

"I'm one of Mrs. Harris's maids, sir."

"And where is my wife?"

"She had to leave, sir."

"She had to leave?"

"Yes, sir. She borrowed my dress and left. Said she had to meet with a man, sir."

"What the devil?"

He hadn't meant to shout, but he failed to rein his voice properly. As a result he not only shouted, he boomed.

"Please, sir!" The young maid's lower lip trembled.

Brendan took a deep breath and spoke in a softer tone.

"Do you have any idea who the man is?"

If anything, the softer tone sounded sinister to the terrified maid. "No, sir."

"So she's gallivanting about dressed as a parlor maid, meeting some mysterious man?"

Nodding, the young woman looked down at the carpet.

"Did you see which direction she was headed?"

"No, sir," she whispered.

"Very well, then. Thank you."

He turned to leave, realizing that the maid would be forced to remain in the room. Her attire had left without her.

"Good-bye," he said.

"Yes, sir."

And he left in search of his wife.

He was nowhere to be seen.

Celia rubbed her upper arms—it was more than chilly in the afternoon air, and she hadn't had time to find her cloak.

Who had she seen? She stood looking up toward the window where she had been just a few minutes before. Then she glanced in the direction she saw the man run. For a few moments she debated whether she should return to the warm rooms or try to follow the man.

It was indeed cold. But finding out who had harmed—possibly killed—Amanda was far more important than a little discomfort.

Shrugging off all thoughts of the weather, she began to walk quickly down the alley. There was a possibility he was still nearby, remote though it was.

All she needed was a single glimpse. And she was determined to do her best to have it.

In the span of two short days, Brendan had managed to misplace his brother-in-law, gain a wife, and just as promptly lose her.

As he walked up Broadway, he slowed his steps, lost in thought. Other pedestrians shot him annoyed looks as they were forced to pass the large man who had so abruptly slacked his pace. Yet the few who lingered on his face for even the briefest of moments found their annoyance replaced by curiosity at the handsome, well-dressed man who blocked foot traffic.

A shabbily clothed man wearing fingerless gloves and a sandwich board that read "Tumbling Chinamen—Five! Extraordinary! Refreshments! Exotic wonders! McAllister's House of Amazements!" brushed against Brendan's shoulder. The sign left a streak of white on his cloak, but Brendan didn't notice.

It had just occurred to him that he had somehow lost himself. His actions of the past few days had been of another man, someone he didn't trust. Someone he did not understand.

He had lost control of his life. And from where he stood, on bustling Broadway, with shopping emporiums, and pushcarts offering roasted corn and every segment of society represented in the dozens, he was not likely to regain control.

Yet there was a curious familiarity to the feeling. Only once before, when he was a very young man, had he experienced the same sense of tumbling, the same clutching at air as if waking from a dream of falling off a cliff.

It had been the worst months of his life, that time. Worse even than the death of his mother or father, worse even than the shattering news that his younger sister had been killed.

London. That was where he had been, a city of energy and commerce, yet with a curiously odd sense of antiquity. In New York there was a vital perception that the rules were being made and remade daily, that almost anything was possible. A single man could, by wile and wealth, move into any circle, limited only by his own imagination.

In London all had been set and rendered in stone for centuries. So when the elegant daughter of a duke set her sights on Brendan, he had fallen immediately and completely under her spell.

For just over three months Brendan allowed his business to slide as he entertained and was entertained by the most fashionable of London circles. In his few private moments he wondered why this beautiful creature had set her eyes upon him, but then he would shrug off the doubts and allow himself to experience emotions he had never considered. He would marry her, he decided.

And just when he was to meet with the old duke himself, she seemed to vanish. His notes were returned. His inquiries brushed aside. The very people who had so welcomed his presence days before avoided him at the clubs, snubbed him on the streets. Invitations no longer arrived.

It was then that Garrick had told him all, that his enchanting creature had found herself a gentleman of less means but more pedigree. Twice married, his previous two wives had died, and now this widower was again seeking a bride.

Business became Brendan's life then, to the exclusion of all else. That he could control. The numbers in a column either added up or they did not. There was either profit or loss. While there was an element of risk in every venture, it was a risk that could be reasonably calculated in advance.

Not so with love.

Thus he decided that he would not allow himself to be thrust into a position of vulnerability again. Not this time. Yes, he would do his duty. Perhaps it was better this way. He was attracted to Celia, the woman who was now his wife. But that was as far as he would allow it to go. He calculated the risks, and they were not intolerable. They would have a few children. They would eventually live separately. Perhaps he would indeed leave her on this side of the Atlantic in the near future.

The main consideration now was not to lose control. And he had stopped it, thankfully. After that morning, with the scent and feel of her still more vivid than anything he could recall, he was now able to step back and view the situation as the man he was, as a man of business.

That was as it should be.

Therefore, he would approach his impetuous marriage with thought rather than emotion. There. He felt more in control already.

No longer was he in a tumbling freefall.

He deliberately turned toward her home on Washington Square. In the clear-sighted brilliance of day, he realized he should simply have her old clothing sent over. There was no need for a seamstress, no need for a woman so accustomed to relatively humble circumstances to be elevated.

Then he would find Garrick, with or, most likely, without her help. He would again have his business partner and his most trusted friend. All would be as it should.

Taking a deep breath, he congratulated himself. She would be a most economical housekeeper. When children came, he would not have to worry about employing a governess.

That was what marriage should be. That was as it would be.

Impossible, Celia thought to herself.

She had lived in New York all of her life. Still, there

were some areas she had never visited. The streets in the lower part of Manhattan were confusing, twisting and haphazard roads that changed names and character every few steps.

It was beyond cold now. Late afternoon, and she was still wearing the thin wool dress. So silly, she smiled to herself. But she knew she would recognize the cap and coat of the man who had been standing outside of the boardinghouse if she saw him. She was absolutely certain.

She wasn't cold. Her brisk pace had helped keep her warm, her arms crossed. No one gave a woman dressed as a parlor maid a second glance, not with so many other people milling about, intent on their destinations.

There were more carts in this part of the city, close to the docks. The salt air tickled in her nostrils, but it wasn't unpleasant. Not in the least.

Perhaps she could get used to travel by ship. Now that she was his wife.

Again she smiled, glancing both ways before crossing the narrow street.

All she needed was a glimpse of the man. She had a good memory, she'd always had a good memory.

Then she saw the wharves themselves. How long had she been walking? It didn't matter, for now she stood in the ocean breeze and watched the ships with their mighty sails and the masts that seemed to reach the very heavens, scraping the clouds. How they all jostled for position, these vessels from all parts of the world, from England and China and Ireland and Spain. And the crews, exotic as the cargo, with the different nationalities and races represented with a strange combination of arrogance and nonchalance.

Celia felt an urge to laugh with the sheer delight and wonder of it all, of the excitement which she now—because of Brendan—would be a part of.

How marvelous life could be!

Blinking against a sudden burst of sunlight, she watched a massive bale being lowered with ropes and pulleys to the wooden dock, while just yards away a ship was unloading hogsheads and barrels. The possibilities of what could be in those chests and boxes was unlimited. There could be silks from the Far East, gowns from France. Perhaps fine sherry or port from Spain, or beautiful lace from Ireland.

Maybe there were tulip bulbs from the Netherlands, or wine from Italy. Everything imaginable from all over the world was before her, right then.

It was as if her whole life had just docked, had just arrived. Now all she had to do was open the boxes bursting with delights known and yet untasted.

And it was all due to this marvelous man.

No longer would she be a financial burden to her aunt. She would have her own home.

Lifting her face to the sun, she realized it was time to go back, to return the maid's dress.

It was time to reunite with her husband. Together they would find Garrick, together they would discover the truth of Amanda's death.

And together, they would build a new life.

There were still people milling about the house off Washington Square, but not nearly the crowd that had been there the previous day.

Brendan walked straight up to the house and pulled the bell. After a few moments he saw the curtain on the long slender window bordering the front door pulled back, and a single eye peering at him. The curtain went back into place and the door opened just slightly.

"Come in, hurry," he was instructed.

Once inside, Aunt Prudence, who owned the eye that had been peering at him, grabbed his arm.

"Oh, thank goodness! Where is she?"

Taken aback, Brendan looked down at the woman. A stray thought entered his mind. Who was she? Had she really been so inexplicably unkind to Celia, or had Celia imagined the flash of anger she described?

Or had Celia simply lied?

"Hello, Mrs. Cooper," he began.

"Where is she? They won't see me, they all insist on her, on Celia. Where is she? Some people are growing angry, Mr. O'Neal. They will pay to see her, but will not be satisfied until she returns."

"I do not know where she is at the moment."

"You don't know?" Her voice was shrill. "How can you not know?"

Aunt Prudence reached out to clutch his arm, then pulled back.

"I came to have the rest of her clothing sent over to the rooms I have rented. Perhaps you will be good enough to have them packed, and I will send a boy to retrieve them."

"But she must return, don't you see? Oh, dear. She must return."

Then he saw Patrick standing just over the threshold, beyond the stairs.

"I will see what I can do, madam," he said stiffly to Aunt Prudence as he raised an eyebrow to Patrick. The young man understood the meaning, and nodded once toward the parlor.

Brendan looked down and smiled. "May I trouble you for a cup of tea?"

She glanced up, and seemed perplexed by the request. Then her good manners took over, replacing the strained frenzy of just a few moments earlier. "Why, of course, Mr. O'Neal." She smiled as if still the coquette of four decades earlier. "Please, make yourself comfortable in the parlor, and I will have tea and cakes sent up directly."

Just the act of normalcy seemed to comfort her, put her on more solid footing, and she patted his hand before going toward the kitchen.

Patrick slipped into the parlor through the door behind the screen. "Sir," he said, and looked down.

"What has been happening here?"

"It's been a madhouse," Patrick admitted. He seemed flustered, his hands jammed deep into his trouser pockets. "There were people here all night, women crying they wanted to see their dead loved ones, men pounding on the doors. The newspaper folks haven't left, and that one man from Mr. Greeley's paper has made himself a particular nuisance. If Miss Thomason, I mean, Mrs. O'Neal, could only come back for a bit, I do believe things would settle down."

"I'm afraid I don't know where she is at this precise moment, Patrick." Almost to himself, he added, "Nor do I know where my brother-in-law has gone."

"Mr. Stevens, sir?"

Brendan looked up.

"Yes." Patrick shifted, and Brendan smiled. "Have you by any chance seen Mr. Stevens?"

"I, well . . ."

"Please, Patrick. He seems to have disappeared. I'm quite concerned about him."

"I, well, I really cannot tell you, sir."

"You mean you will not tell me, don't you?"

"It is close to the same thing, begging your pardon."

"Patrick, this is important. Mr. Stevens has been most distraught."

"That he has."

There was a loud pounding on the door, and Patrick jumped. "Another one. All night, all morning, the same pounding. I'm about to jump out of my skin. If only Mrs. O'Neal would return. They would stop, I know they would."

"This must be a terrible burden to you, Patrick. A houseful of women nervous as cats, you the solitary man. Their voices, chattering away. Turning to you to help them against the crowd outside. And what are you to do about it?"

"You're right, sir!" Patrick cried. "It's been dreadful!"

"I suppose if Mrs. O'Neal did return for a spell, and placated the few you allowed, well. Perhaps this madness would just go away."

"That's precisely my thinking, sir! Mrs. Cooper, why, with the tricks we have rigged, she could do just as well. But we need Miss Celia to help her just a bit, until the people get used to her. Then all would be right. I know it."

"Patrick, I have a proposition for you."

"Sir?"

"If you would tell me where Mr. Stevens is, or when you last saw him, I will persuade Mrs. O'Neal to return for as long as it takes. How would that be?"

Patrick looked at O'Neal, then shook his head. "I cannot, sir. I took a vow."

"A vow? Do you mean that you promised my brother-in-law that you would not reveal his whereabouts to me?"

"Not exactly. It is a little more complicated than that."

"How can it be more complicated? This is a simple question, Patrick. I will just ask you, do you know where my brother-in-law is?"

Patrick hesitated, weighing the question. "I suppose I do."

"Very well then. Perhaps if I ask you questions, you can respond as you see fit, for I would not wish you to break a vow."

Patrick looked down, his shoulders hunched for a moment before straightening. "I can't see anything wrong with that, sir."

"Excellent! Then may I ask, is Mr. Stevens in good health?"

"Yes, sir. That I can assure you."

"Well, that's something." Brendan rubbed his chin. "And is he nearby?"

"Well, he is not far away."

"When was the last time you saw him?"

"Quite recently."

"Patrick, please. I need to have more specific information than this. He is my brother-in-law, and I am concerned for his welfare. I fear that by employing Mrs. O'Neal, and with your expert tricks, I may have done damage to him. He was already distraught."

"Oh, he seems fine, sir. We all think so."

They all think so, Brendan repeated to himself.

There was a group, then. He pretended not to have heard that piece of information.

"Everyone is in agreement?" Brendan asked casually.

"Yes." Patrick nodded.

"Well, I thank you. You have put my mind much at ease."

Patrick grinned, pleased with himself.

"So you haven't noticed a vast difference in him?" Brendan's voice was gentle. "Since you first met, I mean?"

"Well, of course he was a newlywed then, all excited about his wife. She was beautiful, he would always say. Begging your pardon."

"No, that's fine. And that would have been when he first arrived, then?"

"Yes, fresh off the boat they were. They were the greenies. I was the old hand."

"How glad they must have been to have had your help, Patrick."

"I think they were," he said fondly. "And I remember when . . ."

The parlor door opened, and Aunt Prudence entered, followed by the younger maid, who was carrying a full tea tray.

"Patrick, could you go down and talk to Hannah? She's all in a dither over the man who tried to enter through the kitchen this afternoon. You should have seen it, Mr. O'Neal. He came in feetfirst, just as bold as brass he was. So Patrick, below." Aunt Prudence gave him a look that indicated he should be below.

"Sorry, madam," Patrick said, his eyes slightly wide. He did not say anything as he began to leave, an expression of mortification creasing his forehead.

"Forgive me," Brendan said, addressing both Aunt Prudence and Patrick. "I will ask to be excused from tea, although I do thank you. Instead, I will return with Mrs. O'Neal as soon as possible."

It took a slightly perplexed Aunt Prudence a few moments to understand what Brendan had meant. And Patrick, as he left the room, nodded at Brendan, still uncertain if he had said too little or too much.

Now all Brendan had to do was find Celia, find his brother-in-law, and get on with his life.

14

*B*rendan slammed the door to his furnished lodgings with more force than he had intended.

That would not do, he reminded himself. He would remain remote, unaffected by the woman. He had just spent the better part of an afternoon scrubbing thoughts of her from his mind. More accurately, from his emotions. Now she could not touch him in any way. And that was how it would remain.

Slamming the door would suggest he cared about her, that she had the ability to provoke anger or disquietude, and that most certainly was not the case. She had no power over him. Her existence would not alter his life one dash, except on those rare occasions when he would require her presence, such as the propagation of an O'Neal heir, or the occasional ceremonial function.

It was time to let her know the situation, the unvarnished truth. The tone of their life together, or apart, would be established now.

Celia, who had been lost in dreamy thought since

her own return, wearing the newly repaired dress, reading from the stack of books on a side table, jumped when the door slammed, her expression an almost comical reflection of surprise. Then she smiled, a warm and languid softness in her eyes.

"I've been reading a most wonderful book," she began. "It's by an author you may know, a Brendan O'Neal."

Then she held up his own book, his most private thoughts. It was the book where he jotted down "What I know" and "What I don't know," the pages he filled in with the most vital moments of his life.

"Oh, Brendan, this is wonderful. I feel as if I know you. The part about Amanda." Then she blushed. "The part about me. I, too, am confused. I do not know where my feelings come from, or where they will lead. In my own head the second column is also nearly blank."

She had found it! No one had ever read that book, he had never allowed anyone to see it. How foolish he had been to leave it unattended in his room.

She continued speaking. "I've been thinking about Garrick, where he might be. There are a few taverns on the outskirts of the city that may have the feel of the public houses in England Garrick had so favored."

Then she waited for his response.

How strange, she mused. She had missed him while they were apart, yet she felt a growing closeness to him in those hours. Is that how other married folk felt? Sometimes she had seen her mother look out of the window, eager for the sight of her father returning home after a long day of work. As a child she had never understood the need to see someone, although she always was pleased to see her parents. There had been an assumption in her young mind that loved ones always returned home, no matter what had transpired in the ensuing hours.

Now she knew differently. After her parents' death, she had learned that people do not always return. And after the words her aunt had spoken to her, those bitter and hateful words, Celia also knew that even when you think you understand the feelings of another, sometimes you do not.

After this morning, after sharing a closeness and bond with this wonderful man who was now her husband, she realized a whole new universe of possibilities beyond the confines of her childhood home, of her own little sphere.

Brendan was home, and she had so much to tell him, so much to share.

Brendan was home, and she felt a sense of joy well within her. This was her new life, her future.

But he did not see her expression, deliberately looking past her. There was no reason for eye contact, for contact of any sort.

"I'm so glad you're back," she said lightly, savoring the masculine perfection of her new husband. And she would tell him about seeing Amanda, and together they would share the search for Garrick, and for the man who likely had been responsible for Amanda's death.

But Brendan said nothing.

"Where have you been?" she continued, curious as to what caused the steely formality of his stance, the flatness in his deep brown eyes. A thatch of dark hair fell over his curiously lined brow, and she longed to touch it, to brush it away and hopefully ease the strain that seemed to be there.

Still silent, as if she did not exist, he pulled off his gloves, tossed his greatcoat and hat on the settee, and walked over to the brandy decanter. With deliberation, he turned his back on her and poured himself a large portion, then drained it in one swallow.

"Are you not well?" Her voice was one of tender concern. "It was cold today. May I get you something to help you warm yourself?"

He would not acknowledge her, his broad shoulders as much of a barricade as a massive stone wall. He poured another brandy.

Rising from the chair, she stepped over to him and placed a hand on his right shoulder, her fingers dwelling, almost touching the bare, vulnerable skin of his throat. But she did not. There was something precarious in the air, a strange and uncomfortable hum between them. And she had no earthly notion of where that unpleasantness had developed, if it had been something she had said or done earlier, if it had been something that arose from within Brendan himself.

"Brendan?"

Slowly, as if he would extend that single gesture to infinity, he put the glass of brandy down and looked at the gentle white hand that was resting on his shoulder. There was such contempt in his gaze, such palpable distaste, that she withdrew her hand and backed away.

"What is wrong, Brendan?"

He remained motionless, and she felt an unfamiliar sense of alarm, a fear in the pit of her stomach.

Attempting to keep her voice even, she swallowed before speaking. Perhaps this was not the best time. He may have had difficulties in business, maybe a disagreeable encounter with a merchant or coachman. But she needed to tell him what had happened.

She needed to somehow engage him in conversation. Anything, anything at all, was preferable to this excruciating frost.

"I saw Amanda today, Brendan. Here, in this very room. She pointed out the window, and she said the person responsible for her death was outside. I ran outside as quickly as possible to see who it was, but I could not."

It was as if he was in some distant place. There was nothing in his stiffness to indicate he had heard her. And then, finally, he spoke, his voice cold and flat and dead.

"You needn't playact for me, madam."

Celia was confused. "Playact?"

The words surged out as pure venom. "Playact. That is your trade, is it not? You would wish me to believe you have the power to rouse the dead, to make my own sister appear. So now you claim she speaks?"

"She didn't really speak." Celia tried to keep her voice from wavering. "It was as if I heard what she was saying without really hearing. It was in my mind. She put her thoughts into my mind."

His hand clenched around the brandy glass, then relaxed. "And now she follows you about? My own sister, who you have never known, follows you from your parlor to this house? Am I to believe you? Can you not realize how loathsome it is for me to hear you bandy Amanda's name about with such wanton abandon? To you she is a prop, a bit of clever business to help stage you and your aunt's little circus. To me, she was my sister, my last remaining relative."

"But I . . ."

He did not hear her response, he could not hear anything beyond the thundering ringing in his ears.

Calm, he told himself. *Control. Do not let her in, do not allow her access to any part of you.* She was still speaking, her voice rising. She was worried, frightened.

And with a peculiar, vivid focus, he suddenly realized something. She had tricked him into marrying her.

It was so obvious he almost laughed out loud at himself, even as her velvet words spilled out onto the corners of his consciousness.

What a fool he had been!

Of course he had been a ripe target, this foreigner who had been dealt the double blow of the loss of his father and sister within a half year, and then the apparent loss of his brother-in-law. She worked her wiles, and worked them well, expertly. And the reason had been equally as obvious to everyone except for him: Money.

The oldest reason in the world had employed, using a variation of the oldest profession in the world. Didn't it always come down to one or the other? In his case, it had been both.

How very perfect it had been for her, for them. They must have schemed and delighted in the ease with which Brendan O'Neal capitulated.

Another thought came to him. Those three men, those ruffians who seemed to harass her for her late uncle's debt, had probably been employed by her. She had been so frightened, so brave, and he had rescued her. She had played the victim, he had so conveniently played his own foolish role.

Calm, he repeated to himself. *Do not allow your fury*

to show. That would give her power. Later you can allow it to wash over you. But not now.

She had stopped speaking. He cared not what she had said, for it didn't matter. It all made sense to him, what a colossal idiot he had been. For the second time in his life a woman had made him a buffoon.

At last, when he spoke, it was with an eerie composure. "As I stated earlier, I do not yet understand the trickery you employed to gain this marriage."

"Trickery?" She could barely breathe. Had he not heard what she had just said? She had detailed her feelings, her tumultuous emotions, of how she wished to embrace him as her future. But he had not heard. All she could do was repeat the vile word he had used to describe the sum of her being. "Trickery?"

He did not offer any indication she has spoken, and continued without missing a beat. "Clearly now there is a chance a child may arrive. In that event, this marriage will be in name only. If that is not the case, then we will follow the plan as outlined in yesterday's letter. A swift annulment when I return to London."

"How can it be?" The room seemed to tilt for her, and she reached back to grasp the edge of a chair for support.

"It is a simple enough concept. I intend to live as I did before, as I have always lived. It has worked quite nicely thus far. Indeed, I believe it would be prudent for you to return to your aunt's house. I have a carriage waiting below."

"How can we have a marriage in name only after what happened today, this morning?"

He remained dispassionate, as if they had been discussing the weather. "That was an error, and I apologize.

It will not happen again, unless of course it is strictly planned for the purpose of children."

"No."

"No?" It was the first time the coldness gave way for just an instant, replaced by simple incredulity. When was the last time someone had questioned him about anything, much less a simple proclamation?

"No. I refuse to those terms."

It took every ounce of his self-discipline not to raise his voice. He refused to display any emotion, and therefore he did not.

Once again, he was himself. Once again, he was in control. "Madam, you have no choice in this matter."

"I most certainly do."

"In case you have forgotten, you are my wife. Under both British and American law, this makes you my property."

Her knuckles whitened on the back of the chair as the words took a moment to filter through her haze of shock and confusion.

Who was this man, this person? It was as if there were two Brendans, one kind, the other cruel beyond reason.

And then came her moment of clarity, a brutal bolt of awareness that shattered the pink gauze that had enveloped her since the morning.

All of the other emotions that had been coursing through her evaporated. The fanciful, girlish thoughts died like a blossom tinged with acid. Her imaginings of a life with this man, of the awakenings she had experienced since that morning, vanished.

This was her worst nightmare, what she had always avoided. This was precisely what she had feared, to become one of those quaking creatures who cowered before their brutish husbands. All of those women who had come to her, seeking absolution from monstrous spouses now dead and buried, men whose hold on their wives—literally as well as spiritually—lessened not at all with their deaths.

"No!" Her voice startled both of them with its ferocity.

And then his lips curled into a parody of a smile, those same lips that had traced her with passion earlier.

She had mistaken passion for possession.

In her mind she cried, *Oh God, no. Please, please not this! Please, God, anything but this.*

But when she spoke again, her voice was firm, steady. It was the voice of calm and absolute reason.

"No." Stiffening, she released her grip on the back of the chair and stood straight, her shoulders squared. "You, sir, will never own me. Nothing about me, ever, will be yours."

There was a flash in her eyes, a spark, and against all of his deliberate rationale, all of his hard-won restraint, he felt the powerful stirrings of desire.

"The subject is closed," he announced. He had to get her out, had to remove her from his sight. Even from a distance of several feet he could sense her fragrance, more compelling than any perfume. His body began to react, recalling that morning, his blood pounding, traitorous and undisciplined. "Downstairs is your carriage. Good evening, madam."

There was no choice. She had to leave. Her chin raised, she, too, avoided his gaze, just as he had moments before when he had first entered the room.

Moments before, a lifetime before.

She would collect her coat downstairs, to cover herself, for the creature warmth she had not required before. But now, now how very much she needed it.

Without another word, she left the room, closing the door gently, without a slam, without a sound.

Her soul was shattered and splintered with violence. But in silence.

And on the other side of the door, Brendan listened for her footsteps descending the staircase. But he heard nothing. She had retreated in complete silence.

Instead of the triumph he had expected, he felt a rush of fatigue, of crushing despair. It would pass, he told himself. It would pass.

His hands reached for the back of the same chair she had been gripping earlier. And now it was his own powerful knuckles that grew white.

Celia's reentry into the house at Washington Square was as routine as it was crushing.

There was precious little acknowledgment of the recent past. It was as if she had stepped out to visit a friend, or perhaps to the flower market.

Aunt Prudence had been expecting her. "Hello, my dear," she said, holding the door open wide.

Celia squelched the urge to scream, to run.

"Hello, Aunt Prudence," she replied automatically. There was nothing else for her to say.

She was abandoned by everyone. All she had was herself now. But that was fine, she thought. That was all she had ever really had, she just hadn't known it.

"You must be so exhausted, my dear. Come inside, and after supper you can get some sleep. We have a big day planned tomorrow."

Her gaze hollow, she just looked at her aunt, this

woman with whom she had lived for so many years, and this woman whom she had known so very little.

The older woman sensed the hostility. "Celia." She reached out to grasp her niece's hand, and Celia simply did not have the energy to pull away. "I said some hurtful things, some awful things. I don't know what caused me to do that. It is most certainly not how I feel. You must know that you are the daughter I never had, my own child."

It wasn't worth arguing. Celia nodded simply to be able to leave, to go up to her own room.

"Shall I have dinner sent up?" Prudence asked cheerfully.

"Please," she replied. Then she climbed up the steps.

Would she be climbing these same steps for the rest of her life? With the same dull, bone-deep melancholy?

Was this all there was, all there would ever be?

And then, with a deadening sense of despair, she realized that it probably didn't matter anymore.

Celia managed to numb herself emotionally by the next morning. She would not feel, she told herself, because all of the pain she had ever suffered had been a result of caring.

All day she remained cloistered in her room, the shutters closed and the curtains drawn. The hours passed with a curious sameness. She did not pick up a book, nor did she reach for her needlepoint. The hours ticked and tocked, and Celia stared ahead, not really seeing, not really caring.

Once she looked down at her hands, startled to see the gleaming wedding ring on the left ring finger. With anger she tried to pull it off, to remove the mockery of a symbol, but it would not be released. It remained obstinately fixed on her finger, like a small golden shackle, leaving the flesh around it raw and reddened from her efforts.

Although her aunt had told her with great excitement who was going to be there, she did not really hear. As if in a dream, she had dressed herself, prepared. She would go through with the charade, simply because she could not find a way out. At least not yet. *Later*, she thought. *Perhaps later.*

Now she was ready. She would go downstairs as always, although it had seemed years ago since she carried on with the dull routine. They would speak of their loved ones, dab the moistness from the corners of their eyes, and she would listen with sympathy and then Patrick and Aunt Pru would perform their tricks.

Yet something strange was happening. Even as she dressed she sensed a peculiar tingling. It continued, growing in strength as she began to descend the stairs. Stopping, she looked at her hands. They seemed no different, nothing out of the ordinary. Yet they felt as if a million tiny pins were dancing on her palm and along her fingers. Then the sensation seemed to climb up, over her wrist, coursing over her forearms, even under the dark green sleeves of her gown.

Perhaps she was ill, she thought with detached curiosity. It made little difference.

Her aunt met her at the foot of the staircase. "Oh, Celia! Such very important gentlemen and ladies are within!" Lowering her voice, she continued, "So many wished to be here, but they worked it out amongst themselves who were to be the first ten to witness your powers." She glanced over her rounded, lace-cloaked shoulder. "Even Mr. Frederick Douglass has sent someone to tell him what occurs! He's right there at the table, a man from the *North Star* abolitionist paper. He's right in the parlor, seated just as civil-like as you or I would be."

Celia just stared at her aunt, not really comprehending the words, her hands and arms still tingling. Prudence continued listing the people of importance in the parlor, people who were there to judge Celia, to determine if she was a fraud. Part of Celia heard the names, all of them familiar. The other part seemed to move as if on some unseen person's volition. *Otherworldly*, she articulated in her mind. She felt as if she did not belong here, nor did she belong anywhere. Only her body seemed to remain stubbornly earthbound. The rest of her felt as if it could float to the ceiling, perhaps beyond.

Prudence patted her cheek and she entered the parlor slowly, allowing her eyes to adjust to the dimness of the room. The parlor was darkened, as it always was before a session.

Just another session.

Now she looked around the room, at Mr. Robert Sweeny, the reporter with the *Daily Telegraph*, at Mrs. Lucinda Kuhn of the Woman Suffrage Society, and at the representative of the Reverend Beecher's church over the East River in Brooklyn.

The man sent by Frederick Douglass was next to Mrs. Kuhn and splendid with his high cheekbones and his magnificently untamed hair. He nodded once at her.

The room seemed to swim, and she straightened her shoulders.

"Welcome, each of you." She smiled, clasping her hands together so they would not tremble so obviously.

Celia was dressed simply, in green wool with cream trim at her throat and wrists, her luxurious hair pinned simply at the nape of her neck in a figure eight.

Altogether, there were ten people in the parlor, with Patrick tucked away awaiting his cue, but Aunt Prudence standing just behind Celia.

And then she saw him. In the corner, well away from the table and relaxing in a wing chair, was Brendan.

"Good afternoon and welcome," she stammered before realizing she had already greeted them.

Why was he here?

To humiliate her, she thought. To jeer and be as unpleasant as possible. To add to her misery.

Well, that would not happen. She would not allow him to keep her off-balance.

A sense of power swept through her, even as the strange tingling continued. She would make this the most convincing session she had ever held.

Better yet, if at all possible, she would make this real.

Amanda had come before, and she would come today.

Serenity mingled with her newfound power.

"Please, let us all gather at the table. All of us, except for Mr. O'Neal," she said.

O'Neal, who had begun to get out of the chair, stopped. Even in the faint light of the dimmed parlor she could see his jaw tighten as he hesitated an instant, then resettled into the chair.

There had been some debate as to whether this experiment should occur in the evening or daylight, and in the end it was determined by the man from Mr.

Samuel Morse's office—who was there to decide if Celia was worthy of receiving the prototype of Mr. Morse's new spirit communication machine—that the experiment should occur in daylight.

An eerie silence spread throughout the house, a hush of expectancy, as if the very walls were waiting to be tested.

"Good afternoon," Celia began once again after a slight pause.

Now she could see their faces, the individual features of those gathered around the parlor table. Her aunt stood back just slightly, an expression of trepidation mingled with that unique glint that always came into her eyes when the possibility of money was involved.

The others were far more difficult to read, their expressions neutral, although Mr. Sweeny seemed more openly suspicious, stroking a thin mustache and hiding the barest of grins. And Mrs. Kuhn, a woman one would commonly describe as handsome, with a no-nonsense posture and a gold eyeglass pinned to her breast. These were not believers. The room was filled with skeptics, every one of them.

Especially, of course, Brendan O'Neal.

"Let us gather around the table and clasp our hands," she began. "I beg of you, do not leave the circle, do not loosen your hold on your neighbors' hands, no matter what you see or hear. No matter what your experience may be. The circle must remain unbroken. And let us think of those who have passed over, those you wish to speak with."

Mr. Sweeny raised an eyebrow. "What of Mr. O'Neal? Shall he not join us at the table?"

Celia did not look back at the topic of discussion.

"Mr. O'Neal is here for reasons of his own, although what they may be I cannot guess. He is supreme amongst nonbelievers, sir. And I fear his presence in the circle will corrupt the entire proceedings."

"I must protest," said Mr. Sweeny firmly but politely. His tone was one of suspicion mingled with humor—he did not believe one jot in all of this spirit hysteria, and he was vastly anticipating a sensational series of articles debunking the admittedly lovely medium as nothing more or less than an accomplished actress. "I understand Mr. O'Neal happens to be your new husband."

That was the last thing Celia wished to be reminded of at the moment. But she maintained her composure. "Yes," she replied, unable to come up with a sensible enough phrase to qualify the situation. It seemed inappropriate to mention that the marriage would be in name only, that she found him the most vile and reprehensible of beings, and that she felt it an unqualified shame that Mr. O'Neal was on this side of the netherworld rather than with the unfortunate souls to whom she would soon speak.

She could almost feel his smirk. So she repeated very calmly, "Yes."

"Well, madam." Mr. Sweeny nodded toward Brendan. "I do not wish to cast aspersions on anyone, but I believe I can speak for all of us when I express my concerns that Mr. O'Neal may have a vested interest in this afternoon's outcome. And as such, it may very well be most difficult for us to accept anything that occurs without blemish if Mr. O'Neal is allowed to remain outside of the circle. Is everyone else in accord with me?"

The others exchanged glances, and Mrs. Kuhn, in a surprisingly forceful voice, said, "Indeed, Mr. Sweeny.

My own thoughts were very much in harmony with yours. Mr. O'Neal? Do you have any objection to joining the rest of us in the circle?"

Before he could reply, Celia offered another suggestion. "Perhaps Mr. O'Neal would be kind enough to excuse himself altogether from our presence. He may be interested in taking a long, pleasant walk, or joining his esteemed brother-in-law in some distant amusement."

Brendan stared at her, realizing that in a very roundabout way, she had just made a request that he, for want of a better phrase, get lost.

"Thank you, sweetling," he replied with such a honeyed voice that she found it difficult not to reach for something—anything—to throw at him. "But I would be most pleased to join your enchanted circle." Turning to the others, he smiled his most charming smile. "You see, my comely bride has been summoning my younger sister of late." He paused. "Both my sister and the summoning can both be described as late."

Mr. Sweeny grinned—clearly he now had a most marvelous line for his first article.

"However, my dear." He nodded toward Celia. "I have a few things I wish to discuss with Amanda as well."

With that he made rather a show of pulling up a chair, placing it between Prudence and the man from Mr. Morse's office, and settling into his position, twice winking at her with his cultivated affability.

She would not look at him, not allow him the satisfaction of thinking he had rattled her nerves. Instead she turned her full attention to the gathering at hand.

Something needed to be said, something out of the ordinary, for this was not simply a routine session. Every one of these individuals was waiting for her to prove something that in the entire history of mankind had thus far been unprovable.

"I realize that for all of you, this is a most unusual experience, perhaps even frightening. You have heard much of this new science of spiritualism. But it is the oldest belief in the world. We long to know our contact with loved ones will transcend the experience of death, will remain firm and true forever. I may not succeed in proving that, not this afternoon, maybe never. I simply request that you keep your minds and hearts open."

They did not respond, although all were giving her their full and most polite attention. "If it makes you more comfortable, you are all here for an experiment. Just as I understand some of you have explored the events that occurred with the Fox sisters, you are here to witness whatever happens or whatever does not happen. And rest assured that no matter what you conclude, what you feel compelled to write or decree, I will accept your decision. I will not frequent your doorsteps, or use your distinguished names on posters pasted to walls or fences."

They all smiled, distant, remote smiles.

Brendan was seated slightly to her left shoulder, so she was unable to see his reaction without being obvious. Yet she felt it, knew he had arched a brow and carefully observed his fingernails.

"Very well then," she continued, in command now in spite of his presence, or perhaps because of it.

And she glanced over to where she knew Patrick was posted. Their cue had been preset, and when she said the words "Very well," he knew it was his turn to perform.

The session began.

The tingling throughout her hands had not abated, but now her entire body felt alive and poised for something, although she did not have the time to ponder the sensations flowing through her. She asked the gathering to close their eyes, to free their minds of their everyday woes and concerns.

Instead they were to think of those they loved who were no longer alive.

As she spoke the words, a fresh sense of urgency made what she was saying more potent somehow.

"They are with us now," she said without the usual melodramatic pauses the clients had come to expect. "Although they may have passed over into another world, their love remains. But that love is no longer tinged with the imperfections and vexations of this world. Now their love for you is intact, whole. Pettiness has vanished, the small hurts or even the larger calamities of life no longer taint the purity of exquisite love. It is distilled into its most glorious form."

Mr. Sweeny's mouth quirked, his eyes still closed.

"Very well," she said in a loud enough voice for Patrick to hear. It was automatic, this pretend. This trickery.

Trickery. The exact word Brendan had used to describe her. And he was right.

She looked at these people gathered at the table. Although she knew little of them, other than Brendan and her own aunt, something had compelled them to be there, at the table, at this very moment.

It was hope. No matter how jaded and sophisticated they may have seemed, and may actually have been, in their hearts they all harbored a kernel of desire that this was real. She could only imagine what losses each had suffered, how deeply wounded they had been by the mortal separation of human affection. Perhaps there was business left unfinished, words left unsaid.

Even the cynical Mr. Sweeny, beneath his cocky veneer, must secretly wonder if it would be possible to communicate with the dead.

And even Brendan, she realized with a start. Even he must have allowed his thoughts to imagine, for why would he have brought Garrick to her in the first place?

Somewhere yet lurking in the cervices of his soul was the small Irish boy who had been told tales of fairies and goblins, a child whose mother had died and who must have longed with all of his might to see her but one more time.

All of these thoughts came to her in an unexpected flash.

Even Aunt Pru must want to believe. Poor, disappointed Aunt Pru, a woman who had been either misled by fate or, even more crippling, entirely ignored by it.

They all had hope. And no matter how expert Patrick's inventions were, these people would not be fooled. She would not fool them, not now. Not this time.

"Think of the ones you miss so very much," Celia said softly. They were forced to strain to hear her words. "For they are here. And they miss you every bit as much as you long for them. But they are at an advantage. They are at peace, and they know that love continues."

The prickling in her hands became even more pronounced, as if something of great power was coursing through her, using her body as a means of conduction.

Yet something was genuine. Somewhere between the trickery and the blind desire of faith lay the truth.

"Please come to us," she pleaded as she closed her own eyes. She thought of her mother, her father, Uncle James. She recalled friends from childhood who had perished, the laughing faces of youth taken away so suddenly, so utterly. Only the random vagrancies of chance had preserved her own life thus far, the same chance that had spared everyone else at the table.

The same chance that had taken Brendan's sister.

The room was cold, as it always was without the benefit of a fire or any sort of heating. The strange stillness seemed to envelop them all in an expectant silence.

And then came the fragrance, the familiar scent of Amanda's perfume.

Celia did not open her eyes to see what Brendan's reaction was. She was barely aware of the aroma. Instead she was intent on her own thoughts, on the odd swirling she sensed around her. It was impossible to define where the air began, where her limbs ended. As if she could float, as if she had become one with the very essence of the room and of what was happening.

No one else was with her then, only Celia—a Celia not bound by the rest of the known world.

Another fragrance emanated from an unknown place and encompassed everyone gently in its singular musky overtones. Horses, Celia thought vaguely. It smelled of horses and hay, of saddle leather and stable soap.

The scent was not familiar to her, but that mattered not. The swirling seemed to intensify, and then there was a warmth that drove back the chill of the room, a warmth that seemed to caress and move about like some benevolent entity.

Still she kept her eyes closed, as did the others. A noise then, a hum as of a great mass of something vibrating, joined in the symphony of the senses. No one spoke, none of the people at the table so much as moved.

Celia could barely breathe. Something was poised to happen, something of great importance.

There was a gasp, a feminine gasp, and Celia wondered if it could have emanated from her own mouth, but then in her detached awareness she dismissed the notion.

Something was about to happen, something was on the verge of breaking, a thundercloud near to bursting.

"David!" a woman cried. It was Mrs. Kuhn, Celia realized, it had been she who had gasped. "My David, oh David," she sobbed.

"Celia," someone whispered so close to her ear she thought she would feel the warmth of another being, but there was no such warmth other than the gentle feverish feel of the room itself. "Tell him, you must tell him."

The accent was a softly lilting one, lovely, Celia thought. A beautiful sound. Amanda.

"Tell whom?" Her voice came out as a shout. "Amanda, where are you? And whom shall I tell—Garrick?"

"Amanda?" It was Brendan, an unfamiliar edge in his speech.

"No, no," the ghostly voice whispered in her ear. "Tell Brendan. Tell him."

"Tell him what?" Celia again felt as if she had broken the silence of eternity, her words booming.

"Tell him that I forgive him. When we were children I fell and cut my face, and all these years he had been pointing the finger of blame at himself. But it was me, all my fault. I fell over the fairy ring, I tripped over the fairy ring . . ."

And then there was a colossal thud, a bang that seemed to shake the house to its very foundations. The door to the parlor flew open, slamming against the wall, the sound of broken glass tinkling to the floor. A great beam of light struck the parlor, shattering the swaddled dark that had been there.

In the white ray of light was a black silhouette, the unmistakable figure of a man.

Someone screamed, whether it was a man or a woman it was impossible to tell, so animal-like was it in its shrill intensity, its primal terror.

Then came a silence almost as horrible, and the silhouette spoke.

"Oh, sorry. I was looking for . . ."

"Garrick?" Brendan said, rising to his feet.

Celia and the others blinked, confused.

"Brendan? I was looking for Miss Thomason." His features were obscured by the backlight, yet the confusion in his voice was evident. "I knocked but no one answered. I do hope I haven't come at an inconvenient time."

Again, there was silence, until their eyes adjusted to the sudden flood of light from the hallway, from the afternoon sun. Brendan stood as the others glanced uneasily at each other.

The séance was over.

15

Mrs. Lucinda Kuhn was trembling.

"It was him, it was my David," she said in a flat, unemotional voice.

"Your David?" Mr. Sweeny asked, the color beginning to return to his cheeks after a stiff brandy. "Who is your David?"

"My son," she answered, the breath and words coming from her throat in one thickly deep rush.

"I did not see anyone," stated the gentleman from Samuel Morse's office, scribbling into his small pad of paper. "As far as I am concerned, this experiment was most inconclusive. Decidedly inconclusive."

"It *was* David, my son," she reiterated, her voice firm now. "He was but fourteen when he died. I know I saw him."

"I regret to admit that I, too, saw no one other than this gentleman." Sweeny jerked his chin toward Garrick Stevens.

The gentleman from the *North Star* had already left, as had several other observers, all convinced they had indeed seen something extraordinary, but not quite certain exactly what that something was, or what it meant. None of the usual props had been used, no floating instruments or jumping vases. Patrick had not had the time to even begin his work when Garrick Stevens inadvertently but so abruptly interrupted the séance.

Celia remained in the chair at the table, her hands folded in her lap. And she watched Brendan. She watched her husband.

Brendan and Garrick were talking in voices too low for her to hear, but each speaking intently, nodding and frowning as they exchanged such urgent words. And in that moment she saw someone other than the engaging, distracted young widower she had met days before. There was something else, something different about him.

And she knew then, watching them, the almost boyish relief in Brendan's features, the expression of distance on Garrick's.

"He killed her," Celia whispered to herself. Of course! Why hadn't she seen that before? It was so obvious now.

"What was that, Mrs. O'Neal?" Sweeny glanced up from his own pad, where he had been taking notes on the room. He leaned forward. "Please, Mrs. O'Neal. I do not wish to miss a word. Lord knows this piece will be thin enough as it is, with too much description of the parlor and your attire and not enough on the substance. So for the love of ink, Mrs. O'Neal, repeat what you said."

Garrick turned slowly and stared at her. He appeared thinner than before, his sticklike neck protruding from his collar, the jutting Adam's apple bobbing when he swallowed.

He looked at her, and she inhaled sharply. Celia clasped her hands together tightly, vowing not to glance away in discomfort.

She wanted him to know, if possible, that his secret was now shared by at least one person.

That he had killed his wife. That she had not perished as the result of an accidental explosion, but that it had been a most deliberate explosion.

Amanda had been murdered.

Suddenly Celia could not catch her breath as she stared, unblinking, at Garrick Stevens, her chest rising and falling with ragged speed.

He smiled at her. A strange, distracted cast came to his pale face. Their eyes met, and Celia thought he saw it all there, that she knew everything. There was guilt there, too, a lingering guilt that she hoped would dog his every moment of joy for the rest of his life. And she saw that he was aware of her knowledge.

Then he grinned at Brendan and back at Celia. "What did that gentleman just call you, Miss Thomason? He seems to be under the illusion that you are Brendan's mother."

Mr. Sweeny, ever the newspaperman in search of a sensational story, sensed an opportunity. "Don't you know, Mr. Stevens? Miss Thomason is now your sister-in-law, the newly minted Mrs. O'Neal."

Garrick's lips wavered, as if uncertain of the truthfulness of the statement. There was a brief instant of blank astonishment, disbelief. Yet that raw, bewildered glint remained even as the rest of his features settled into practiced affability.

"I am perplexed, Miss Thomason," he began. "What is this, a jest?"

"I fear not," said Brendan before anyone else could speak. "We are wed."

It was said with the air of a doomed man reciting the means of his ruin.

Garrick Stevens missed a single beat before turning to his friend. "How happy I am for you. Brendan." His hand warmly pumped Brendan's. Then he turned to Celia. "And you, madam." He stepped toward her. "Now you are my sister."

Celia allowed him to plant a moist kiss on her cheek, closing her eyes, imposing a distance between them.

"Did not anyone else see my David?" Mrs. Kuhn asked, her voice strong and certain. Her gray eyes were bright, her decisive features set and determined.

Finally Celia turned her head away from Garrick, and her expression softened when she saw Mrs. Kuhn's hope, her fear that perhaps she did not see her son.

"I am afraid I did not see anyone, Mrs. Kuhn, other than Mr. Stevens. But I did get a fragrance."

Mrs. Kuhn rose to her feet, planting her palms on the table. "Exactly! Tell me, what did you smell?"

Celia was about to answer when Mr. Sweeny stopped her. "Wait a moment. Although the others have gone, I believe we should all write down precisely what we experienced, sounds and smells and sights. That way we will not be swayed by one another, not have our imaginations provoked."

"I for one saw nothing," Brendan stated.

"Then why did you say the name 'Amanda'?" Mrs. Kuhn asked. "Was that not the name of your sister?"

"Yes, Amanda was my sister."

"Please, please!" urged Mr. Sweeny, pulling off pieces of paper and handing them out to the others. "Write down everything you experienced. Do you have pencils or quills?"

Mrs. Kuhn ignored the reporter. "I had forgotten about David's scent. After a day of riding he would come into the house and smell of horse and hay and green."

"I smelled that, too!" exclaimed the man from Mr. Morse's office. "I thought I had imagined it, but I sensed a distinct fragrance of horses, and something else."

"Saddle soap." Mrs. Kuhn nodded. "David always smelled of saddle soap after a ride."

"Please, I beg of you! No more! Confine your statements to paper . . ."

"I thought I smelled perfume as well," ventured Mrs. Kuhn. "A woman's perfume."

"Amanda's," said Celia. "But did anyone else hear her speak?"

"No!" Mrs. Kuhn all but shouted. "What did she say? Did you hear my David speak?"

"Only Amanda." Celia tried to gauge Garrick's reaction. He did seem to pale just slightly, even more ashen than his usual complexion.

"What did she say?" Garrick asked. When Celia did not immediately respond, he took a step closer.

"She said nothing, Garrick," Brendan said wearily.

Mr. Sweeny threw up his hands in despair. "Will no one write down what they saw?"

"Please." Garrick's upper lip began to perspire, even in the cold of the parlor. "Did she speak of me?"

The parlor door opened and Aunt Prudence entered, followed by Eileen with a tray. "Tea," chirped the older woman, as if this had been a mere afternoon social. "Now tell me, Mr. Sweeny, if I provide the particulars, will you mention the upcoming demonstration we are planning? It will be splendid, sir!"

Then she paused and looked up from the tea service. The air was rich with tension, and the smile faded from her face. No one seemed to have taken note of Amanda's entrance.

"Tell me," repeated Garrick. "Did she speak of me?"

Celia shook her head slowly. "No. She did not. She said something for her brother, for Brendan."

"Well, what was it?" Mr. Sweeny asked. "Was it concerning her death? A secret she took to her fiery grave?" With a glance at Garrick and Brendan, he mumbled an unapologetic "Sorry."

Celia looked up at Sweeny. This had turned into a circus. She had comforted no one that afternoon. Certainly not herself. Nor had she convinced anyone that what had happened was genuine. Especially not Brendan, the person she most wished to convince.

And now she was convinced that Garrick Stevens had killed his wife.

"Excuse me." She stood. "I need to think."

"Is that entirely necessary?" asked Sweeny.

"What did she say?" Garrick all but shouted, wiping a hand over his brow.

So why hadn't Amanda simply spoken directly to her brother? For he would not believe the words, not coming from her. But it no longer mattered.

"She said that it wasn't your fault, Brendan."

"What wasn't my fault?" It was the first time that afternoon he had addressed her directly, looked at her without accusation.

"The time she tripped over the fairy ring and cut her

face. She said she was following you, and that it had been her own fault entirely."

Sweeny waited a moment, then his face fell. "That was it? No profound wisdom, no proclamations? The Fox sisters always relay proclamations of great wisdom from beyond. Nothing of that sort?"

Celia shook her head and took one more look at Brendan, who was still seated, his features unreadable.

She walked away and did not look at anyone as she passed.

Upstairs. She needed to go upstairs, but not to her room. She needed to get away from everyone, to make some sort of sense.

The one room in the house with a lock was Uncle James's cluttered office garret, and that was where she went. No one followed her, for which she was grateful.

She closed the door behind her, and turned the lock. Alone at last, secluded from the world.

The office was thick with dust and books piled high. They had spent hours there, in that office, searching for the deed to the house, for all of the vital papers needed after her uncle died. Of course the deed had not been found, for he had already signed away the house to moneylenders. And no other papers of importance had been located, except for an old family Bible that documented births and deaths for the past few generations, and the notice they had received after her parents had died. Celia herself had made the notations in the family Bible when Uncle James passed away, filling in the blank next to the date of his birth.

For the first time since she had first come to live there as a child, she fully understood why her uncle had so treasured his private enclave. He had been clever, she thought with a thin smile, not to make the room more attractive, for it was a small, dingy, haphazard place that only someone who needed to escape the relative order of the rest of the house would find welcoming.

Pushing aside a pile of papers, she sank wearily into the wooden chair at the desk. There was not an inch of free space; every bit of every possible surface was taken up with oversized books, scraps of papers, oblong documents, rolled maps. The rabbit's den of a desk was jammed with broken quills, empty ink bottles. A ruler with blue and black ink splotches held up one of the desk drawers, keeping the drawer in place and preventing anyone from opening either that drawer or the one below it.

She closed her eyes, her temples throbbing. Everything she had touched of late had become a calamity. It was only just that she ensconce herself in this calamity of a room.

A strange sense of calm spread over her slowly, as if the dust and muss of the place had a soothing, narcotic effect. It was so peaceful there, all other sounds muffled and distant. So very peaceful.

"My dear," she heard the voice whisper. Perhaps she was asleep, for she knew the voice immediately. She was imagining Uncle James, not an impossible fancy, considering she was in his special place.

"Oh, Uncle James." She sighed. "Why did you do it?"

Since it was her daydream, there was no cause to elaborate. Nor any need, for her uncle's voice seemed to understand.

"I never intended to die, Celia. That was my misfortune. I had fully planned to rectify the situation before I passed on, you see."

"Aunt Prudence blames me," she mumbled.

"No she doesn't. She has always been a self-centered being, although one I loved from the moment I saw her. She was the belle of New York then, and she never understood that every belle must someday fade. She loves you yet. But she is unhappy now, my dear. You are an easy target for her to vent her spleen upon."

"Mmm," Celia replied, the exhaustion creeping over her.

"Before you rest, my dear, please listen to me. There is something for you in this office."

Again she smiled wearily. "The paperweight made of a ball of glass surrounding a turkey head?"

"I'll have you know that was Benjamin Franklin's very own turkey, the same one he—"

"I know, I know. The same one he was thinking of when he wished to make the turkey our national bird. He lost out to the bald eagle. I wonder who has that paperweight?"

"Listen, Missy." That was the tone Uncle James always took when he scolded her. He hadn't called her Missy for years. "Listen carefully. Look in the red morocco-bound atlas."

She was drifting to sleep, comfortable and safe in her locked office.

"Do you hear me?" she imagined her uncle said.

"Yes, Uncle James. The red atlas."

"Good. Now in there you will find a key. And under the window seat of this room, beneath the plank of wood and the pillow, you will find the box that the key fits. Are you listening?"

Drowsy, she was so very drowsy, and finally she had found a place to sleep. "Key in atlas," she murmured. "Box in window seat."

"Very well," the voice said. "And, Celia?"

"Mmm?"

"All is peaceful here. All is beautiful. Your dear mother and father have watched you and loved you from this place, and they have set you on the right path."

As she fell asleep, she had a smile on her face, and tears running down her cheeks.

Celia awoke with a start. Someone was knocking on the door.

Disoriented at first, she opened her eyes to darkness. How long had she been sleeping?

Fumbling to the door, she felt for the lock and turned it. There stood Eileen, oil lamp in her hand.

"Miss? I mean, Mrs. O'Neal?"

"Yes, Eileen. I must have fallen asleep."

"Mrs. Cooper wishes to know if you desire supper."

"What time is it?"

"Why, it's nearly nine in the evening."

"Has everyone gone?"

What she really wanted to ask was if Brendan had gone, but she didn't wish to dwell on why that was important to her.

"Yes, ma'am. Everyone has gone."

Celia stood for a moment, wondering what to do next. There really wasn't anything for her to do except to have supper and go to sleep in the same bed she had slept in every night for almost two decades. That is, with two notable exceptions.

She needed to ask. "And what of my husband?"

Eileen shrugged. "He said very little. Shortly after you came upstairs he left."

"Did he mention where he was going?"

The oil lamp made their shadows seem sinister on the landing. "No, ma'am. He left, and then everyone else left. Mr. Stevens seemed most upset."

"I'm sure he was," she said between her teeth.

"Ma'am?"

"Nothing, Eileen. Thank you. I'll follow your light downstairs."

With one look back at the office, she went down for a cold supper, wondering what had caused her to have such peculiar dreams.

Brendan knew there was something very amiss.

Garrick's peculiar behavior could no longer be dismissed as the product of grief. No, there was something deeper than that. He had seen it clearly, the panic on Garrick's face when he thought Amanda may have spoken from beyond.

Of course it was all humbug. But Garrick's reaction was genuine.

And then again there was the matter of what Amanda had supposedly said, profound words from beyond the grave. That it had not been Brendan's fault, when she had tripped as a child.

How ridiculous. Wouldn't she have uttered something concerning a more recent event? Specifically, her own death?

It made no sense. None at all.

Following the séance, for want of a better word, Brendan had claimed work to finish and left the house off Washington Square. Then he went to his offices on Water Street, where the disreputable taverns were already in high spirits.

No wonder his office space had come so cheaply, he thought, not for the first time. The establishments on Water Street were legendary, from Joe Allen's concert saloon—a polite euphemism for house of ill repute. The story was that Allen, a former divinity scholar, insisted that a Bible be placed in clear view in every chamber in his "saloon."

Surely she would have said something else, his sister. Perhaps about their parents. Or about other times, more profound times. Not about an insignificant childhood tumble, one he had all but forgotten about.

He passed by the notable locations of Water Street, observing the other passers-by as he walked. This was not a district where one would stroll without being very aware of one's surroundings.

There was a dance hall where patrons were routinely robbed or murdered, although that slight inconvenience did not seem to discourage the other patrons, who waited in patient lines for the dubious privilege of gaining entry. Each tavern was more unsavory than the last rickety frame structure, with doors wide open to the elements, each one with its own peculiar stench.

He passed the Hole-in-the-Wall tavern. In his short few days here he could claim a nodding acquaintance with One-Armed Charley, the proprietor of the place, and his faithful hostess Gallus Mag. It had been simple survival that prompted him to be friendly to these characters. Mag, who was at least two inches taller than Brendan, had gained her nickname in celebration of her fashion invention of hitching her skirts well above her knees with galluses, or suspenders. Often she had smiled at Brendan as he passed, crooking her finger or pursing her lips.

He always passed that spot with a sense of relief, for it was common knowledge that Mag was fond of biting off the ears of unwelcome customers and preserving them in pickle jars behind the bar.

What a fool Celia must think him! Not that the notion of Celia thinking him a fool was troublesome, for it wasn't. Amanda recalling her own tripping over the wall indeed!

He remembered that day, when she received the small scar below her left eye. The sight of her wound sent him into a panic, but she did not cry. Instead she had smiled, and now, thinking back all these years later, he realized she had been glad of the attention. For he had been ignoring her all that day, pointedly ignoring the little girl following his every step. And then he jumped over the wall, and she tried to follow.

That was when it had happened. On the wall.

Celia claimed Amanda had said the incident had not been his fault, when of course it had been. He should have been watching after his sister, taking care of her. But he had tried to escape his duties then. Just as he had tried to escape his duties later, when she was a young woman and his father, by then a confirmed recluse, had abdicated his duties.

So Brendan, focused as he was on matters of business and not of a woman just entering society, had passed her on to others. It mattered little who, from distant relations in London to paid chaperons he failed to thoroughly investigate before handing over their new charge, his only sister.

The one person whose welfare and happiness should have been his primary concern.

But it was not. Nor had her welfare ever been his concern, even from the time he had learned of her existence. He had wished her ill before she was born, hoping that the mystical beings he had imagined at Castle Sitric would take her away and leave him alone. He had implored the fairies to remove her, and they had.

It had just taken them longer than he had originally thought. It had taken over two decades and the crossing of an ocean to accomplish the deed.

Finally the fairies had complied.

Then he stopped, just steps away from his office.

Celia had said that Amanda forgave him for the day she had tripped over the fairy ring. In his memory it had been a wall, one of the hundreds of stone walls dotting the property. She had scrambled behind him, and only when he heard the dull thud of her toddling into the wall did he reluctantly turn around.

All these years he had recalled that incident with more frequency than he realized, so very aware of the moments that led up to the fall. Then of trying to help her, attempting to comfort this small, wounded thing, using the hem of her skirt to dab the cut. Hoping the bleeding would stop. Hoping the punishment he received would be swift and not too severe.

Even then his principal thoughts had been on how the incident would impinge on his own life. He never thought about that cut leaving a permanent scar on his sister. Never really gave a second thought to that.

And suddenly he saw her that day, the blood on her dirt-streaked face. She had been smiling at him, beaming like the most content creature on earth.

Instead of tears he received an embrace, her arms encircling his neck as she kissed him, her tiny white teeth flashing as she laughed.

Then he remembered. It had not been a wall. It had been a fairy ring, the magical stone circles attributed to fairies. Folklore spoke of them as meeting places for the sprites, where they could gather and be protected from the world outside of the ring.

It had been a fairy ring, but all these years he had envisioned a wall. For he, Brendan, had been climbing a wall at the time. Amanda had been running to him, stumbing over the smaller stones of the fairy ring.

But no one knew that. He had even told Kenney the butler it had been a wall, told his father it had been a wall. Only one person seemed to realize it had been a fairy ring, and that had been Amanda.

And there was no way anyone else could have discovered the truth. Even Garrick had been told the story through Brendan's eyes.

Only Amanda knew. And only Amanda would realize the impact her few words would have, the flood of guilt her seemingly insignificant message would release.

Only Amanda.

"Good God," he mumbled aloud.

And he realized something he had known for some time now, something he had avoided every bit as successfully as he had avoided responsibility for his sister.

That the visions had indeed been Amanda.

And Celia was not a fraud.

He had never known such fury.

At first he was just going to issue a warning, much as he had intended that other time, when Amanda had died. But this was far beyond that. No, compared to the rage coursing through him now, that incident with Amanda had been but a trifle.

And it was her fault as well, they way she had batted her eyes at him, just as Amanda had done. And like Amanda, who had promised so much with those eyes, she would betray him. Celia and Amanda were cut from the same traitorous cloth. Of that he was certain.

He might have found happiness with either of them. Indeed, he was sure he was on that path with Amanda, but then she had uttered those hateful words, that she could never love him.

That there was someone else.

He didn't mean for it to happen, but it did, that explosion, the fire. This, however, would be different. This would be deliberate.

He had watched O'Neal approach his office, had seen him walking on Water Street. The building with the office was on a corner, which was lucky, for the fire would have a much better chance of getting started that way, with the wind coming off the river to feed the flames.

There was a lull in the street's activity, as there often was at this hour. He was about to approach the O'Neal Shipping office, his burlap bag clenched in his fist, when three sailors emerged from a tavern.

He pressed himself against the wall, deeply hidden by shadows. The sailors were talking, all three intoxicated. They took forever, laughing and punching each other on the back and exchanging disjointed information about women with names such as "Squinty Jane" and "Half-Mad Mary."

"Hurry," he hissed, as if that would hasten their conversation. But soon they staggered on, their voices raised, their caps tilted.

As luck would have it, the street was again quiet.

Later, when he thought back on what he had done, he remembered how swiftly the old wooden steps became a torch when he touched the match.

And then he ran.

The clanging of the fire bells woke the entire household.

Half asleep, Celia placed a pillow over her head. Why did the fire wagons always make such a racket? But they clattered away, among the shouts of the firefighters and the hooves of their horses.

At last she fell back to sleep.

The first thing Celia did that morning, even before going down to breakfast, was slip up the steps to her uncle's office.

Of course it had all been a dream the afternoon before. But still, she wanted to see if her dreams had spoken the truth.

The room was cold, and she rubbed her hands together and pulled her shawl closer.

The red leather atlas. Where was it? She had seen it months earlier, when they had been going through her uncle's papers. She distinctly remembered placing it on a shelf, flat, because it was too large to fit on the shelf the proper way.

Then she saw it. The atlas, just as she had left it. For some reason she was nervous about opening the leaves. It was heavy, and dirty. She sneezed as she opened the front cover.

And then she smiled, for there was nothing. As she had assumed, she had simply had a dream. But it had been pleasant, that dream. The words of Uncle James, even his voice, had seemed so clear.

She was about to close the atlas and slip it back onto the shelf when she paused, and opened the book to the middle.

The center of the volume had been hollowed out. And in the middle of that hollowed-out space was a key.

For a few moments she just blinked. Perhaps she had seen this before, and forgotten. That was possible.

The key was very ordinary-looking, just a black key with a clover design on the top.

She looked over at the window seat. Was it possible?

The cushions came off easily, and then she felt for some way to remove the wooden base. There was nothing to hold on to, so snug was the fit. Then it came loose.

Some of the white paint flaked off in her hands. She was almost afraid to see if there was anything there. Almost afraid, but not quite.

With a silent prayer, she lifted the seat. And in the well, where she had always assumed was solid wood, was a box.

It wasn't anything spectacular. In fact, she recognized it as the fireproof sort of boxes her father used to have. It was metal with a domed lid, no ornamentation. And, of course, the box was locked.

She took the key, and it slipped into the lock easily. And then she opened the box.

There seemed to be some papers, all sorts of papers, stuffed into the box. Taking the box, she settled into the desk chair and rested it on her lap.

The top paper was a note in the familiar hand of Uncle James.

My dear,

I can only assume that since you are reading this, I have passed from this earth. Do not grieve for me, as I have lived a long and pleasant life. And chief amongst my most pleasant memories is you, my niece yet so much more.

But enough of those sentimental drivelings. These are the things that were provided for you by your parents in the event of their death. Naturally, I did not open this box until we learned of their tragic fate. But you must realize they loved you very much, and had provided for you handsomely even in death. You may wonder why it is I never told you about this, your rightful inheritance and, should you wish it, your dowry. There are three reasons for this secrecy. One is your aunt, my own Prudence. Although I love her a great deal, I am not blind to her flaws, chief amongst them being vanity. She would have considered the enclosed sum to be her rightful property, since she never felt my income grand enough for her taste. Thus I did not reveal the existence of this inheritance to her, to you, or to anyone.

The second reason is unfortunately clear to you by now. I am in debt, badly so. Although I hope to settle my debts before I pass away, there is an unfortunate chance that I will not be able to do so. This is yours, Celia, not mine. And therefore I ask you not to use this sum to relieve my own financial burden. Since I am dead, you should listen to me, Missy.

This is the last chance I will have to make demands of you!

The third reason is a little less clear, even in my own mind. I have long been aware that you do not wish to marry soon, if ever. And I understand your hesitation. Therefore, I felt that the general knowledge of this dowry (or what would have remained had our Prudence discovered it) would make your single state—for I do not like the word "spinster"—impossible. Gentlemen both of means and without would be knocking at the door at all hours, and I confess the thought of all that bother was not a pleasant one for me.

One final word. I do not disagree with you on your reluctance to marry. But marriage, my dear, to the right man and under the right circumstances, can indeed offer us a glimpse of paradise. If you find love, Celia, do not squander it, for it is far too precious a commodity to risk. Do not squander love, my Celia.

And now I hear your aunt making tea, and Patrick going off to one of his secret meetings. Poor boy doesn't know I'm aware of his doings, but I am most aware! Good night, my Missy. You deserve happiness, and it is my hope—as it was the hope of your parents—that you find and cherish it.

For a long time she simply stared at the paper, not really rereading the note, but seeing occasional words stand out. *Inheritance. Dowry.*

Then she put the letter on the desk. Beneath her uncle's letter was another note in an unfamiliar hand.

Dearest Celia,

I am sorry for what has happened, for if you see this letter it means your mother and I have somehow perished. Please, my sweet child, do not be angry with us for being so foolhardy in our travels. We longed above all else to come home to you, but whatever prevented that outcome was no one's fault. It was the will of God, something with which we cannot argue. So grow up magnificently, my Celia. Your mother and I are watching, and I know we are proud of you. One day we will all be reunited in a better place. But until then, may you lead a long life full of love and joy, for that is what you always gave to us.

She had never seen her father's handwriting before. Again she stared at the writing, the curves of the letters. Her own father had written this.

There was an uncomfortable lump in her throat as she realized something. All of these years, she had assumed that her parents didn't return from their trip because somehow they didn't wish to.

But now, with this note, she knew otherwise. They had loved her, her mother and father and Uncle James. Instead of having survived a childhood devoid of love, she had been lavished with it. Her parents loved her still, as did her uncle. And Aunt Prudence, well.

In spite of herself, Celia smiled just a little. Aunt Prudence would always be Aunt Prudence.

Almost without any expectations she removed the rest of the paper from the top of the box. It really did not matter, for now, at last, she had her inheritance, the legacy of the letters. Anything else was almost secondary.

Well, almost.

Under the papers, beneath drawings she had made as a child with her mother (and she remembered them, each drawing!), there was a small blue satin box. She opened it by pressing a small gold button, and the lid popped up. And she gasped.

Her mother's diamond ear bobs! How she remembered them dangling so gloriously from her mother's ears. They were exquisite, with a large diamond set at the top, a smaller diamond on the bottom. But everyone had assumed they had been in the luggage that was lost after they died, or that perhaps she had been wearing them, or . . .

But here they were. With a gentle finger she touched them, feeling the cool, smooth surface, watching the sunlight from the window bounce off them.

Her mother's ear bobs. What a glorious treasure. She sighed. So unexpected, but so very beautiful. Still holding the box with the jewels, she continued rifling through the papers with her other hand. There were condolence notes from friends and relatives. How wonderful to see them now, to read about how well loved her parents—and Celia herself—had been.

And then she came to another box, black velvet and oblong. Inside were bills issued by the Merchants' Bank on Wall Street. The bank was still there, more prosperous than ever. Good old American currency. Idly she added them up, still tilting the ear bobs so they caught the light.

Then she stopped.

"Impossible," she said aloud.

She must have counted wrong. Surely she must have counted wrong.

Again she added up the total, and the ear bobs very nearly slipped from her grasp.

"Thirty-eight thousand five hundred and eighty-seven dollars?"

In blank amazement she sat, stunned, in the office until she heard a commotion below.

Taking a deep breath, she returned the box to the window seat, not knowing what else to do with it. She kept the key, slipping it into the waistband of her day dress, a deep maroon one at least four years old.

How many new dresses could she buy?

What an extraordinary thought!

This would take time to comprehend.

Brendan. She thought of Brendan. "Do not squander love," the note had said.

And she knew, as she had known since the first day she had seen him standing on the front steps, that she loved him. They were married.

There was hope.

She wanted to see him. Now. She was financially free, and somehow that made her wish to see him even more ardently.

She had yet to tell him of what Amanda had said, of the warnings. Perhaps this would help him believe enough to love her. She looked down at her wedding ring, and impulsively kissed it.

All of their misunderstandings had been childish, so childish. But that would change.

She absolutely knew they had a chance. It would not be easy, of course. But still . . .

The commotion downstairs was growing louder. What on earth could it be, and before breakfast? Perhaps Hannah had burnt the toast again, a capital offense to Aunt Prudence.

She had been loved by her parents, by others. And now, she would be loved by Brendan.

Unable to ignore the din any longer, she went downstairs, careful there was no sign in the office of what she had found.

There was a sobbing from the parlor, and Celia realized it was Aunt Prudence. She hadn't heard sounds such as that since Uncle James had passed away.

"Aunt Pru?" She entered the parlor, and Garrick stood up. His pale face was streaked with black, his clothing torn and filthy.

He looked straight at her, his eyes unwavering. "I'm afraid I have some terrible news," he began.

16

*C*elia did not believe the words.

Garrick Stevens was speaking, but what he was saying made absolutely no sense.

Stevens seemed distracted, pushing his hand through his thinning brown hair. "I was going over to the office on Water Street, to go over the books. It was to be something of a surprise, you see. For once I was going to really buckle down, straighten out the ledgers. I've neglected them terribly, made a mess. I don't know why. Perhaps I've never been good with numbers. Maybe that was it. A mess, a complete mess. At university I did well simply because the theories were just that, theories. But in the real world, well. That's a different story. Why, even the most basic of . . ."

"Please, what happened! You said there was a fire at the office," she all but shouted.

Aunt Prudence continued her solitary crying, head down, her large, rounded shoulders heaving.

"Oh, yes. The fire. I went there, and already the flames were leaping from the windows. I tried, Mrs.

O'Neal. I went in, but the smoke was so thick. Oh, God, how I tried to save him! Amanda and Brendan, it doesn't seem possible. The same way, the exact same way . . ."

Celia just stared at him, hearing the words but not able to comprehend their meaning. Eileen and Patrick stood in the doorway, Ginny—Patrick's younger sister—behind them, with Hannah, her hand over her mouth, her eyes wide and pale-lashed.

"He's dead, Celia," blurted Aunt Prudence. Then she continued to sob.

"Are you sure?" she asked Garrick, not believing. Not really.

Because he had just said that Amanda and Brendan had gone the same way. Impossible. She would have felt something, wouldn't she? Deep down she would have sensed the loss, the trauma. They were married, for whatever that was worth. There was some sort of bond there. He had kissed her, and more. She would know if something had ended his life.

Wouldn't Amanda have warned her about the fire?

She looked over at Aunt Prudence, who was wailing as if her own life had been ruined. Maybe it was, in her eyes. Brendan had represented security, stability, to Aunt Prudence. To her, Brendan was the living embodiment of a safeguarded future, for a wealthy man cannot allow his wife's only living relative to starve, or even unwillingly miss a meal.

Her thoughts ran riot. Wouldn't she *know* if something dreadful had happened to him?

But she hadn't known about her parents when they died. The letter telling of their accident had stunned her as much as it had stunned anyone. Indeed, she was still stunned all these years later. And she had failed to sense the impending death of Uncle James, sick though he was.

There was no warning of fire from Amanda. Then Celia stiffened.

There *had* been a warning.

Celia had been told not to leave Brendan's side, a piece of advice she had not ignored, just been unable to implement. And the way Amanda had appeared during the wedding, a twisted grotesque thing, had been frightening.

That, too, must have been a warning.

"I am going to the fire," she stated to Garrick, shrugging off her shawl and walking over to the cloak rack that held her coat and bonnet.

"That is not a wise idea," Stevens said flatly. "It may be a rather gruesome sight."

"Have they found anything? Any proof that he's hurt? He may not have been there at all."

"When I left, the embers were still burning. No one had been able to enter yet. Please, Mrs. O'Neal. By now they will be pulling him out and . . ."

"I am going, sir."

Garrick followed her, his arms almost reaching out to touch her but not quite. "Please, do not put yourself through this. Let me help you. Allow me to perform any of the unpleasant tasks that may lay before you."

"Have you checked at the boardinghouse on King Street?" She was tying on her old bonnet, the one she had slipped on and off without thought for so long, but now her fingers felt thick and heavy, fumbling with the bow.

"Yes, of course. And he wasn't there."

"Why would he have gone to the office at that hour? It makes no sense."

"It was my fault. I had made a disaster of the books, rendered them impossible to read. Can't even remember what I was doing, why I made the judgments I did. He knew he had hours of work before him."

Garrick did not seem shaken by the assumed death of his brother-in-law. Instead he was oddly more concerned with the shabby state of the O'Neal Shipping records. Why was he so preoccupied with records that would be destroyed by now?

Nothing made sense.

All she knew was that she had to go there, to see what had happened with her own eyes.

"Then I will accompany you, Mrs. O'Neal," Garrick stated.

Hesitating, she looked up at him, the glazed eyes, the unnatural pallor of his waxy complexion. She did not feel comfortable being in the same room with this man, much less traveling across town with him. There was something terribly wrong with him.

Would he murder her just as he had murdered Amanda?

"Thank you for your offer," she stated coldly. "But I would prefer to go alone."

"Very well. Then I will remain here, and see if I can be of any help. Perhaps I can do something in this house."

The thought of Garrick staying behind was even more alarming.

"Actually, sir." She attempted to smile fetchingly. "I would appreciate your company."

That seemed to please him, and she assumed that he

wouldn't dare try to do anything to her, not in broad daylight. Not when the entire household knew where she was going and, more specifically, with whom.

Aunt Prudence was still in her cocoon of grief, her face now covered with a handkerchief conveniently edged in black, a relic of mourning for Uncle James.

Celia had to leave, to get out of the house before they hung the black bunting and funeral wreath.

Outside the day was gray, a mist hovered over the park like a soft cloud. As Garrick looked for a carriage, she stared at the park, at the iron fences outlining some of the gravel walks. Before she lived there someone had attempted to put on a military display with a smartly turned-out regiment. But someone had forgotten that Washington Square had been a potter's field, where hundreds of unclaimed souls lay buried. Or if someone had remembered what it was, they had most certainly forgotten what was likely to happen if hundreds of men stomp on hundreds of layered, shallow graves.

As a result the splendidly attired men sank into the ground, some of the men screaming with horror, kicking with their parade-polished boots, scrambling to escape. Why did she think of that now?

Garrick seemed to be having trouble locating a carriage. It was strange that he was having such difficulty when Brendan never seemed to have any trouble at all hailing a vehicle.

At last one rounded the corner, and Garrick—narrowly escaping physical harm—managed to commandeer it.

He helped her into the carriage, his fragile hand outstretched to assist her.

Was it possible that someone so frail could have killed his wife?

She settled against the back of the seat as he entered from the other side.

It took no strength to strike a match, especially if the gas jets had been left on for any length of time.

"Water Street and Dover," he instructed the driver, announcing the address as if there should be a question mark at the conclusion.

There was a moment's hesitation on the driver's part. This was not a savory location. Then the driver cracked his whip against the side of the carriage, and the wheels started rolling.

How different it had been to ride with Brendan, his easy command of every situation. Even in the carriage, the feel was so vastly contrary to riding with Garrick Stevens. For one, she had far more room now.

An involuntary smile curved on her lips as she recalled her failed attempts to keep away from him, of clinging to the carriage door. But no matter how small she tried to make herself, she could not escape Brendan, she could not avoid physical contact, his shoulders pressing against hers, the heat of his body.

Stevens was fidgeting, his heel rising and falling like some sort of grinding machine. He alternated between looking out the window and pulling at his cuffs. Then he busied himself with unwinding a single thread from his trouser knee, all the while the other knee pumping like a steam engine.

Once the thread was successfully pulled, he applied his skills to a bit of something invisible that was soiling his elbow. Whatever it was vexed him a great deal, and he hunched over, arm bent round his torso to provide a more advantageous view.

Poor Amanda, Celia thought. To marry a man in one's first flush of youth, hoping to awake in the arms of the groom of her dreams, only to have him become a dull, twirling top. And then to have him end her life.

His head lowered over the bent elbow, the forearm and hand flaying limply in Celia's face.

"Excuse me!" she said, unable to bear the contortions any longer.

He glanced up, his face questioning, eyes too large and too dark. "Oh," he said, lowering the elbow. "Sorry."

And *this* was Brendan's best friend?

Finally he seemed to calm down for the last portion of the ride, so she could compose herself, ready herself for whatever lay ahead.

The passing scenery was growing ever more sinister, with streets winding into narrow alleys, wood frame buildings—some from Colonial times—sagging, with tired-looking shutters and missing front steps. Most were taverns now, the doors open even in the damp winter air, the stench within making the cold seem almost welcome.

Then she could smell the unmistakable scent of a fire, of charred wood and ash and the strange dampness, heavy and pungent, that always marks a recent fire.

The carriage stopped, and Celia stepped out before Stevens had a chance to assist her.

There was a corner lot with a few piles of timber.

"That was the office," Stevens explained unnecessarily.

There was a very large man in a fireman's coat and

hat, kicking the wood aside and ordering water poured over the occasional glowing ember.

"Sir?" she said, approaching the man.

He looked up at her, an enormous man. With the added height of his hat he was close to six and a half feet tall, and his girth was every bit as impressive.

"Yes?" he replied, then turned to another member of the brigade. "No, no, McBride. Not like that. Use the whole bucketful." Then he turned back to Celia. "Yes?"

There was an insignia on his cap, "The Americus Engine Company," featuring a ferocious-looking Bengal tiger, claws drawn.

"Excuse me." She had to look up at him, the tiger and the fireman both showing their teeth. "This was my husband's office, and . . ."

"Name," the man barked.

"Celia," she said.

"Your husband's name is Celia?"

"No, no sir. I mean I am Celia, Mrs. O'Neal. Have you . . ."

The man swaggered off, ordering some other men about. He couldn't have been any older than Celia, but his arrogance almost vibrated.

She turned around and Garrick Stevens was standing with his hands pushed into his pockets, just staring at the remains of the building.

"Excuse me," she said, following after the fireman.

Another man came up to the large one. "Boss, I found this."

Without hesitation the large man took the item, whatever it was, and slipped it into his pocket.

"Sir," Celia said, her tone frosty. "Was that yours?"

Very slowly the man turned and grinned. "It is now."

"My husband," she said, her dislike of the man growing with every passing second. "Have you found any body?"

The grin remained. "Ah. So you don't know where he was last night? Rest assured, we haven't found a body. As far as we can tell, the building was empty."

Until she heard those words, she hadn't realized how terrified she had been.

He was alive!

She clamped her hand over her mouth and closed her eyes tightly, saying every prayer she had ever heard uttered at once. Finally she could breathe again.

"I presume that *is* good news," the man said.

She nodded at the hateful, glorious man who had just delivered such wonderful news, even as he engaged in a little unlawful pillage.

Then he looked more closely at Celia, at the fine features and the silken complexion, her dark eyes and the delicately pointed chin.

And hair, an abundance of thick, rich hair was under the bonnet.

"I'm running for assistant alderman next year," he announced.

Celia had been about to walk away. She had the information she needed.

But she stopped.

"I said I'm running for assistant alderman of the seventh district next year." It was not merely an announcement. It was a boast. "Tell your husband that the Big Six put out the fire as soon as possible. Tell him to vote for me."

She nodded.

"That's what they call us, the Big Six. Fire company

number six, otherwise known as the Americus Engine Company. That was my idea. And the tigers."

What a strange man! His face was elongated in spite of the plump cheeks, his eyes curiously sunken. An odd nose, like a lumpy potato, was positioned above flaccid lips.

And he wore a sparse, moth-eaten—looking beard on his chin.

At that point she realized, with a laugh, that not all large men appealed to her. Only Brendan.

He returned the smile, assuming it was for him. "Thank you, ma'am! And don't forget, my name's Tweed. William M. Tweed. Tell your husband to vote for me."

"Boss?" shouted another fireman.

And Foreman Tweed of Fire Company Number Six went to the fireman's assistance, confident he had made yet another conquest of the fetching Mrs. O'Neal.

Garrick seemed astonished that Brendan had not been killed.

"But the flames," he kept saying. "They were higher than the rooftops. How could he not have been killed?"

"Because he was not in the office," she repeated for the third time. "He was no more in the office than you were. That is why we are searching for him now. Wherever he was, he may not be aware that the office is destroyed. We are searching for him, just as he was searching for you earlier."

She had hoped that would prompt him to explain where he had been during the missing days, but it did not.

Garrick blinked, shaking his head and looking out the carriage window. "But the flames . . ."

"Oh, lands." She sighed, giving up.

Several times he turned to her, his face an almost pathetically happy grin. "He looked for me? You and Brendan were worried?" Then he would continue, "But the flames."

She wasn't sure if Garrick had been putting on some sort of show for her, to demonstrate his innocence—even though no one had accused him of anything thus far. Or if he was truly addled. Several times she had glanced at him from under the rim of her bonnet, and even without his knowing she was watching he had seemed preoccupied, unfocused. She was no longer frightened by him, for he was too scattered to be a threat to anyone, except perhaps to himself.

They had checked the Astor House, and Brendan had not returned there, although the clerk who had been on duty the night she had tried to finagle Brendan's address gave her a distinctive double take. Garrick said he was exhausted, and Celia certainly believed him, so he remained behind in his luxurious rooms, complete with running water.

By now it was bright afternoon, and she decided to walk over to the King Street boardinghouse. Mrs. Harris herself, in blue taffeta stiff enough to keep watch on its own, answered the door. The bright smile faded from her features the moment she saw who it was.

"Mrs. O'Neal," she pronounced the name.

"Mrs. Harris," Celia replied. "Is Mr. O'Neal within?"

"No, he is not."

A sudden bolt of alarm ran through her. What if he had indeed been hurt—or worse—in the fire? Perhaps they hadn't found him yet. Maybe he was under one of the ash-covered timbers Tweed had been kicking with his oversized boot.

"Mr. O'Neal left this morning soon after breakfast," she said with great satisfaction. "He was here all night, Mrs. O'Neal. Seemed to enjoy breakfast a great deal . . . Mrs. O'Neal!"

Celia had jumped up and hugged the woman, leaving her slightly off-balance.

"Oh, thank you, thank you," Celia cried. Tears she hadn't known existed now began to stream down her cheeks, heavy and warm. "He was here, all night?"

"Yes, he certainly was," Mrs. Harris began.

"Do you happen to know where he went after breakfast?"

"Well, let me see. He took a big book with him and some pencils. That's all I know."

"Thank you, Mrs. Harris," she mumbled, joyful that Brendan was well.

Brendan sat on the small hill overlooking the Hudson River.

It was astonishing to him that within walking distance, albeit a long walking distance, was this place of beauty and nature. The city seemed a million miles away then, and the only sounds he could hear were sheep and birds, someone's dog barking.

At first he just stretched out on his back, the ground cold yet comforting beneath him. The sun was gentle, warming him so that he no longer needed his gloves, and he unbuttoned his greatcoat and tilted his face to the sky. How glorious it felt.

And then he looked down at the book he had brought, and opened it, looking over what he had written the night before, examining the work he had done until dawn. There were the familiar two columns.

"What I know" and "What I do not know."

Under the first column was a simple list. He knew that Amanda forgave him, that Celia was a genuine spiritualist—at least when it came to Amanda. Also that Amanda's death was still suspicious, that Garrick had been acting strangely, that the O'Neal Shipping ledgers were in a shambles, and that he did not seem to care a dash about business at the moment.

And last on the list, that he was in love with his wife.

It had come upon him the night before with such sudden certainty that it had taken his breath away. He'd been walking down sordid Water Street, of all places to realize something so sweet and pure.

Instead of attending to business he went right back to the boardinghouse to think. To brood.

Images flashed in his mind like small, perfectly executed paintings. Celia smiling at him at the Astor House. Celia in her wedding gown. Celia waiting for him to return home.

All Celia.

Then he read the list in the other column, "What I do not know."

What had happened to Amanda, where Garrick was spending all of his time. How he could possibly make sense of the books here in New York.

And finally, was it too late for Celia to love him back?

That was the question that had kept him awake all night.

He had been horrible to her, fiendish beyond words.

Never in his life had he behaved in such an appallingly cruel manner. Indeed he had been so horrendous, there had been times when he himself had almost exclaimed, "What a brute! A monster!" Part of him had wished to step aside and explain that this was not the real Brendan.

The real Brendan had been lost somwehere between childhood and now. The real Brendan was someone he himself did not know. There had been glimpses, yes. Rare and fleeting, like a movement seen from the corner of the eye. He existed, though. Celia had caught a glimpse, perhaps two.

But something had happened. Amanda's words, for he knew without a doubt they had been from Amanda, had released him. She never did blame him, and although he would always blame himself, the knowledge that Amanda, wherever she was, did not despise him had set him free.

And for the first time he could remember, he no longer despised himself.

That is why he had played with Celia as he had. Because there had been times, so many times, that he had looked into her eyes and seen a hint of redemption, an echo of forgiveness. He had felt he did not deserve it, not then, not ever.

Thus the easiest, least thought-provoking way to react was as he did—despicably. He was so busy thinking up new ways to misbehave that he had no time to question his conduct.

It had been an exhausting game. The effort to be unkind to Celia had been grueling, and at times he was simply unable to continue. At those moments he longed for the minutes to continue into hours, into years. Under the smallest gesture of softness she would blossom, expand and glow like a magical flower. Then he would see what it could be like, if only it were possible.

But always, his hardness would return with a redoubled effort, with a sharpened vengeance.

His fists clenched as he closed the book and looked at the river, at the ships and small boats dotting the water.

And again, the question plagued him, searing the very corners of his heart, his soul.

Was it too late?

17

Celia didn't mind returning to Washington Square this time. There was no shame, no head hanging low. After all, Brendan was safe.

The moment she saw the house, Celia began to laugh. Aunt Prudence had been busy in the ensuing hours: There was enough black bunting and a large enough mourning wreath for a state ceremony. Before entering she began to tear it down, jumping up and grabbing it with both hands, yanking the black cloth to the ground, enjoying the sound of the cloth ripping.

She was taking down the wreath, the ghastly thing, when Aunt Prudence opened the door, resplendent in her most impressive widow's weeds.

"Celia," she hissed. "Shame on you! You and Mr. O'Neal may have had your difficulties during your brief union, but still you should have some respect for propriety."

"But he's fine, Aunt Pru." She smiled. "He wasn't at his office, he was at the boardinghouse."

"Are you certain?"

"Of course. Mrs. Harris told me he had a full breakfast this morning."

"Are you sure he is alive?"

Celia stepped into the hallway. "Yes, of course. How else could he have had breakfast?"

Aunt Prudence pulled off her black lace cap. "I don't know. In all honesty, with all of the peculiar comings and goings of late, being deceased no longer seems to interrupt anyone's social schedule. I'm going upstairs for a lie down." And wearily her aunt climbed the steps.

Eileen, also clad completely in black, came from the kitchen. "Ma'am, I am so very sorry," she began.

But before she could finish her condolence, there was a knock on the door. The maid curtsied, then answered the door with only the slightest of starts.

"Ma'am, it is your dead husband come to visit." Then she returned to the kitchen.

"What did she just say?" Brendan O'Neal asked gruffly as he stepped into the hallway.

How wonderful he looked! Everything about him was spectacular, from the tall hat in his hands to the dark gray cloak. His lush hair, dark brown with hints of red in the sunlight, was slightly tousled from either his hat or the wind, and a single curl fell over his forehead.

And then there was his face, the features so well defined. His nose, she decided, was perfect on him, but only on him. With another face it would be too sharp or too large. He slipped off his cloak without her help, and gestured to the coat tree.

All she could do was nod, when what she really wanted to do was to fall into his arms.

"Madam," he began. Were his eyes always that bright

and alive? They seemed to have an inner light, something special and unique. "We have some unfinished business."

No, oh no, she thought, although she kept her face impassive. He was going away. He wanted to annul the marriage as soon as possible.

"It is concerning our contract," he continued.

A small dash of hope crept into her heart.

"Yes?" She kept her voice as gruff as his. She had learned that he did not like her to be soft or gentle.

"It occurs to me that no matter how impressive your demonstrations have been, they have not solved the problem of my brother-in-law."

"You're right!" Celia exclaimed, then forced a frown. "Of course you are within your rights. We must address this issue, mustn't we?"

"Yes," he ventured. "And I expect you to be thorough in your duties."

"Naturally."

"We must not rush through this."

"No. That would be a terrible thing."

For several moments they stood looking not at each other, but in any other possible direction. Brendan studied the curve of the banister, and wondered if he should start counting the poles leading up the staircase. Celia focused on an umbrella stand that was said to have come all the way from China.

Did they have umbrellas in China?

"I think . . ." she began.

"We should . . ." he began at the precise same moment.

"No, you go first," they both said.

Then he smiled, and she returned the smile without thinking how much he disliked it when she smiled.

"Well." He straightened and looked down at his shoes. "Maybe there is something in your Green Book to help us."

"I had been thinking much along the same lines," she said with an attempt at boredom that registered as anything but boredom.

"Good." He looked up at her. "I've been very worried about him." There was no bravado there.

"I know," she said, longing to touch his arm but not wishing to repulse him. "I have a difficult question for you."

"Is it about Garrick having something to do with Amanda's death?"

"It's . . ." She stopped. "How did you know?"

"Because I've been wondering the same thing. It's an abhorrent thought, is it not? Like something from a Greek tragedy."

She noticed some movement in the parlor. One of the servants was cleaning, although she couldn't see who. "Would you like to go upstairs to my uncle's office? The Green Books are there, as well as some privacy."

"Excellent idea." He gestured for her to go ahead of him, to lead the way.

Celia was exceedingly self-conscious knowing he was directly behind her, watching her backside sway. By the time they reached the fourth-floor office, she was slightly out of breath.

"Here." She paused, holding the door open with one hand as she brushed a wisp of hair from her cheek. He looked down at her, his expression uncertain, as if he wished to say something, but he refrained.

Instead he simply entered her uncle's office.

"It's a bit of a clutter." She stepped over a box. "You may be able to clear a space over there, by the stuffed woodcock."

Wordlessly, he did just that.

"So tell me," she said once he was settled. "Do you think it was Garrick?"

"I don't know," he said. "Some days I feel certain of it, other days it seems impossible. I do believe he is keeping society with some people. And he's most secretive about it."

"Indeed?"

"Furthermore, I believe your Patrick may know something about his social life."

"Patrick?"

"Yes. I asked him about Garrick once, and he implied that . . ."

Celia gasped and jumped to her feet. "Uncle James's letter!" she almost shouted.

"What letter?"

Then she faltered for just an instant. He was there, inches away from her only security in the world. As her husband, the money in the box—along with the letters and her mother's ear bobs—were his property.

This was too important. This might help solve Amanda's death.

"Celia?"

Then she smiled.

Slowly she took the key from the waistband of her dress. "Do you mind?" She touched his leg and he stood, not sure where to go and what she was doing.

Deliberately she removed the window seat cushion, then the plank. And then, of course, she removed the box.

His expression questioning, he remained silent as she opened the box and pulled out her uncle's letter. "It's in here. Just a moment," she said, scanning the paper. "Here it is. He mentions Patrick having his meetings. Uncle James knew everything that went on in this house."

He watched her eyes go over the words, longing to get closer, to feel the warmth of her. Then he looked at the paper.

Some words stood out. "You have an inheritance," he said conversationally.

"Yes," she admitted. "I just found out this morning. It's over thirty thousand dollars, and my mother's diamond ear bobs."

He said nothing.

Taking a deep breath, she added, "By law they are yours."

And then he pulled his attention from the paper to her face, their eyes inches apart. Reaching out, he caressed her cheek lightly, something he had wanted to do, something he could not stop himself from doing. Tracing the side of her face, he smiled. "Celia," he said softly. "I would not dream of touching that. It's yours."

"But you are entitled," she repeated. Perhaps he had not understood what she had said.

All he did was shake his head. "It's yours," he said, then returned to the paper, leaving her to wonder what sort of man was this Brendan O'Neal.

By the time he left the house, they had both agreed to follow Patrick that evening, for it was his night off.

"So I'll meet you here then," she concluded, whispering as she handed him his hat and gloves.

"No. I will do this alone, Celia. It may be dangerous."

"Precisely. You'll need me to protect you."

At that, one dimple appeared on his cheek as he tried not to smile. "There will be no argument, Celia."

"I'm not arguing, I'm going with you."

"No."

"Brendan, I am the New Yorker here. I know how to follow without being detected. How do you think I found you at Mrs. Harris's establishment?"

"I had assumed you handed a letter to the desk clerk and then followed the messenger boy from the Astor House."

"For your information I . . . How did you know?"

"It was just a guess." He grinned.

"Please, though. Let me come. I promise to stay out of the way if it seems there might be danger."

He regarded her for a moment. What if it was indeed too late for them, if he had already ruined any chance of their future happiness?

In that case, this could very well be one of their last times together.

"Very well," he said at last. "But at the first sign of danger . . ."

"I'll run," she said.

This time he was unable to suppress the smile, and she felt her knees weaken just a little.

"Where are you going now?" she asked, curious.

"To the office. The ledgers are a mess and . . . what's that expression?"

"I'm afraid I have some bad news."

"What sort of bad news?"

"Last night, when you in your boardinghouse, the office on Water Street burned to the ground."

"Are you joking?"

"No, of course not."

"I was almost there," he said, all humor gone from his features. "At the last moment I decided to go back to my rooms. But I went as far as the steps."

"Do you think this has anything to do with Amanda?"

"I don't know." He shook his head, lost in thought.

Placing a hand on his arm, she said softly, "Garrick came by here this morning to tell us. He claimed to have tried to rescue you in vain."

"What on earth would he have been doing on Water Street at that time?"

"He said he wanted to work."

"Garrick?"

She nodded.

For a few moments he seemed to be lost in thought, then he turned to her. "Celia, when Garrick came and told you about the fire, did you think that I was . . ."

Impulsively she took his hand. "Yes," she said softly. "At first I did."

And then she placed his large, strong hand next to her face. Before he could ask her how she had felt, she kissed his hand, her eyes liquid.

Swallowing hard, he closed his own eyes. "Thank you," he said, so low she wasn't sure he had spoken.

With a smile he put on his hat and gloves. "On the bright side," he said, as if nothing had just transpired between them, "the books were a mess. This is probably going to make things a lot easier."

And then he left.

Celia watched him leave, a decided spring in his step. Here was a man who had just realized someone had probably tried to kill him the previous night, and that someone was very likely his closest friend, brother-in-law, and murderer of his sister. Yet he was walking with the jaunty air of a man who had just been handed a treasure.

Celia did not realize it, but that was precisely how he felt.

She stayed close by his side as they followed Patrick, walking through the twists and turns of upper Manhattan, the places that were still farmland, the occasional grand house and the scattering of shacks.

Patrick turned around once or twice, as if sensing someone was behind, and then they would slip behind a tree, or pretend to be entering a tavern. At last they came to what seemed to be an old abandoned house. Lights were blazing from within, shifting and moving as people milled through the rooms. Patrick walked straight to the door, and after conversing with a shadowy man, he entered.

"What do you think this is?" she whispered.

"I have no idea."

They watched as other men entered, pulling beside a large hedge so they could not be seen. Several men paused, talking before they went through the rickety gate, and Brendan leaned very close to her ear. "They're Irish."

"How can you tell?" she replied. Even in the darkness she could see his eyes flash. "Oh, of course."

"You stay here. I'm going to try to go in."

"I'm going with you."

"No women are being admitted. You stay here."

She couldn't argue with him. Only men had made their way up the winding little walk, past a fence that hadn't seen paint since Washington bid farewell to his troops.

From where she stood she had a partial view of Brendan. He walked up the path with complete authority, then exchanged words with the man at the door. Almost immediately he was let into the house.

Now she couldn't see anything.

As quietly as possible, she crept up to a closer shrub. More people entered. She could hear voices now, some raised followed by a few shouts or murmurs.

Just a little closer, she thought.

With a swift dash she was at the side of the house, right by a window, the glass old and thick with brush strokes, distorting the figures and the lanterns within. Inside the place was empty but for a few chairs, but nobody was sitting. They were all on their feet, moving closer to a center room.

But from her vantage point, she could see little else.

Moving to another window, she could finally see into the center room. It took her eyes a moment to adjust to the shifting inside. She thought she saw Patrick, but wasn't sure.

And then, a head taller than most of the men, she saw Brendan, attempting to blend, but not making much of a success of it.

She could hear the words now, talk of liberty and freedom, of famine and revolution. Someone mentioned the name Daniel O'Connell, and there was a round of cheers. When another man yelled the name

Brian Boru, the applause was deafening. Clearly, she thought, it was better to be a dead Irish king than a live Irish politician with this crowd.

But there was no Garrick. She scanned every face, every slouched figure, but she could not find the one person they were looking for.

And then she recognized someone. It was the onion-nosed man who had come with his two companions to collect the debt from Uncle James. As she suspected, the other two were there as well, shoulder to shoulder as if they had been stitched together.

She inched forward to hear more clearly.

The onion-nosed man was speaking at the front of the room, the others gathered around in a horseshoe shape to listen. "And so I tell you lads," he said with a thick Irish accent. "We have the power to end the famine, to free Ireland! All we need are the funds, laddies. The hat is being passed. Be generous, for they are starving even as we stand here."

A large floppy hat was being handed around, and every man was digging deep into his pockets, men who seemed as if they could use some help, men who did not appear to have anything to spare.

The onion-nosed man was smiling and nodding, urging them on with his hands gesturing, give, give.

And they did give.

He didn't have an Irish accent when he had appeared at her house. Of that she was sure, nor did either of his friends.

"May I speak?" The voice was firm, authoritative and exquisitely familiar, and Celia felt her stomach knot.

What was Brendan doing?

She held her breath, cleaning a small circle in the glass to get a better view.

The other men encouraged him to go to the front, and Celia saw the onion-nosed man's genial smile falter, then return in greater force when Brendan was by his side. He even reached up and clapped his back, and Celia bit her lip at the withering look Brendan gave the man.

"Friends. I am Brendan O'Neal of Dublin." There was a general round of applause. "I agree with all that is being said here. The situation in Ireland is indeed dire. The starvation there is nothing short of horrific. And I also agree that a free Ireland will be a better Ireland."

There was another round of cheers, and the onion-nosed man nodded with either relief or accord. "But gentlemen," he continued, "do we know exactly where all of this hard-earned money is going?"

A slight silence before the onion-nosed man stepped forward. "Rest assured, my friend, it is all going where it is needed."

"To your boss?" Brendan countered.

Then there was a murmur. "Of course not. It goes directly to Ireland. Why, this shipment will be there in time for Christmas. Think of the happy wee little faces . . ."

"How will it get there?"

"Excuse me?"

"The funds. And come to think of it, what good will money do in Ireland? They need food, staples. A handful of coins will be of little value when there is nothing to buy."

"Yes, well, you must understand this is a complicated matter." The genial smile was twitching.

"I realize that. But again I ask you, how will the funds get to Ireland?"

"Well, by ship, of course. How else?"

"But it is late November, sir," Brendan said. "No ship will run across the Atlantic until spring."

The crowd was completely silent now. "We have a special boat, you see." Somehow the onion-nosed man had just lost his lilt.

"Fascinating, sir," Brendan said, arms crossed. "And what part of Ireland are you from."

"Oh, well. We traveled about a great deal when I was a wee laddie. So I would say I am a citizen of Ireland, an island without boundaries, whether or not I am lucky enough to be embracing that fair land."

There was no applause. And that was the line that always drew applause.

"What county were your people from?" Brendan persisted.

"My people? Well, they traveled too. All over. Our love of Ireland was such that we were always in search of the fairest stream, the deepest green hills, and the most beautiful lassies."

Again no clapping.

"What county were you born in, sir. Surely your mother remained in one place long enough for that event."

There were a few chuckles, but the others were staring in confusion.

"I was born in County Clare," he said at last.

"Were you? What was the closest town?"

"I do not remember. I was just a lad." No laughter.

Brendan just stared at him for a painfully long moment, then he turned back to face the crowd. "Gentle-

men. This man is Cyrus Fuller, also known by a string
of aliases. He is a native of the green hills of Pennsyl-
vania, and is employed by a certain councilman whose
name I will not divulge at this point. This, gentlemen,
is a thief. I met him recently when he was attempting
to collect on a large loan from a single lady. He ac-
costed her in a most vile fashion, threatened her welfare with his two companions there. The poor lady
lived in torment and fear. Why? To secure payment for
a loan that had already been paid by the lady's late
uncle."

Celia's hand slipped on the windowsill, but she
righted herself.

"I protest, sir!" the onion-nosed man proclaimed.

"In a moment, Cyrus. Now, this issue of Ireland is
too important to all of us to be used by a cheap crook
with a bad Irish accent. We need to pull together, to or-
ganize. Yes, funds are important, but not as important as
our unity."

"How can we trust you?" shouted someone from the
crowd.

There was a mumbling of agreement. Others just
glared at the onion-nosed man, who was growing uncomfortable up front. His two companions had slipped
out some time ago.

"How can you trust me? I don't know. You must use
your judgment. But let me tell you this. I am the owner
of O'Neal Shipping, the largest concern of its sort in
London and Dublin, and soon New York. I need good
men, steady workers. I will pay well, and I am a fair em-
ployer. But more to the point, I believe we should
gather in public places, with the consent of the city itself. We have nothing to hide. And I will not pass a hat,

but we will work with merchants and politicians to send relief to Ireland as swiftly as possible."

The excitement in the room hummed, and even Celia got caught up in the momentum.

And that's why she failed to hear the footsteps behind her.

18

~~~~

She was slammed to the ground, her face pressed into the dirt and grass, her breath knocked out from her body.

Dazed, she could still hear the sound of Brendan's voice inside, the cheering response, the applause and hoots and the happy shouts. But it all seemed so very far away.

He was heavy, the person on her.

"Please," she heard herself say.

And then he turned her over, holding her hard against the ground.

"Patrick!" She could see his features clearly. "Oh, I'm so glad it's you! I was frightened for a moment but . . ."

He was simply staring at her, his eyes narrow. "You're just like her now. You look the same."

"Who are you talking about?"

"Amanda."

Her wrists were pinned down, and she could feel his knee against her side, sharp and painful.

"How did you know Amanda?"

"I loved Amanda."

Good God, she thought. But she tried to smile kindly. "You loved Amanda?"

"Yes!" As he spoke he lifted her slightly and smashed her back into the ground.

"How . . ." Celia began, but was unable to continue. The twisting on her wrists was becoming unbearable.

"Just this way, Celia." His tongue rolled over her name. "She was peeking in the window, looking at Garrick. Just as you were looking at Brendan. She was even dressed the same."

"Did you speak to her then?" It took all of Celia's will not to cry out in pain. Her wrists must be close to breaking, she thought distractedly.

"Yes. And at first she was sweet and kind, so willing to help with the cause. We thought they were good for a lot of money, you see. But then that sniveling Englishman got scared. He thought something was wrong, and then Amanda thought so, too. Do you know what he was going to do?"

"No," she rasped.

"He was going to plan his own relief fund for Ireland. Just to please her! But that would have cut into our business, you know. They would have all of the high and mighty folk, the ones with plenty of jewels and all. So I was sent to warn them. To warn him, really. And I hoped that he would die."

"Why? Why would you wish that on anyone, Patrick?"

"Because then I could be with Amanda. Because then we could be together as we belong. Then she said something terrible to me. Something terrible."

"What was it?"

"That she loved her husband. She told me that, right to my face when I had come by to give her an evening bouquet of flowers. I used to do that, you know. A morning bouquet and an evening bouquet. Then she asked me not to do that anymore. And when I asked why, she said she loved her husband."

He was no longer aware of her now. "I meant to kill him, but when she died, it was almost as good. Almost. And Garrick will die soon, too."

"He will?"

Then Patrick smiled, a horrible grimace that stretched viciously across his teeth. "The opium. It wasn't hard at all, you see. He was weak. And when Amanda died and he was all alone, I took it upon myself to let him sample the opium. I've never seen anyone take to it so! He cried once, and said when he was numb, the pain wasn't so bad."

Celia felt her throat tighten in spite of the terrible agony of her wrists. Poor Garrick. That explained so much, the ledgers, his behavior.

"Last night I tried to kill him, you know. I almost did."

She didn't need to ask who he was talking about. A thought rushed through her, how close Brendan had come to disaster. How very close.

"Then we will be together."

She had to do something. Now. Keep him talking.

"What about the times we saw Amanda? Were you not frightened she would be angry at you?"

Again he grinned. "Nah. Don't you understand? She came there to visit me! She couldn't stay away, even when she was dead. It is better that way. You'll see. It's so much better that way."

Frantic to escape, she tried to jut her knee up to dislodge him, but her heavy skirts kept her pinned down, immobile.

He simply showed more teeth, and then he leaned closer, closer, pressing harder. And he held her wrists down with his forearm, thus freeing his hands.

"Here we go now, Celia," he said pleasantly. "You'll see now. And just think, you already have a friend waiting for you. Then it will be you and Amanda and me. Always."

And his hands circled around her throat.

No! She tried to shout, but she couldn't make a sound. Then she couldn't breathe, nothing would come, no air.

Still she struggled, and he seemed to gain strength as she felt hers ebbing. Her eyes rolled up and she could see the edge of the house, the window from where she had been watching Brendan.

But he would be fine. Just fine.

Her lungs were burning, and she heard strange gurgling sounds. Were they coming from her? Was that possible?

Then she felt herself cease the struggle. She felt herself let go, just let go. Away from the pain. Away from this monster.

Brendan would be fine.

Just as she felt herself slip to someplace else, a soft place, she heard a growl, like a Bengal tiger.

"No!" It was not human.

Her eyes closed, and then, magically, the weight was

off her, lifted high and, she imagined, tossed across a hedge. Her vision was a small slit between her almost closed eyes.

"Celia? Miss O'Neal?" She recognized the voice. She tried to say his name, Garrick, but no sound came forth.

She heard the unmistakable sounds of a fight, of fist pummeling flesh, dull thuds and grunts.

And then she was being cradled by someone very large and very gentle. He held her close to his chest and she heard the pounding of his heart as he gasped.

"Celia, oh God. Tell me it's not too late."

No words would come from her throat, but she opened her eyes, and he made a strange moan and held her so tight it was almost painful.

But it was pain of the most glorious kind.

She was aware of some men leading Patrick away, of the crowd scattering, men casting glances over their shoulders as they left.

Garrick was still there, slumped against a tree trunk.

Then Brendan leaned back to get a better view of her face, and when he did that she smiled.

And so did he.

"Thank God, Garrick," Brendan said, half to himself. "If you hadn't arrived the moment you did, if you hadn't pulled me down from the bloody podium . . ."

"It was Amanda," muttered a still-bewildered Garrick. "She came to me, to me, Brendan. Told me where to go. How would I have found this place otherwise?"

"I know," soothed Brendan, smoothing her hair. "I know."

And Celia smelled it then, the perfume. "Brendan?" she tried to say, but her voice was still a croak.

Suddenly she was there, standing before all three of them. She was no longer twisted or grotesque. Now she was a vision of peace, of love.

"Amanda," Garrick sobbed.

And she shook her head and smiled. *You will be well, Garrick. I did love you, and you will again find the love you deserve.*

Brendan just stared, and she looked at him.

"Thank you," he said to his sister. Nothing else.

Celia tried to speak, but Brendan just held her close, protecting her, embracing her with his love.

"Oh, Amanda," repeated Garrick.

She was beginning to fade now. *Good-bye*, came her words. *Do not squander love.*

As she diffused, Celia tried to speak. "That was in my uncle's letter," she said. But no one could understand her scratchy throat.

Now Amanda was gone.

Celia repeated herself, stronger this time. "My uncle said that," she was able to say clearly.

Brendan looked down, at first just listening to her voice. Then his eyes crinkled into a smile. "Your uncle said 'Do not squander love'?"

Relieved, she nodded.

"It's engraved in your wedding ring, Celia. My mother's ring."

Her eyes widened in wonder, and he nodded. Then he kissed the top of her head, somehow the most wonderful thing anyone had ever done.

"And we won't," he concluded.

*   *   *

Garrick went back to his hotel and Celia and Brendan returned to the boardinghouse.

He insisted on carrying her up the three flights of stairs to his room, and she allowed him to without a complaint, gratefully wrapped in his arms.

Epilogue

The sea air was crisp, warmed by the spring sun.

Celia stood on the deck, wrapped in a long blanket and clutching a hot cup of tea. The view was infinite, water and sky and waves as far as she could see. It didn't seem possible that anything else existed, that anything else had ever existed.

And then strong arms came up from behind her, encircling her in strength and pure love. "In a few hours we'll be able to see the west coast of Ireland," he said.

"I cannot wait," she said, turning her face up to his.

"Are you feeling better, love?" His hand slipped to her thickening waist. The baby would be born at Castle Sitric in just a few short months.

"I'll show you the fairy rings," he said softly.

"Do you believe in them again?"

"I do." He smiled and held her close, both looking out over the water. "Maybe I never stopped believing. I just needed to be reminded. Needed to know in which column to put them. And they are now firmly planted in the 'What I know' column."

Garrick came out on the deck, his complexion the shade of pea soup. "Are we any closer?" He gripped the railing for dear life, his knuckles white as he listed back and forth in almost perfect opposition to the ship's rhythms. "Oh, please tell me this infernal rocking will stop soon."

"Actually, no." Brendan winked at Celia. "We've decided to go to South Africa instead."

"That is not funny," he replied, his cheeks puffing out once or twice, rendering it very funny indeed. And then he dashed across the deck.

"Poor Garrick," they both said at the same time.

The crew was busy with ropes and sails, most of them recruited from the United Irish Brotherhood. In the cargo hold were the usual items for trade, plus a full load of nonperishable food items to distribute, as well as crop seeds that could fare well in the sometimes problematic Irish soil.

"I hope they don't follow me over, Brendan."

She didn't need to explain who.

After that night at the meeting, the crowds at Washington Square were even thicker, more needy. And since that night, Celia O'Neal was once again a spiritual fraud.

It was gone, whatever had visited them so briefly and wondrously. Amanda had not returned, no matter how Garrick pleaded on his knees. And little by little, he had managed to find his own way. The opium had been more difficult than any of them had imagined, but he was no longer a slave to it. The color had returned to his cheeks—that is, until this journey.

"They won't find you, Celia. I've seen to that."

She cocked her head. "What did you do? Poor Aunt

Prudence has high hopes that we can open a new salon in Ireland."

"Poor Aunt Prudence is enjoying her newfound wealth too much to think beyond the latest Paris fashions." He laughed. Then, more soberly, "That was wonderful of you, Celia."

"She deserved it. My inheritance plus what you paid me for helping Garrick. She needs it more than I."

"Even after the hurtful things she said and did?"

"Brendan, she only said those things because she was frightened. You above anyone else should understand *that.*"

"Ouch."

"But really, what did you do to make sure they won't follow us?"

He did not speak at first, scanning the beauty before them, the promise of forever.

"Do you remember that little document I had you sign?"

"The one that professes me to be an utter and shameless fraud? With my bold signature across the bottom?"

"That's the one."

"Lands, Brendan. What did you do with it?"

"My guess is that at this precise moment, subscribers to New York's most respectable newspaper are savoring every word."

"You sent it to the *New York Post?*"

He nodded, and after her first flush of embarrassment, she began to grin.

"It was the only way, Celia," he explained.

"I know."

He took the teacup from her hands and placed it gently on the deck. "How do you feel, love?" he said huskily.

"Marvelous." She sighed. "Every day I feel like a bride, fresh and new and full of awe. Joy is a wonderful thing."

"May you feel this way forever, my bride."

And just then, for the first time, wrapped in her husband's arms, she saw the vivid green of the Irish coast, and she could only guess what new enchantment lay around the next corner. Forever.